Praise for *If I Loved Y...*

D0626485

"[Robin] Black delivers real emoti........................ pause. . . .
I want to shout about how just when you thought no one could
write a story with any tinge of freshness let alone originality about
childhood . . . . about marriage . . . about old age, Black has done
it. . . . Will Robin Black win [the PEN/Hemingway Prize] for this
book? If I were a judge, she would."

—ALAN CHEUSE, *Chicago Tribune*

"*...oved You* is a 'Fantastic Voyage' into the bloodstream of the
......an species. . . . Maybe it's midlife maturity, maybe it's raw talent,
but *If I Loved You* leaves you longing for more."

—*San Francisco Chronicle*

"[*If I Loved You, I Would Tell You This*] offers the kind of storytelling
that's so deft, so understated, and so compelling that you have to slow
down to savor each vignette. . . . Black's characters are conventional,
l... ..ople we know—the soccer mom, the teenage daughter, the guy
ne.. door—but their tales vibrate with aberrant energy. . . . A nervy
new writer to watch."

—*O: The Oprah Magazine*

"F...... ..ck stakes out some of the emotional territory occupied by
....nro, Amy Bloom and Lorrie Moore. . . . A nuanced portrait
of the heart that repays careful reading."

—*Financial Times*

"In every story, [Black] creates wonderful little images, sees symbols,
doub...ction."

...hia Inquirer

"[Blac........

X000 000017 3337

—*Vogue*

If I Loved You,
I Would Tell You This

Robin Black's stories and essays have appeared in
numerous publications. A finalist for the 2010 Frank
O'Connor International Short Story Award and a
recipient of fellowships from the Leeway Foundation
and the MacDowell Colony, Black is a graduate of the
Warren Wilson MFA Program for Writers. She lives
with her family in Philadelphia.

If I Loved You,
I Would Tell You This

Stories

ROBIN BLACK

PICADOR

First published 2010 by Random House,
an imprint of The Random House Publishing Group,
a division of Random House, Inc., New York

First published in Great Britain in paperback 2010 by Picador

This edition first published with a new story and reading guide 2011 by Picador
an imprint of Pan Macmillan, a division of Macmillan Publishers Limited
Pan Macmillan, 20 New Wharf Road, London N1 9RR
Basingstoke and Oxford
Associated companies throughout the world
www.panmacmillan.com

ISBN 978-0-330-51179-7

9 8 7 6 5 4 3 2 1

A CIP catalogue record for this book is available from
the British Library.

Printed in the UK by CPI Mackays, Chatham ME5 8TD

Visit **www.picador.com** to read more about all our books
and to buy them. You will also find features, author interviews and
news of any author events, and you can sign up for e-newsletters
so that you're always first to hear about our new releases.

For Richard

Contents

If I Loved You,
I Would Tell You This

The
Guide

AT SEVENTEEN, Jack Snyder's daughter is slender-faced and long of limb and still able to startle her father with her seeming certainty about everything she thinks. They're driving along roads he doesn't yet know, on their way to meet her first seeing-eye dog, and she is wearing polka-dotted sunglasses, a long jean skirt, and a shirt with the words: "If you can read this T-shirt, maybe YOU can tell ME what it says." A kid from her school ordered them, in the dozens, and Lila bought three in different shades. "You're sure they aren't identical?" she questioned her mother at the time. "I don't want my teachers thinking I never change my clothes."

"Believe me, Lila," Ann Snyder said. "I don't want your teachers thinking you never change your clothes either."

As Jack scans the road for signs, Lila is proclaiming to him in those certain tones of hers that if it weren't for being quite so blind and having to have one, she'd definitely never get a dog. Never. Never ever. And her father is trying to follow her, trying to respond appropriately; but thoughts of Miranda Hamilton compete with the girl's words. Miranda Hamilton unbuttoning her jeans the night before, sliding them down her thighs, stepping panty-clad from the denim pooled at her feet. Miranda Hamilton unbuttoning his suit pants, leaving them bound around his legs until he kicked them off. Miranda's cropped blond hair fading into soft, colorless down along the back of her neck. Miranda laughing as she filled her mouth with bourbon from Jack's glass and held the fluid there, smiling while it drizzled from her lips until he kissed her and swallowed it himself. Miranda whispering to Jack, her mouth still whiskey damp, just to lie back, lie still, while she moved her hips in something close to perfect circles over him. Just lie still. Just lie still. Just lie still.

"Really, Dad, they're so obsequious," Lila says, and Jack has to remind himself what they're talking about. Guide dogs. They're talking about guide dogs. "The whole alpha-male pack-mentality thing. Cats don't give a shit about anyone, right?" Her father swerves around a pothole, and senses her sway beside him, unprepared. It's an early-spring day and they are into the long weeks between the damage done by ice and snow and the repair work to come.

"That's certainly their reputation," Jack says. "Cats are undomesticatable. Too wild."

"I find that infinitely more appealing."

Jack nods silently, an assent he knows his daughter cannot see.

"Maybe I could have the first ever seeing-eye cat." Lila crosses her arms. "Some real haughty feline with attitude."

"You mean like you?"

But his daughter shakes her head. "No." She turns her face toward the breeze of the open window, lifting her sunglasses. "No," she repeats. "I'd want a guide cat who really doesn't give a flying fuck." She draws an audible breath through her nose. "Manure?"

"We're in farm country now." He says it quietly, as he looks around outside. Rolling hills of tilled soil settle dark brown against the clear blue sky. Occasional red barns dot the land, appealing in their melancholic disrepair. The scenery is picture-postcard beautiful, but he keeps that to himself. For now, anyway. Later in the day, maybe after dinner, he'll call Miranda. And he'll tell her all about how lovely the landscape looked; and then maybe he'll tell her once again how painful these moments of unshared beauty can be. Standing in the farthest reaches of his backyard, he'll hold his cell phone close against his mouth so he won't have to shout and he'll close his eyes as he describes to her again how solitary he so often feels with his sightless daughter by his side. How among all the things for which he might feel guilt, there's always this one mountainous inequity: that he can see and Lila cannot.

"Is it pretty?" Lila asks.

"We're out in the sticks. It's okay." He pictures Miranda pacing her kitchen, phone in hand, running an exasperated hand through her hair. *This isn't your strength, Jack. You have to learn to let go.*

"Yeah, I figured as much." Lila turns her head his way. "Are there cows?"

"A little way back there were. Black Angus, I think. Big and dark."

"Sounds nice, Dad." But Jack only murmurs a neutral

sound, and Lila turns away, facing forward again. "The thing is," she says, "I just can't imagine raising a dog and then giving it away. Even if I don't much like dogs, it still sounds like an elaborate form of masochism."

"It's a . . ." But Jack can't find the word he wants, and he's pretty sure he's just missed their turn. "Dammit, I think we're lost. No, wait, this must be right. It's a good deed," he says. "It's something these guide dog people want to do. He's your dog and they know that from day one. So they don't get attached."

"Yeah, right, Dad. Do you really believe that? That you can just tell yourself not to get attached? You don't seem so thrilled about me going to college. Why didn't you just tell yourself not to get attached?"

"Very funny." But she's right, of course. Who is he to assume anyone can tell themselves what to feel? He's always been unable to tell his heart a goddamned thing. "Very clever, Lila," he says. "But it's the system. It's how this guide dog business works. And since we benefit from the system for once, I'm not going to argue with it. Here we go. Sharp turn left . . ." He gives her the warning and at the edge of his vision sees her brace herself for the curve, hands gripping her seat. "Hang on, babe. This looks bumpy. Dirt road."

"I think I can handle it. Bumps in the road are my speci-al-i-ty." Lila has her head turned to the open window again, holding the door, her thick dark curls flying in the breeze. "Maybe there's something wrong with me," she says, "but I actually like the smell of manure."

"No." Her father draws in a deep breath of the sour, full air, savoring the simple fact that they're smelling the same thing—a relief from all the sights they never share. "I agree with you, baby. It's a strangely pleasing smell."

"And, by the way, so is skunk."

"Absolutely," he agrees, remembering the pungent, oddly twisting scent of Miranda's sweating skin. "Absolutely," he tells his daughter. "So is skunk."

Lila was six, playing in the garage of a neighboring family the Snyders didn't really know, when an aerosol can of orange spray paint blew up in her face; and for a long time after that, many years, Jack was stuck on that one simple fact—on the tenuous, fleeting nature of the acquaintance-ship. Almost as though the same accident, with the same result, in the home of a close friend would have somehow made more sense. But none of it made any sense, of course. He knew that. You could turn the thing around, replay it endless times—and you would. You would. And you would. And you would. But none of it made any sense at all. There you are one fine October day, living your life pretty much as you had planned, your lawyer's shingle hanging up, white and shiny, outside your solo practice downtown; tranquilly married to your wife of eight years, whom you've managed still to love, though so many of your friends have clearly, even openly, tired of theirs; doting on your six-year-old daughter whom you adore, with the not so secret sense that she's a little prettier, a little smarter, and a lot more special than other people's kids; enjoying your smug, self-congratulatory thoughts about the way fatherhood refo-cuses priorities. Long gone are the days when you were known as a bit of a skirt chaser, back in the single years; the days when anything held the same appeal as tossing a ball in the backyard with your kid. And then a fucked-up aerosol can of orange paint blows up in your daughter's face. In the garage of a boy she doesn't really know.

The first few weeks flew by in waiting rooms filled with cold cups of coffee and shifts of relatives taking turns. Bits and pieces of news were conveyed by strangers who came to him fresh from delving into his child's face. Some good: the eyes wouldn't have to come out. There were deep cuts on her jaw, but they would fade over time. She had been knocked unconscious by something that had fallen off the wall—a wheelbarrow, Jack eventually found out. And this was excellent news too, the doctors said. This would limit Lila's memory of what they called "the event."

But then in the center of it all, whatever salvage might be found among the wreckage, there was the conversation, the now-inevitable talk Jack began having with his daughter, six years old and emerging so untidily from all the anesthesia, all the painkillers, emerging so he could tell her, not once but many times, that she would never see again. Six years old, he would think as he spoke the words. She doesn't understand forever. She can't imagine what "never again" really means. And of course a part of him didn't want her to, as he sat on the edge of her hospital bed, touching her continually so she'd never feel alone in the dark, caressing her constantly—for himself as much as her. So neither of them would feel alone. While Ann stood just outside the doorway, listening as though she were eavesdropping, retreating even then into the fears that would engulf her as if less frightening than real life turned out to be. And Jack repeated the truth to his girl—because that's what the psychologists had cautioned him to do. Never lie. Never lose her trust. But have the conversation again, again and again, until the child understands, as no six-year-old should have to do, exactly what forever really means.

"This is it," he says, pulling into a long, rutted drive.

"Nice place?"

Looking up at the small ranch house, set on stilts, Jack frowns at the empty flowerpots that line the porch rail. An old bicycle leans against the front window. "Not really," he says. "Not somewhere I'd want to live, anyway, though someone else might find it quaint, I suppose." He should be used to being her eyes. He shouldn't even notice doing it by this time. But in the car, as he peers at this nondescript house, he can feel himself resisting her questions, as he does more and more when there's a matter of taste involved. Is he handsome? Are the flowers pretty? Nice place? Does she understand how often these are matters of opinion and not of fact? Realize how likely it is that if she could judge these things for herself they might disagree? Does she ever guess how very injured and myopic a filter he has become?

"It's a small place," he says. "It's reddish and a little run-down."

A tall woman steps out onto the porch and waves what looks like a powerful arm. Jack waves back, out his window.

"Come on," he says to Lila. "It's showtime. Look's like she's here."

"Giddy-up," she responds, lowering her glasses again. "As long as we made the trip, let's do this thing."

When he told Miranda how much he hated the idea of Lila getting a guide dog, she accused him of balking at letting Lila grow up. She said he was resisting the idea of her transferring her needs and her dependencies onto someone else—even a dog. "Same old, same old, Jack," she said. "You are way too attached." Jack was visiting the café where she worked, catching her at odd moments between her customers. "You're so identified with her. It would be good for you both if Lila could lean on someone else."

But at home that night over dinner he tried not to think about that, dismissed it as psychobabble, only said something vague about feeling unsure, not having a gut sense that this was the right move to make. Introducing such a huge change into their lives. About it being a long-term commitment—a phrase that caused Ann to stare pointedly his way. *Exactly what would you know about keeping commitments, Jack?* Lila claimed to hate what she called "the whole geeky blind-girl thing with the dog who snarls at everyone but me." And Ann eventually confessed to having her own concerns, to a recent fear of large dogs, which caused Jack to throw his own exasperated look at her: *Exactly what is it that you aren't afraid of, Ann?*

In the home of a blind child, it turned out, a marriage could easily enough dissolve in unwitnessed pantomime. Ann and he could be giving each other the finger through every meal, for all Lila knew. And at times, they had come pretty close.

"It isn't the most important consideration, I understand," Ann said in her quiet, steady tones, so suffused with control that the effort itself was like a second, twining voice. "I probably shouldn't have brought it up."

"Poor Mommy." Lila reached across the kitchen table to pat her hand, and Ann moved it for her to find. "Who said parenthood wasn't hard?"

The college counselor at school was adamant, though, and ultimately persuasive. "It's the best way to do college," she said. "It's the best way to do adulthood, in fact," she added, reaching to pet the heavyset creature lying beside her feet on the gray carpet, as Jack watched Ann shift in her chair, away from the dog. "You don't want her living with her parents for her whole life," she stated—startling Jack— as though that were clearly true.

She handed Ann a card with two agency names, and Ann then passed it on to Jack, a move he recognized all too well. Everything from phoning for take-out to planning vacations to calling in someone to see if their lacy-leafed maples should be sprayed—all these were increasingly his to do, as his wife retreated ever more steadily into her phobic state.

"Would you like to compare coping mechanisms?" she'd asked him once, when he let fly his rapidly growing anger at her rapidly shrinking world. "Yours versus mine? What's her name, again? Amanda? Miranda? Would you like to have this conversation? Or should we just keep trying to help each other stumble through for a few more years? For Lila's good?"

Stumble. It was the obvious answer. They would stumble through, of course.

Jack picked one agency over the other by no more scientific means than the fact that the first one's phone was busy; and the agency whose phone wasn't busy put him onto Bess

Edwards. "She has her own methods, but they work," the agency man said. "She's a dog woman through and through." Jack repeated the phrase to Lila just to hear her laugh and describe what she thought a through-and-through dog-woman must be like.

"Hairy, of course, and always licking herself between the legs."

But on the phone Bess Edwards sounded only sensible and experienced. "I've done this four other times," she said and told him it would take her another three months to have the dog—a nine-month-old Lab named Wally—ready to meet them. Then it would take an unknown number of sessions for her to train Lila. Saturday morning visits to her home, about an hour away. "I do this my way," she said. "It isn't orthodox, but it's worked so far."

Meanwhile, Jack should mail her a few of his daughter's socks, preferably worn, and tell her just a little about the home. Are there stairs? Is there a yard? Traffic noises? Other pets? Other children? She reeled off the questions and he shot the answers back.

"Are you a single parent?"

Jack felt himself hesitate. "No, there's a mother too." The phrase sounded ridiculous. "I have a wife," he said.

"I will need some money for his food." She named a sum that sounded low.

"What about your services? We must have to pay you for this."

"No," she answered, after a noticeable pause. "This is just something I do. I couldn't possibly take money for helping the blind." And Jack flinched a little at the phrase: *the blind*. The words conjured images of ragged, sorrowful men wearing worn and filthy sacks. The blind leading the blind—in the Snyder household they'd made every version of joke possible from that line. Jack had never laughed. Even at the ones he himself had made. The blind leading the blind—to certain doom. In the momentary quiet, he waited for Bess Edwards to go on, to volunteer some connection, tell him that a relative of hers had been sightless, tell him a story about why this was something she would do.

"I guess I believe we all need to be involved in acts that make us feel a little decent," she said instead. "Don't you?"

"Well," he said, after yet another pause. "It certainly is a noble goal."

"Bess Edwards," she calls out now, as, arm in arm, Jack and Lila approach her rickety porch. She's a little older than he is, he sees. The other side of forty-five. Somewhere in there. "Call me Bess. You must be Jack." He nods, with a little smile, as he guides Lila up the two painted steps. At the top, Bess gives him a gripping two-handed handshake and Jack notices her dark blue eyes, vibrant against the brownish, lined skin that looks as though she's never passed a moment in the shade. A healthy-looking woman, discounting all the warnings about the sun. Strong and fit. A single long, black braid hangs slung over her shoulder. "And this must be . . ."

"I'm Lila." Jack watches as his daughter extends her slim arm into the exact proper spot and Bess Edwards grasps it. "I'm the blind one," Lila says, her eyebrows arched just above the black screens of her glasses, all loveliness and charm, using her company manners—much like her home manners only without even the small trace of vulnerability Jack could occasionally detect. She lifts her chin, Grace Kelly at her aristocratic best, and in the clear, natural light, Jack can still just make out the silvery skin along her neck where the cuts had been.

"I'm glad you told me that." Bess Edwards's tone is more humorous than he'd expected. Unfair of him maybe, but he hadn't counted on a woman who put doing something decent on her list of daily deeds to participate in Lila's kind of jokes. "I wouldn't have wanted to be mistakenly training your father on the dog." She throws him a conspiring, bemused kind of look. "Why don't you both come in and sit down. I'll go get Wally ready."

While she holds the screen door open, Jack places one hand lightly on Lila's back. "Step inside . . . one small step up . . . okay, about four steps to the couch." Passing Bess, he feels their bodies brush and mumbles an "Excuse me," to which she offers no reply.

"Dog," Lila whispers, barely audible, two steps in. "I smell dog."

"You smell your dog," Jack corrects, as the faint odor hits him too. "Get used to it."

"Poor Mom. She'll die."

"She won't die." Jack can hear his own impatience. "She'll just have to deal with it."

"Have to deal with what?" As he turns he sees Bess standing just inside the door as the screen creaks shut, her arms folded at her waist.

"My wife is allergic to dogs," he lies, orienting Lila to the couch and watching as she sits. "But if it's a problem, she'll just take some medicine."

"I've had families deal with that before," Bess says. "It's pretty unpleasant, but it's manageable. I've even heard of people allergic to their own guides." As she speaks, she steps farther into the room.

"It's why she's not here," Jack adds, sitting in the shabby armchair beside the couch, trying to banish images of Ann and what she might be doing at this moment. Staring out their front window, alert for intruders. Examining and re-examining the cans in their pantry for signs of swelling or suspicious dents. Or quite possibly still just lying in bed by the phone, anxious, immobile, and alone.

"Hmmm." Bess shifts her eyes to Lila on the couch, her legs crossed at her ankles, the sunglasses still down. "Well, she probably should come out here sometime," she says. "Just to meet Wally, before moving-in day."

"That shouldn't be a problem." As he shrugs the subject away, Jack sees Lila's mouth tense. "Lila heads out to college year after next. The dog won't be living in the house for very long, anyway."

"I'll be right back," Bess says. "Just let me get him harnessed up and all."

She walks past Jack and through the room. There's something about the sway of her hips as she steps away, the braid swinging over her shoulder, falling straight down her back, something unexpectedly sexy. He glances over to Lila—almost as if to be sure she hasn't seen him checking Bess out. Her lips are still curving down, the lower one sticking out in an unmistakable pout.

"What's the problem?" he asks. "You look upset."

"I feel bad about lying. About Mom."

"You didn't lie. I did."

"You know what I mean." She shifts back a little on the couch, still looking troubled. "You could have just said she's scared of dogs. There's nothing so weird about that." She fills her cheeks with air and puffs it out—a mannerism of hers that predates the accident, a thread connecting her, connecting him, to those days. "A lot of people are. It isn't like it's some shameful thing." And then a moment later: "Really, Dad, is it? Is it something we have to cover up?"

Is it? Or is it just his own weariness with Ann's concerns? "No, I suppose it isn't. You're probably right."

"Now what do you tell Mom? That she has to come here and pretend to be allergic to dogs? And pretend not to be scared? How's she supposed to do that?"

"I don't know, Lila. Maybe she won't come here."

"She will come, though. She will if I need her to."

"Okay, then she will. We'll handle it when it happens."

Jack watches Lila's face fall back into thought.

"What if the dog doesn't like me?" she asks, uncrossing, recrossing her legs. "I'm not exactly an animal person."

"If you'd seen our hostess, you wouldn't worry." He hears his own nervous release of a laugh. "I can't imagine the creature who won't do exactly what she says. And that's including you."

"Really? What's she look like? Is she pretty?"

Jack stares over toward the door through which Bess has disappeared. Yeah, she's pretty. Not girlish pretty like Miranda, with her small tight body and mischievous eyes, but attractive, without a doubt.

"Oh, I don't know," he says. "I wasn't really looking for that. She's tall, I suppose. She has a long braid, black hair.

And she's kind of muscled up. She doesn't look like she puts up with a lot of crap."

Lila frowns a little at that and lifts the sunglasses, rubbing her eyes. In the background Jack can hear a dog bark. He sees her flinch slightly at the sound. "My master's voice," she says. She turns her head so he sees her now in profile, and sitting there on Bess's worn couch, she looks a lot like Ann. A lot like Ann did when they were young. The same pale complexion and angular face. The same strong, straight back. Even her half-closed eyes remind him of how Ann always seemed to keep herself a little hidden, a little obscured, back when her need to have Jack guide her through the world felt emboldening to him still, made him feel big and strong. Back before it became a burden. A long, long time ago.

He stands up, begins to move through the room. He steps across Bess Edwards's faded carpet, past her upright piano. It could almost have been another man's life, he thinks. Though of course it wasn't. As recently as last night, after the trick with the bourbon, and after he'd followed Miranda's instructions, just lie still, just lie still, just lie still, after she was done tracing those heavenly halos with her hips and they'd fallen into two separate bodies once again, he found himself thinking, as he did from time to time, about that boy whose family they didn't really know. The one who'd told his daughter to shake the can of paint as hard as she could. Beside him, Miranda was blowing long, narrow streams of smoke from the one daily cigarette she'd allow herself, and Jack was telling her he couldn't even remember the kid's name. Not Tommy. Not Billy. But something like that. Something plain and seemingly harmless. Something common and deceptively benign.

"You'd think it would be burned into me, that name," he said. "But it's gone."

Rolling onto his side, he pulled Miranda's patchwork comforter up around his naked waist, and he told her for the first time about the day the boy's parents came by the house, only that once, leaving enormous, bright flowers and a long, rambling letter on the porch. A letter in which they wrote about the wheelbarrow that had been hanging on the wall, and about how they wished that there was anything they could do. How they wished they knew the Snyders better, and wished that the Snyders knew them well, knew what decent people they were, so the Snyders could understand how terrible they felt. And how terrible the boy felt too—whatever his name—how terrible they all felt that this had happened in their home. Because pain that is shared, their letter said, can be pain that is lessened. They knew that was true.

He'd found it tucked among the flowers and thrown it in the trash, after reading it just once.

"Did you ever talk to them, Jack?" Miranda asked.

"No." And he didn't go into any more than that. But he could remember how when they had come to the front door they rang and rang and rang, seeing the lights on, seeing a car in the drive, and he didn't answer the bell. Because they were upstairs together, he and Ann, making love to one another with all their might, still thinking they might be on the same side, still thinking that the other story might be theirs. The one in which pain that is shared is pain that is lessened, just like the boy's parents said it was.

"No," he said to Miranda. "I never did speak to them. I never saw the point."

As she stubbed out her cigarette and rolled onto her elbows, close enough that he could feel a little of her heat shift to him, he reached over and drew a gentle line up and down her bare, pale back. "I was never a big enough guy to let them off the hook, I guess."

"Even the kid?" she asked. "He had to be carrying a shitload of guilt. You had to have felt sorry for the kid."

Jack didn't respond, aware of his fingertips, rough against her smooth skin.

"I guess it isn't your strength."

"What?" Jack looked her way, his hand stopping, then resuming its long trail. "What isn't my strength?"

But she only shook her head, a silent no, a partial shrug, and lowered her face onto the pillow so he could keep his fingers moving easily all the way down her back, up to the base of her neck again, just to where he could feel the silky, downy hairs. Up and down. Down and up. A straight line over the knobs of her spine.

"So tell me then, Miranda, what is my strength?"

But by then she had fallen asleep. For a few moments, he watched her breathe, studied her unconcerned rest. Then he rose to dress and stepped quietly out her door, the question still hovering, unanswered, in the air.

Jack hears his daughter sigh, a theatrical, gusty sound, and turns to see her feeling at the face of her watch. "What's your hurry?" he asks. She's perched on the edge of the couch, bouncing impatiently.

"It just seems like a long wait," she says. "How complicated is it to get a dog ready?"

"You should know by now, Li. Everything turns out to be more complicated than you think."

"Tell me about it, Dad."

"I'm sure she'll be ready for you soon," he says. But her face stays tense.

Jack looks away. A picture of Bess smiles down from the mantelpiece. Bess kneeling beside a big, dark dog. He walks over and picks it up. She's wearing the same grin she gave him on the porch, over Lila's head, a grin that looks as though she's in on something fun. As if she'd be ready to manage whatever came her way. An easy, open face. Maybe the face of someone who does something just to feel decent from time to time.

"Okay, Lila." If Bess notices Jack holding her picture, she gives no sign; and he puts it where it was. "Wally's all ready, out back. Why don't you come with me." She turns Jack's way as she walks toward Lila with an arm ready for her. "Jack, if you like, you can come out to the back porch. I'm going to take them pretty far out, where I have a path. I don't want him meeting you the first few minutes, but you can watch. Just give us a little time. There's some coffee in the kitchen. If you don't mind rummaging, feel free to find a cup. Kitchen's a mess, but milk's just where'd you'd expect, in the fridge. I'm not sure about the sugar, but it's there somewhere."

"Sounds good. I'll poke around."

Lila turns in her father's direction and he smiles, certain that he'll see her smile too, that odd exchange of expressions they so often have, that she never sees. He stands silently, waiting for the grin, waiting for the flash of humor and the line he knows will come. The joke she has to make. He can almost supply it for her, knowing her nervous patter so well. Something about being leader of the pack. Something about being top dog, maybe. Something to which he can reply, "Very funny, Lila. Now go get to work." But instead he sees her mouth relax into a child's tentative lips.

"See you in a little bit, Dad," she says, and turns away.

Bess's kitchen is small and cluttered, a far cry from the scrubbed hygienic laboratory Ann inhabits, and nothing like the near empty, seemingly unused room in which Miranda grabs bottles of liquor and microwaves frozen food for them after sex. Among Bess's things it takes him longer than he can believe to find the coffeemaker, which is full, as promised, but hidden behind bags of white and whole wheat flour, loaves of bread and mason jars of who knows what. He opens and inspects three cabinets before locating a mug. The one he chooses advertises a local folk art museum—one of the many places he's told himself he ought to see but hasn't managed to yet. Because he can't take Lila; there'd be no point. And he's promised Ann not to be seen in public with Miranda, to show her that much respect, anyway. "Just don't make a spectacle out of us. And please don't let my daughter know. That isn't asking too much, is it, Jack?"

No. No, it wasn't asking too much. He's been very careful to do as Ann asked. Lila knew nothing, he was sure, and Miranda has only seen Lila once, a few months earlier, back in the fall. Jack picked her up at the café after work and on an impulse, his impulse, they drove across town to Lila's school, just in time to watch the kids boarding the late bus for home.

"That's her," he said, pointing out his lanky daughter, curls pulled back into a messy knot. She was walking arm in arm with her best friend, Gabrielle. The blind leading the blind—personified. He was grateful to Miranda for not making the joke. "That's my Lila," he said. "The tall, pretty one in the red T-shirt."

And for some moments Miranda looked silently toward the girls. "But they're wearing the same shirt," she finally said. "In different colors."

Jack saw that she was right. Sure they were. They often were. "Yeah." He nodded and he started up the car. "On any given school day . . . One kid made a fortune selling them."

"What does it say?"

He told her.

"Funny," she said, as he pulled out into traffic.

"Yeah, funny," he repeated, some seconds later. "I guess it is."

Jack fills the art museum coffee cup, though he doesn't really want the coffee. He steps out the screen door onto a small wooden porch.

Behind the house is an open field, and twenty yards or so away there's a dirt track where Bess and Lila stand, close together. At first Jack can't see the dog, but as the two figures step apart, he finds him there. His broad, tawny back is bound by the harness, no ordinary leash, even from that distance, but the unmistakable constraints of a guide dog at work. The stiff lead is in Lila's hand and Lila looks suddenly blinder to Jack than she has for years, as though something about the image has been completed, the last piece of a puzzle snapped into place. From two dozen yards away, his daughter is visibly blind. For all the world to see. And for a moment, he stands still, snagged on the paradox of being glad that at least she can't see herself like this.

"Jesus," he says, out loud. "Jesus Christ."

Eleven years. It's been eleven years. You have to let go, Jack, Miranda would say. You have to let her go. He sits onto the steps, slowly, his hand behind him as if to be certain the wooden surface will be there, as though he is the one who must feel, to be sure. And then, without noticing, he begins sipping at the coffee he didn't want—but there's a chill in the air and the warmth feels welcome after all. Holding the cup close to his face, he watches through the rising steam. Then he reaches into his jacket pocket and pulls his glasses out, the ones he has always needed for distances but didn't wear for years and years after the accident, not until Miranda gave him holy hell for the notion that walking around in a blur would somehow help his child.

Lila begins to move, very slowly, the dog many steps ahead. Then Bess joins her, says something, and Lila stops, starts again, pulling the animal closer to her side this time. She walks another ten feet on the track, then stops. Then pulls him close, again. Every once in a while, Bess Edwards pats the dog. And after she does that a couple of times, Jack sees Lila begin to do the same thing. He watches as his daughter's face moves very close to the dog's and her hands run over his ears and nose. Her lips are moving; her head is tilted to the side. Bess Edwards take a step away from them. Soon she looks up at him and waves. Lila just keeps talking to, touching the dog.

Wally. The animal's name is Wally.

"Jack!" Bess calls out and he can almost feel himself materialize as Lila's head swivels, seeking him.

"I'm over here. I'm over here." Jack raises his arms overhead and waves as if toward his daughter, who waves back, in the right direction—more or less. "Looking good, Lila," he calls. "I like your new friend."

"Wally?" Her voice cuts through the air, banishes his invisibility, calling him back to her again. "I'm not so sure about the name," she says. "I think he's more of a Hubert, myself."

"Get to work!" Jack has his hands cupped as a bullhorn around his mouth. "You still have a lot to learn."

"Are you kidding? This is a breeze."

When Lila turns away, Jack settles back onto the step. He watches the scene, and tries to take it in. This is the creature who is to become his daughter's eyes from now on. Jack's replacement in a way, he understands. Just like Miranda said.

The dog barks, as though in response to Jack's thoughts, a deep, confident bark. This is who she must trust completely now—even when others turn out to let her down. Wally. The companion she'll have for years and years. Because her guidance counselor talked them into it. Because Ann handed him the card. Because the other phone was busy. And because Bess Edwards is a woman who thinks that we should all do something decent now and then.

"It's the best way to do adulthood," the counselor said about her own guide.

It probably is, Jack thinks. It probably would be for anyone. He looks at his watch. Just past ten. Miranda should be rolling out of bed now, sleeping late the one luxury she cares about. He thinks again about their conversation, about the way the question of his strengths was left hanging in the air.

"I can't remember his name," he said to her.

More lies.

The kid's name had been Oliver. Oliver Franklin. A skinny little boy with dark blond hair and eyes that filled with tears all too fast, that October afternoon. A little boy who cried much too easily when Jack stepped into the child's yard and found him—caught him—tossing a ball up into the air. Playing, alone. Playing with a ball. Throwing it up into the sky, and knowing how to catch it as it fell. Knowing where to put his perfect little hands and catch the falling sphere. Every goddamned time. "It might have been Bob," he said as they lay side by side. "Except I don't think it was. It was something like that, though. Something simple and harmless-seeming like that."

He'd been light as nothing, and Jack had just picked him up in his arms. Just the work of a moment, lifting him and carrying him behind the hedge. Away from any adults watching them. Away from the sight of the child's house, where the mother must have stood, fixing dinner, or maybe sat, resting for a moment in front of the TV. Away from the garage, where it had happened. Away from the wheelbarrow. The can of paint.

Shake it harder, Lila. Shake it harder.

"Is that what you said to her?" he asked, as he himself shook the boy, digging his fingers into the child's skinny frame. "Is that what you told my daughter to do?"

But his young eyes had filled up all too soon, great rivers of distorting, falling tears, his little shoulders convulsing in noisy sobs.

"Yes," he told Jack, his head flopping in a violent nod, from chest to back, chest to back. "Yes, I did. I did. I told her to. I did."

And that was that.

And there hadn't been any good from that. No good at all. There hadn't been a single moment of satisfaction to be felt. But before he took his hands off the boy, Jack had thrown him to the ground. "Little fucker," he said, as if that might somehow help. And then he walked away. Left the kid lying there. He walked past the house. Past the garage. Down the street. All of that. All of that for nothing.

Because when he got home, Lila still couldn't see.

Bess touches Lila's shoulder and they exchange a few words; then Bess begins to walk toward him. Jack shifts toward the rusted rail, making room for her.

"Lila's doing great," she says once she's close enough for a normal tone of voice. "She talks a good game, your daughter, but she's a good listener too." As she sits in the space beside him, a clean soapy smell drifts his way, and he notices a slight haze of freckles across her cheeks and nose. "She's a nice kid," Bess says. "She asked me how I was going to feel letting Wally go, asked me how I keep from getting too attached. Not every kid thinks in those terms."

"I was wondering that myself. How do you?" Jack is half watching her, half watching his daughter on the field.

"Well, to be perfectly honest, I don't." As she speaks she smooths tiny wrinkles from her jeans. Her hands are broad. A silver ring glistens on her index finger. "I miss the dogs pretty badly when they go. Then, eventually, I get another and start all over. And that helps, I suppose."

"Did you tell Lila that?"

"I told her something like that." Her hands settle on her knees. "With a little less emphasis on the sad part. I don't want her feeling bad." Jack doesn't know what to say, but then Bess picks up again. "She tells me you and her mother are having a hard time thinking about her taking off for school on her own next year. That's understandable. She's quite a girl."

"Oh, I don't know. I think all parents probably—"

"She told me something else, too." She's turned away a little from him now, so Jack can't see her eyes. "She told me you weren't entirely truthful about your wife."

"Huh." He looks out toward Lila, kneeling now in her denim skirt, patting the dog along his flank. "Huh," he says again. "She told you that, did she?"

"You'd be amazed how many people are terrified of dogs." Bess is smiling a little at him again, but he can't quite smile back. "I deal with it all the time, Jack."

"I don't . . ." He can't come up with very much more. "I guess that's right. I guess a lot of people are."

"Your daughter's exact phrase was 'I don't know why my dad was so bizarre about this. As if it were leprosy or something.' "

Jack smiles at Bess's imitation, in spite of himself. Pitch-perfect. He looks down toward his shoes. "That sounds like my girl," he says. "And I'm sorry about the bluff. I don't know why I did that. Really, in all honesty I can't imagine why."

And he can't. There is no real why. Just a further symptom of how messy everything's become. Ann's fears: a symptom. His habitual lies: another symptom.

Bess shrugs. "It doesn't matter, Jack. I'm not pegging you as some kind of criminal because you covered something up." She smooths the fabric along her legs again. All the little wrinkles. All the little disturbances. "It probably just felt private to you, which is fine. But I do need to be a little clinical about all this. Something like a doctor, I suppose." She turns to face him. "I really need to understand Lila's home life—really understand it. If your wife has a dog phobia, even if it's just a minor problem, we'll deal with that. I just have to know about it." He notices her small, off-white teeth that have never been fixed, a little crooked, a little buck. "We can work around just about anything—I just have to know the truth about what I'm sending Wally into. Wally, and Lila too. They have to trust each other. Which really means that we have to, right?"

As he nods, Jack's chest rises and falls in a sigh. He's probably already broken some aspect of Bess Edwards's personal code of decency, he understands. She's trying to be kind, but for a moment, sitting there, he's oppressed by his sense of the bad impression he must already have made. He looks out to Lila, still kneeling in the dirt, her feet sticking out from her long denim skirt, her face right up against the dog's. Never lie to her. Never lose her trust. Maybe that would be an easier mandate for an animal to follow.

"Listen, Bess," he begins. "Lila doesn't know every-thing." Jack closes then opens his eyes. "There's a lot more to our home life than her mother's fear of dogs." He leans over and picks up a small stick. "My wife and I are separat-ing, after Lila goes away to school. It's all been decided. I'm planning on moving out."

As the words come out, something else occurs to him. This woman whom he barely knows is the first person he's been honest with about this. Other than Ann. Even Mi-randa doesn't know how concrete these plans are. "We haven't said anything to her yet." Jack shakes his head. "We've had to give our daughter an awful lot of bad news in her life. I guess I just haven't been able to face doing this. Pretty cowardly, right?" Bess's eyes give no reaction he can read, and for just a second, he thinks of adding something more. Something about how Ann has told him he's the one who has to tell Lila, because he's the one who first gave up on them. Because he's the guy who wants out. The guy who can't keep himself from seeking something resembling pleasure somewhere else. That all he can think of when he imagines breaking this news to his daughter is that other terrible conversation. The one he had with her when she was six. The one in which it felt as though with every word, he personally, Jack Snyder, was robbing his own child of any hope. Bess's eyes are so open to him and so kind, he can easily imagine trying to explain it all to her. Trying to de-fend his decision to leave. To betray. To run away. Going into the petty, the hurtful, the heavy drag down into failure that has brought their marriage to this end. He can feel this desire to confess and then plead his own case swell like a powerful wind gusting somewhere deep inside his chest.

But he stops himself. Closes himself tight against the urge, and for a time, Bess gives no response at all. Just looks away a little from his gaze, and gradually it becomes the kind of moment when the sounds that were there all along are audible, anew. Cars passing by on the distant road. Birds calling out to one another; birds calling back. A plane overhead.

"Actually, Jack," Bess says finally, looking down, "Lila already told me that too."

And with just a quick hand to his shoulder, she stands and walks away.

The first few months of Lila's life, she hollered as if indignant at having been born, maybe as if she saw the injury to come. He so envied Ann back then, the way she could slip her breast into the baby's mouth, the way Lila would settle, the way Ann could know who she was to her. For all those miraculous months, that was what injustice seemed to be, his wife having that, when he did not.

Out on the path now, Lila and Wally are walking around and around and around. There's a moment every time when it looks as though they're heading toward him, but then they stay with the curve, Lila's arm straightened by the unaccustomed pull of the lead. It takes Jack a while to realize she must have lost track anyway, that she can't know where the circle starts or ends, when a full rotation is complete, can't know whether she's facing him or facing away.

He takes his glasses off so that out among the distant blur of green, Lila and Wally are just another distant blur.

Staring at them, at nothing, he can remember how much

it felt like exile those first few months, how he seemed to be invisible to her all that year, how this new, keen, devastating love seemed to bring nothing so much as isolation. And how that changed one night when Lila was crying out, not crying, but yelling for help, for comfort. Maybe it was a tooth, maybe a terrible dream. Ann was either sleeping or pretending to be, so he went in. He found his daughter standing up, just a shape in the nightlight dusk, all her weight thrown against the rail, hollering into the night. He held his arm out, next to hers, and with his other hand he moved her grip so she was latched onto him. He remembers now exactly how she looked as his eyes adjusted to the dark and her little face emerged, curious, trusting, beautiful, as though she were a candle burning through the night.

Just hang on, Lila, he told her then, and she smiled at him, she seemed to understand. Just don't let go.

If I
Loved
You

I.

IF I LOVED YOU, I would tell you this:

I would tell you that for all you know I have cancer. And that is why you should be kind to me. I would tell you that for all you know I have cancer that has spread into my liver and my bones and that now I understand there is no hope. If I loved you, I would say: you shouldn't be so hard on us. On me and on Sam.

Because it may not even be just the cancer.

For all you know we have a brain-damaged son living in an inadequate institution thirty miles from our house. For all you know, we agonized one long, cold winter night six years ago over whether to send him there. But then, broken, exhausted, we finally stood together in our kitchen, staring hard at each other, both of us the worse for scotch, and just knew, just then, at the exact same moment, that we couldn't manage him at home any longer. Not with him so big I couldn't bathe him by myself. Not with him so strong. Not with me just diagnosed and in for my second round of chemo.

There's so much you don't know.

For all you know I have three, maybe four months to live and Sam is up every night trying to figure out how he's going to break it to our brain-damaged son that I won't be coming to visit anymore. And I'm lying right there next to him, hour after hour, trying not to think about the possibility that our boy will be angry at me for this. Or maybe worse, maybe better, that he won't even notice that I'm gone.

You want to build a fence between our homes.

It will be wood, you tell us.

You're tall, and you're young, and you paid a lot of money for that enormous house next to ours. It will be solid wood, you say, with no space or light between the slats. And it will be six feet high and run along the property line you had surveyed just this week.

Understand, you say, I didn't ask the surveyors to add land to my land. It just turns out that the line's much closer to your house than anyone thought. I was every bit as surprised as you.

And for a moment all three of us, you, me, and Sam, stare down at the pachysandra-covered ground.

But if you build a six-foot-tall solid wall, I say, if you build it right where the pink flags are, I won't be able to open my car door. Not without banging into your fence. Not within twenty feet of my front door, anyway. I'll have to park at least twenty feet from my door.

You only nod.

Sam walks along the line, from flag to flag, then says, You're telling me those hemlocks belong to you? You're saying they're not ours?

It turns out they're on my land.

We've been paying to have them sprayed for years, I say. It's been sixteen years. The whole time we've lived here. We thought they were ours.

You say nothing. Sam says nothing.

Why six feet tall? I finally ask. It seems awfully high. It's so close to our house. We'll just see a wall every time we come outside. We're used to looking at the hemlocks. We've always had a view. Maybe they don't belong to us, but we'll feel like we're walled in.

We will be walled in, Sam says.

I need it that tall because I'm going to get an animal. An animal could jump over a lower fence.

We've been staring at these trees for sixteen years, I say. It's going to be a big change. But that isn't the real problem. The real problem is that we won't be able to park in front of our house.

You nod. And then you hand me a letter. Our full names are typed on the envelope—complete with our middle initials. You've been looking through public records. You are doing this by the book. This is no friendly note held in my hand. It's a document.

Here is the part I go over in my head:

When I think about you buying the house, having the land surveyed, finding the property line just about in your neighbors' driveway, telling them you're going to build a wall, a solid wall, right there; this is the part that I still don't understand.

You know nothing about the reasons it might matter to us to be able to park right in front of our door.

For example, in the cancer scenario, I'll grow weak. That's inevitable. Walking twenty feet will feel like a mile to me. Maybe I could do it, make the walk from the car, if we were just a foot or two from the house. But all the way down the drive, all the way from where there's room to open the door, that's just too far.

So Sam is going to have to take out the folding wheel-chair from the back. And wheel me up the drive. And then help me out from the chair and then, when he's settled me in the house, he'll have to wheel the chair, empty now, back down the drive to the car. And every time he does this he'll suffer. Every time, his heart will break. Because one day soon, he knows, the chair will be empty for real.

But back inside the house he tries to make me laugh—by imitating you. We're going to get an animal, he says. An animal! A hippopotamus, in fact.

What's the deal, I ask, with a man who can't just say *dog*?

And then Sam says, Just don't set a foot onto my land. My land, my land, he says in a Scarlett O'Hara voice, his fist raised in the air. And I try to laugh—for Sam. But eventually I have to raise the question of whether it's time for us to tell our son. Because I can feel that there are only three or four more visits left in me. Power is running from my legs like sand down an hourglass. Do we tell Todd in advance? Or will I just be gone one day?

We hire a lawyer.

I don't want to, but your letter quotes township statutes and talks about your rights as a landowner. It's just possible, Sam says, that we have rights too. He looks so worn and haggard as he speaks. He looks as though this is one thing too many. I say, Go ahead, hon. Hire a lawyer. Let somebody else take this on.

Our lawyer sends you a letter. It says that we want you to hold up on construction while we investigate the situation. We want you to give us a chance to see if there's any way around this. The phrase *adverse possession* appears in the second paragraph. We also send you a handwritten note, behind our lawyer's back, saying we don't want this to be a legal fight. Please. We just want you to let us open our car door in front of our house—as a courtesy. We only hired a lawyer because you gave us that document, you made it seem so official. We felt we had to do everything we could.

Your response comes hand-delivered, overnight.

"I have every right to erect a fence on my own property."

It says a bit more. But not much.

There's a conversation that hasn't been had, I tell Sam. The conversation human beings have with each other. He isn't quite treating us like people.

He isn't quite a person, Sam says. He's a creature. He's an animal himself. He's like a yeti or something.

He is! He looks exactly like a yeti. That scowl on his face. The way he stomps around his land. It's inspired, I say. He's the yeti.

And that is what we call you after that.

I suppose it's this ability of yours not to care that intrigues me so.

If I loved you, I would tell how much you're missing because of that. I would find ways to convince you that I exist. I would resist erasure every moment that I could.

For several weeks the letters fly back and forth.

You're amazed that we think we have any rights.

We're amazed that you think rights are what's at issue here.

Sam says he's going to paint a bright red stripe on our side of the line. It'll be wet paint, he says. I'll put it down on the day they're building the fence. So if they set a foot on our property . . . if they set even one foot on our property . . .

I'll sit out there with a shotgun, I say. First one of them steps in red paint loses a leg . . .

I want to scold you in the harsh, caressing tones of a mother to a child. I want to help you, make you understand more about the ways things *should* be than you do, make you think more, give you some imagination. I want you to imagine that I have a life. A life that matters. You should care about my life.

Sam stares out the kitchen window every night when he comes home from work.

I'll miss the trees, he says. I really will.

I don't give an answer.

Why make matters worse?

Another possibility is that Sam is in danger of losing his job.

What if I have cancer, our son is out there in the institution, and, because the boy and I take up so much time, Sam is having trouble putting the hours in at work? They've tried to be patient with him, they know the situation, but the irony is it's dragging on for too long. If I'd died six months ago instead of four months from now, there might not be a problem. They're good guys. They do care. But this is too much.

The fence goes up on a day when we're out.

And you have no idea where we've been.

If I loved you, I would invite you in, sit you down in our kitchen, and I would say to you: You just never know. You, the yeti. You don't know why this matters so much to us, why we care. You don't know what secret pains we have that we haven't shared with you. You don't know us.

But then I would have to admit that I don't know everything either, wouldn't I? Like I don't know why it matters so much to you to build that fence exactly there.

What happened in your life that makes a property line mean so much?

Why do you think you should get what is your right?

You're so uncaring, so unreasonable. It must be a defense mechanism of some kind. I'm sure that it is.

But Sam says that's ridiculous of me. Even to think about you that way.

It's late at night and neither one of us can sleep. I say to him, I'm sure that the yeti must have been hurt. Very badly. At some point in his life he must have been very badly hurt. Or he'd understand our side. No one can care so little about other people unless they've been very badly hurt.

Not necessarily, Sam tells me. Maybe the problem is he's never been hurt. He can't imagine real pain because he's never experienced it.

I can feel his hand reach across the bed for my arm.

Or maybe some folks are just bad.

He wraps his fingers around my wrist.

Maybe some folks are just bad.

My poor sleepless husband.

He says that to me twice.

II.

On the day of the mammogram I was more worried about the technician seeing all the bruises on my arms than about the results. You'll be lucky, I told Sam, if they don't come and arrest you for wife abuse.

I hate to see you look like that.

I was standing in just a bra and panties. The bruises were all different colors, the newest ones purple, the oldest turning yellow. It's not so bad, I said. He doesn't mean it. He doesn't know he's hurting me.

I know he doesn't mean it. I'm not angry at him—you know that. I just hate to see you this way.

It's nothing big, I said. He gets upset. He can't talk to us, so he lashes out.

But I understood that the words were pointless, just filling the air between us with sound. There was nothing I knew that Sam didn't know. There was only this ritual of repeating back and forth what we both already knew.

We kissed in the door and I watched him pull out his car—just behind mine in the driveway. He didn't wish me luck and it never occurred to me that he should.

So, first there was the mammogram, at which I stood with my breasts and my mottled arms exposed. As the technician squeezed my flesh into position I mumbled something about having fallen off my bike. I bruise very easily, I said. Not: My son had a stroke while in utero and is severely brain-damaged. He isn't a bad boy at all, but he has these moments of violence and these are the results.

Not that.

Then came the letter ordering me back for more tests, an ultrasound, the biopsy, the meeting in my doctor's office— this time Sam right there by my side. And through all of this, about three weeks, right up until the surgery, all I could think about was Todd. Not even what would happen to him if I died—I couldn't die, that was out of the question, not on the table for discussion—but little things like who would watch him while I went in for the biopsy, and could I possibly take him to the doctor's office with me and have him there in the room.

It used to seem so simple: you're young, you go through school, you fall in love, you marry, you get pregnant. And then the road takes a certain kind of curve. Your sense of self can disappear.

Todd: cannot speak, cannot walk, barely hears, is blind in one eye. Cannot control his bladder or his bowels. Does he know us? It's never been clear. Until now, I'd always hoped that he did. I'd always hoped that it gave him some kind of comfort to have me and have Sam there with him. But now I'm not so sure that I want that anymore. Now I find myself hoping sometimes he never really knew who I was.

Now, my yeti, I find myself hoping he may be like you. And so won't ever miss me when I'm gone.

There was spread into the lymph nodes. One doctor spoke about saving the breasts and I said, Just do whatever will make this stop. I don't give a shit about my breasts.

New questions arise:

Just how many fifths of scotch were the two of us going through every week?

We tried not to count them in the recycling bin. And eventually we began to throw a couple of bottles into the garbage cans instead, split them up. Maybe Sam would take a bottle or two in the car and dump them somewhere else. It's almost funny.

We were drunk the night we realized Todd would have to be moved. *In vino veritas.* In whiskey are decisions born.

Is this the brave thing to do or the coward's way out?

Sam said, I don't know, honey. I just know it's what has to happen to now. And so do you.

Lawrence House. It's a low-lying building filled with heart-breaks, amongst whom my son looks like part of a crowd. And people like me and like Sam pass one another with guilty looks on our faces. The first year, I went to see him just when I was well enough. The second year, there was no sign of spread. I was off chemo and I went almost every day.

Maybe we could bring him home, I said to Sam. We managed before and I'm feeling fine now. He could come back.

Sam's voice was quiet. He said, I don't know if that's something we should do. Remember how the two of you used to struggle? You were covered with bruises, Ruth. You couldn't handle him at all.

Well, let's think about it anyway. Let's just not say that we won't.

Okay. If you want. We won't say that we won't.

Sam deals the cards, counting quietly to himself. We've kept the same deck beside Todd's bed for all these years.

Fives? I ask.

Go fish.

So I draw from the pile.

No, I say. Not a five. It's your turn.

I look over at our boy. He is staring somewhere else.

My son is eighteen years old. His head is covered with thick black curls like my own used to be and his eyes are the same bright blue as Sam's. He would have been a very handsome man. He would have been something wonderful, I'm convinced. But for the travels of a blood clot to his brain, while he burrowed small and silenced in my womb.

III.

It's been two months now since your six-foot fence went up. Two months, more or less. From my bed, I can hear your children playing on the other side. Sometimes I turn the television up louder just to drown them out. It's a terrible thing to feel yourself hate a child.

Sam didn't want to go to work today but I argued him out through the door.

Nothing will be improved by you losing your job, I said.

He drives my car these days. It was always the more dependable one. It's parked down the drive, near the street, of course—thanks to you. His is stowed in our garage. He argued when I first told him he should take my keys. We went through the game of my telling him not to be silly; it would just be until I felt stronger. It wasn't a big decision at all. Stop being ridiculous, I said. You look like you're murdering me. It's just the better car. You should use it while I can't. I'll be taking it back soon enough.

And so he gave in.

I know that you go to work a little after he leaves—I hear your car door, the ignition. I know the hours you keep, can predict when you'll come home. And I know you have a wife. A friend who visits me, brings us food, brings me gossip, has told me that your wife is very pretty, slender and naturally blond, in her thirties. She stands on the corner in the mornings and puts your daughter on the bus. Then an older woman comes in and watches your little boy, while your wife keeps herself busy, though no one in the neighborhood knows exactly what she does.

There are speculations about you. The new family on the block. There are rumors that you're putting in a pool. But winter is coming now, I know, and it isn't the right time. Maybe in April, when the world has thawed again so the ground will be soft enough to dig.

Sam drives out alone to Lawrence House now, every two or three days.

My last trip was two weeks ago. I said my goodbyes in silence, the language of my motherhood. There were other periods when I wasn't there. There's no way to explain to my child that this is different. And probably no reason that we should, though I still carry this awful fear that he'll think, in whatever way he thinks, that I have given up on him.

I held his heavy head one last time, pulled it gently to my chest, no longer soft.

That day, in the car driving home, Sam was unusually talkative, telling me stories about a new coworker, and then about an old friend. Both of them had done hilarious things—as though everyone Sam knew had taken on an antic side, every situation holding a fistful of punch lines.

And it was funny, genuinely funny. I laughed out loud as he drove us both home.

I don't drink anymore. I lost the craving. But Sam brings the bottle upstairs now and he sits by the bed. Sometimes we watch television. Sometimes we just talk. He pours freely for himself on the understanding that I'm not keeping track. I pick through our lives, recounting good moments, like looking for treasures at the flea market. He listens, sometimes even smiles.

I know you must have heard by now that I'm sick. It's that kind of town, that kind of neighborhood. Our story: the boy who was born so damaged, the mother who won't make it to the spring, it's all well known. We're the kind of family people talk about.

Sam phones me from the office to let me know he'll be late because he's visiting the boy. I tell him that's just as well. I'm feeling tired. But by the time he gets home, I say, I'll be awake.

I say it, but who really knows?

The clock has lost its meaning. My relationship with time is more personal now.

Just take care of yourself, he says. I hate to have you there, alone.

I'll just take a nap.

Just don't go on the stairs.

I won't go on the stairs. I won't even go to the bathroom. I won't get up. I'll just rest.

Just take care.

Just.

It's a word we use a lot now—though in only one way that we might. As though we have lost our knowledge of the other meaning.

Just be careful. I'll just do this tiny thing. Just move my pillows a little higher up. Just don't worry. Just be good to yourself. Just take care.

If you'd just moved the damned fence just a foot . . .

It was the little note of grace that we both needed then.

I sometimes think that when I'm gone Sam will drive his car right into your well-constructed fence. I can picture it so easily: Sam behind the wheel pulling up into the drive, gunning it; and veering left. If the tables were turned, there's no doubt it's what I'd do.

Because who is there left to be angry at? Except you? We used up all the other obvious candidates long ago.

When he gets home, Sam climbs heavily to our room, the whiskey bottle and a glass in his hand. I have been dozing, but am now awake.

I hope he feels bad about what he did, he says.

If he were the type to feel bad, I say, speaking slowly, he

wouldn't have done it in the first place. If he cared a tiny bit about us and our lives he wouldn't have acted as he did. He's indifferent to us. It had all been decided before we met. There was never any hope.

I don't tell him about these now-fading fantasies of mine. The ones that started early on. About trying to reason with you. Trying to make you believe in my life. The simple fact of my existence. I don't tell him that.

I am so close now to being entirely erased. I see things that were invisible to me before.

Sam sits there, and he drinks, a flush beginning to spread through his cheeks.

He's indifferent? he asks. Is that really what it is?

There is a universe of sorrow, wide and dark, in my husband's staring eyes. An eternity built there, constructed over time, forged gradually of the realization that this is in fact our lives. This is what we have been dealt.

It's possible, I say to him, that you were right. What you said about some folks just being bad.

But as I speak, I realize how little I want to say what I have learned. How reluctant I am to admit to Sam what indifference truly means, and has long meant to us both. I do not want to play a role in confirming that cruel universe that dwells inside my husband's eyes. But I do love him. I do. I love him very much. And so to him—if not to you— I speak the truth.

Immortalizing
John Parker

It isn't a new sensation. For the past many weeks, Clara Feinberg has found it harder and harder to paint human faces, her bread-and-butter task. Increasingly, she is struggling with what feels to her like a repugnance to the act. Though it's all very sophomoric. Her own thoughts on the subject sound to her like the voices of pretentious but earnest youngsters debating the meaning of life.

It's morning—again—and Clara is perched on the side of her bed, as though undecided about whether to stand or lie back down. Her hands grip the edge of the mattress, maybe to push her up and maybe to hold her there. She can see herself in the dresser mirror—if she lets her eyes drift that way. It's not her favorite sight, not normally of particular interest to her. As drawn as she is to study others' faces, she would be perfectly happy to go through life without ever seeing her own. Not because of anything amiss about her appearance. For a seventy-year-old woman, she looks better than well, straight and a bit stern and more handsome than ever. Age suits her. But she knows too well what a face can reveal.

As a child, if she caught a glimpse of herself when alone, she would stick out her tongue; and to her own surprise, she does it now. It's an odd sight. An old woman making the face of a spiteful little girl. An oddly upsetting sight. She closes her lips and looks away, looks down to her feet, hanging bare and gnarled just above the floor. She still can't quite force herself to stand. Not yet. Can't quite force herself to dress, to leave the apartment, to walk among the living. Go to work, step into her studio. Smell the paint, the turpentine. Populate the blank canvases waiting there with her people, her creations.

The prospect pins her where she is.

It isn't that she has tired of studying faces. Not at all. How could she have? She still thinks daily about how it felt thirty years ago, how like learning a precious secret it had been when she first discovered her longing to sit for hours and ponder another person's features, to study their very particular texture. It was as though she had found a hidden primal drive in herself, something to align itself with hunger, thirst, sexual desire, the instinct to stay alive. And this drive has never flagged.

But the paintings themselves upset her now. The act of painting them upsets her now.

She forces her eyes to her own image again, holds her face steady, drains it of what expression she can. It's this same eerie stillness she detects in her portraits now. A kind of death. Death, which used to seem so remote, now feels to Clara as though it is everywhere, like the universally disliked relative who arrives early to every gathering and shows no discernible sign of ever going home. She can sense it turning her against her own work, lurking in the notion of permanence surrounding portraiture, skulking around the very idea of catching a person at one moment and documenting them, just then. This is what death does, she thinks, stony-faced, staring right into her own eyes. Catches us all. Stops time.

"Pull yourself together," she says out loud. "You still have a living to make."

And finally, that gets Clara to her feet. She is paid preposterously well for those paintings of hers; and so this recent repugnance must be overcome; and the day, the new clients, must be faced.

As if revealing a precious secret, Katherine Parker states that she and her husband—John—have been married for fifty-one years. Not that Clara has asked. She's asked them very little since they entered the small sitting room adjacent to her studio. And when told how long they've been married, she doesn't offer up much of a reaction. Divorced herself for nearly three decades, she can think of too many reasons, good, bad, and indifferent, why people might stay married half a century to assume that she knows the appropriate response.

"We didn't make very much of our fiftieth. But then when this one came around, I realized I would like to have a portrait of John. That's the gift I want. John, immortalized."

Katherine Parker is a small woman, with suprisingly short hair, entirely white. The wrinkles that web her pouching cheeks run without a break or variation across her pale lips, as though a veil of lace has been etched into her face. When she speaks, her eyes blink rapidly, seeming to seek refocus every time. And the truth is, Clara realizes, she would rather paint her than him. It might be interesting to try to capture this topography of time and the sense of urgency that seems integral to her.

"Not of you both?" she asks.

"Oh, no. I had mine done years ago. I'd much rather be remembered that way. Young, and elegant. Not like this."

Clara nods, skipping over her own arguments with this view. The point, it turns out, isn't youth or beauty. The point is happiness. And to the extent that happiness ever came to her, it came to her late.

She looks over at John Parker on the sofa beside his wife. He hasn't spoken at all. Not a single word. Nor is his face particularly expressive. His skin has an odd smoothness to it, a yellow tinge; his eyes are round, brown, and moist.

He's dull, she thinks, that word stepping out of line, as if louder, bolder than the others in her thoughts. Sitting there, Clara recognizes this as something with which she'll now have to contend. Often, with her subjects, there's a first impression that dominates her ability to see clearly. And here is one, again. This quality of dullness she perceives will have to be continually questioned and examined. In the end she may conclude that it does define him in some way that deserves expression in the work. Or she may not. But for as long as she is painting him, she knows, she will be in a continual dialogue with this word. *Dull.*

"Do you want your portrait painted?" she asks and he startles a bit. Then looks over at his wife. Then he nods.

"Yes," he says.

Clara sits back in her chair and begins to describe the process. How many sessions; how much time she'll need; how much warning if a session is to be missed. And then she names a very high figure, to which neither of them reacts.

"And I'll need to see you alone," she says to him, sensing in herself an annoyance with his silence.

"Oh." It's a small sound that Katherine Parker makes, but an expressive one, an objection. "Is that necessary?"

"Yes, it is," Clara says. She could go into an explanation— she could talk about the relationship between subject and artist, she could talk about any number of things that might justify this, some real, some made up. But she prefers simply to state the condition and not discuss her reasoning. Too much in her life has had to be justified.

"Well, then," Katherine Parker says. "Then I suppose that's what we'll do."

They have only the scheduling left. This is Monday. They'll begin on Wednesday. As the Parkers leave, each shakes Clara's hand, and the wife declares herself so excited, so grateful that Clara has time for this. It's a gift she's giving herself, she says. She rarely does that. But this one is different. This will be something very special.

. . .

IF GEORGE COOPERMAN could tell this story, he would doubtless start with a description of those portraits Clara paints. A psychoanalyst, he would sneak up on the events by walking through an exhaustive analysis of her work, which would lead naturally for him into an exhaustive analysis of her character. She paints like *this,* he would say, she invariably sees other people in *this* particular light. It doesn't matter who they are. The portraits all share these characteristics. And you see, he would say, you understand, that is because she herself is *this* kind of woman. Her work is consistent with who she is. It is the key to who she is. It explains everything that she has ever done. That is how George Cooperman would start.

If Harold Feinberg were telling this story, he would unlikely make much mention of Clara's work, largely because he's never really thought all that much about it, not the work itself, not the way she sees and re-creates the people whom she paints. And also, he still resents the work a bit, still smarts at the way it seemed to make her happier than he ever did. So, Harold would doubtless talk first about the early days of their marriage. He would say that in the beginning she had seemed very intent on having what he thought of then as a proper home. It was 1966, he would say, and things were just beginning to loosen up; but not Clara. Not then. She had her trusty copy of *The Settlement Cook Book* out and opened every night. She had her hair done once a week, so it looked more like a wig than like hair. And whatever happened afterward, whatever she later felt or said, she had wanted the children, wanted them as soon as she and Harold were wed.

Oh, and the sex with her—if he'd had a couple of drinks, and odds are he would have, he would go into this—the sex with her was efficient and somewhat businesslike, but not prudish. He'd been with a few prudish women in his time, and that was never her. But there was an element of practicality to the act that always left him a little unsatisfied. It was all a little too hygienic for his taste. And then he would say that maybe that had something to do with what got into him back in the seventies. All of that infamous cheating he did. He was just looking for something a little more exciting. Not that that was any kind of excuse. Just the truth. He was bored.

But the funny thing is, he would say, the thing he has thought about a lot, is that he probably wouldn't have been bored by the woman she became—after everything blew up. That was when she went a little wild. And of course that was when she started in with the painting seriously. That was when he would come by the house to pick up the children and see her in overalls and a man's undershirt, braless as far as he could tell, bits of paint clinging to hair. Something changed in her, he would say. Something changed, and it wasn't for the worse. Once or twice he even asked her if she would consider trying to make a go of it again, but the answer was always no. It wasn't an unusual story, he would say. At least not in the beginning. Boy meets girl. Boy cats around. Boy loses girl.

In Clara's mind, the story begins in January 1979 with George Cooperman giving her a lift to pick up her car. It begins with the odd realization that she might as well be sitting in the front seat of her own Volvo station wagon rather than his, that the cars are identical inside. Though she remembers then that in her own car she wouldn't be in the passenger seat, not anymore, because since the separation in November, she has always been the driver and never the passenger when in her own car. This is where she used to sit when she was married to Harold.

It starts then for her with this odd mixture of familiarity and unfamiliarity, with a chain of thoughts set off by a particular shade of beige, and by the sensation of being back on the passenger side of a vehicle—riding shotgun, in the dead man's seat, the wife's place—and by the oddness of it being George Cooperman and not Harold at the wheel of the car, beside her, driving to the garage where she has had snow tires put on her car, though it's probably silly this late in the season, another chore that got lost in the mess of the marital collapse.

It starts there, and then it shifts very quickly into discomfort, the scene being *almost* something she knows so intimately. It's that unbidden intimacy that slips in and unsettles her. George has pulled into the wide oil-stained drive outside the garage and they are facing each other to say goodbye. She notices the precise shade of brown of his eyes. She sees how his upper lip is so much thinner than the lower. She understands exactly how she would paint that lip. Having known him for so many years, she is learning too much about him, in only seconds. As though she is seeing him for the first time now.

She hears herself mention Janet's name. *I'll call Janet in the morning,* she says. And he says, *I'll let her know.* And as he speaks, she notices the different tones of darkness in his mouth. He asks her if she wants him to wait and be sure her car is ready, just to be certain she won't be left here alone in this sketchy part of town. But she says that she's already called and checked. The car is ready. She says, *Thank you, though* and opens her door and feels the coldness of the air outside. *Here,* he says, reaching over. *Don't forget this.* And he hands her the pocketbook she's left in the car.

. . .

As CLARA MAKES her way down Locust Street, after meeting the Parkers, she thinks glumly about the husband, John, about his silence and his evocation of that word *dull*. The truth is, she isn't relishing the job. He doesn't seem like a very interesting subject, to her. But then maybe nobody would at this time.

It's a familiar route from the studio home, one she can walk with her mind entirely occupied, one she suspects she could walk in her sleep. Clara has lived for well over twenty years in her town house off Rittenhouse Square. After the children moved out to college, first Daniel, then Ellie, she spent a few years on her own in the big house out in Bryn Mawr. But it never felt like her own home, even then. It belonged to them all, to Clara, Harold, Daniel, and Ellie; to them and to the way their lives had unfolded there, intricately wound together, then pulled apart, in small and larger ways.

Family life. Looking back, it seems like a dance, a four-person minuet comprised of steps toward and steps away, approaches and retreats, ending, finally, with each of them standing entirely alone. By the time she was the sole occupant, the big, cold fieldstone house was more museum than home to her. Even the rooms themselves bore names that no longer applied. Harold's study. The playroom. The au pair's bathroom. Phrases, like old photographs, offering remnants of a different time, relics and evidence.

When she left, she took almost nothing. The children could have whatever they wanted. Goodwill could have the rest. A few boxes of papers, albums, some keepsakes from her own childhood, her mother's candlesticks, her father's pocketknife. Her own paintings, of course. Even the ones she no longer liked. That was all. It didn't occur to her until after the move, everything long gone, that she might have offered Harold a pick at what he wanted. But when it did occur to her, the thought came without regret. Harold wasn't her problem anymore.

The Bryn Mawr house had been done up in a somber, traditional style, the new bride following the old rules. But Clara drenched the place on Spruce Street with color, so it was giddy with color, as though all that mattered was a sensation of abundance. Too much. Too bright. It hardly looked like the home of a well-respected artist. Certainly not of the creator of the careful, muted portraits for which Clara was becoming known. No. It looked more like the set of a children's television show.

"God, it's like a paint store threw up," Ellie said the first time she visited, and then apologized. "I shouldn't have said that. I just don't think I'd be able to sleep in this. That's all I meant."

"To each her own," Clara said. "It doesn't really matter what anyone else thinks. I find it cheers me up."

But now, as she enters her home, Clara herself finds all that imposed cheerfulness jarring. She stands still in her doorway for a few moments—as though there's an obvious next move to make and she just can't remember what it is. This is a familiar sensation, since George's death. She waits and nothing comes to mind. Nothing ever comes to mind. It is the sensation of absence, she knows, disguised as an impulse to act. There isn't a damned thing to do, except see it for the trick it is.

She hasn't eaten all day, and decides to make herself a tuna sandwich—the perfect, semiconscious kind of task. The body moving almost on its own. Bread in the toaster. Can opener from the drawer. Simple, simple, simple. Drain the tuna of its water in the sink. Take out a bowl. Find the mayonnaise, and check the expiration date. Unscrew the lid. Look for a lemon, and throw out the decidedly shriveled one in the fridge. Just enough thought required. The brain occupied, but not challenged in any real sense.

This is the best way to get through these days, she knows. Stay active. But not too active. Stay busy. But not frenetic. She is familiar with the routine. George Cooperman, old friend, lover too, isn't her first loss. Not by any means. This isn't even the first time she's lost George Cooperman, though now, of course, he can't come back. Still, she well understands that grief must take her as its plaything for a while—like a kitten with a mouse. A hopeless matchup.

Clara Feinberg doesn't believe in God; she never has. She believes in time. Omnipotent, surely. Friend and foe both, as deities of all religions seem to be. Determining everything about one's life, from the sudden absence of a man like George to the expiration date on a jar of mayonnaise. For now, time will be an ally of a kind, she knows. At the very least, it will soon take care of this sense of disbelief, this punch to the gut when she thinks of George and remembers again that he's died. Given time, she knows, that will fade. A day, a day, another day, another day, and soon, she'll be used to the idea. She won't like it, but at least she will know it without having to keep remembering again.

She slices the sandwich from corner to corner, and corner to corner again, four triangles on the plate; then she brings it into the other room, over to the window, and she stares outside. Snow is falling, the first snowfall of the season, not yet sticking on the ground. It isn't quite dark, but it will be soon.

She's always loved this time of day. George also loved this time of day. Some of their best hours together had been passed sitting in this room, her living room, both of them reading, waiting for the sun to drop from view, the daylight to fade, staying there, in that early darkness together, not switching on a lamp, not yet. Tacitly agreeing to fight the evening off. Fight every ending off. Live within all transitions for every possible second. But then, as true darkness fell, they would be forced to look up from their books, forced into conversation, into each other's company.

It had all been a great big tease, she understands now. Fighting off the moment of conversation had been like fighting off an orgasm, the delay designed to increase the pleasure.

A streetlight comes on. Clara waits to see how long it will take another to join it. A minute passes, two minutes. Nothing. They must have different levels of sensitivity, she thinks. They must believe different things about what darkness is.

When she leans back against the window glass, she feels the cold there and also the heat of the radiator below, on her thighs, on her rear. At this moment, there is a perfect absence of consensus in the world. The streetlights busily debating among themselves over definitions of night and day, while these parts of her own home argue over whether she should be warmed or chilled.

It's close to ludicrous, of course. Imagining *things* in conversation. Things having arguments. But it's true that she sees the world around her as animated—spirited. Nothing truly dead. Nothing truly dead, except the dead.

. . .

ARGUABLY, IT BEGAN when Clara kept the Coopermans in the divorce. The house, the car, the dog, the children—for the most part—and the Coopermans, who said there was no real decision to be made. Not after what Harold had done to her. He was no great loss to them.

Janet had been particularly vehement on the subject. She called him a cad and a scoundrel and a bounder. She swore that she would never speak to him again, unless of course it was to tell him what she thought. Clara, listening in their living room, sipping none too judiciously at her scotch, had found herself irritated by the vocabulary with which Janet dispensed her loyalty. Janet sounded to her as though she had stepped out of some drawing room comedy.

Harold was not a *bounder*. Harold was not a *cad*.

"He's an asshole," Clara said. "He's a prick."

It had felt important to her at the time. This wasn't some dinner-theater Noël Coward production, for God's sake; this was her actual life. It deserved a coarse kind of discourse to match the coarseness of events. "He fucked all those other women," she said. "Fucked them for years and is fucking them still. And not just strangers, but women I know. He's a shit."

It was only a small annoyance, but it heralded more to come. Maybe it was inevitable, Janet still living the life that the four of them had shared. Married, with children. Married to George. Stability personified, George. No shattered hearts to sweep up and throw away in the Cooperman home.

· · ·

WEDNESDAY MORNING, the Parkers arrive on time, and without Clara having to prompt her, Katherine Parker volunteers a hesitant "Well, I suppose I have to go." She'll be just down the street, she says. She'll shop a bit. She may have some coffee. She'll be back in two hours. She looks at her small silver watch more than once. She blinks toward her husband, and then at Clara. She lists a few more things she may do during this time. She finally leaves.

It's now time to get to work.

Clara has already decided that she'll be damned if she's going to try to make John Parker speak. If it's his habit to be silent, she'll paint him silent, then. And she'll even view his silence as a relief. It's often the most trying part of her profession—the chatter, as she thinks of it. Portraitists and hairdressers, both are expected to talk about irrelevancies when they should be concentrating.

In thirty years of doing this, Clara has not befriended a single subject. Not really. Nor has she painted her own family or friends. She never drew George, much less attempted a full portrait—not even a sketch, for which she's now glad. She never drew him and she has no photographs of him, and the degree to which he exists only in her memories comforts her. Nothing left of their history, outside herself.

In the studio, she seats John Parker on the red velvet armchair. "I'll just be sketching odds and ends," she says.

"You don't have to sit still. Not today. I may take some photographs as well."

His hands are resting on the arms of the chair, loose, not
gripping. And his head is turned away, so she sees him from
a three-quarter view. Clara spends some time, fifteen minutes or so, trying to understand the nature of the line that
runs from his jaw down his neck, across his shoulder, and
then through his left arm. It's oddly difficult. There's a
sense of elongation to him that she hadn't noticed on Monday, and it's hard to capture without exaggerating it.

"The woman who brought me here . . . ?"

It startles her. He's still looking away.

"Yes. Your wife."

"Yes. My wife," he says. "That's right. We've been married more than fifty years." Clara waits to hear more, but
nothing comes. He shifts slightly, so that one hand falls
away from the chair arm. After a moment, she gives up on
the exchange and decides to start acquainting herself with
his face. The smooth skin, the pointy chin. A small, round
nose.

The word isn't *dull*.

It's *dulled*.

This quality she's sensing—much like the lines crisscrossing his wife's soft lips—seems like something he's acquired. Something imposed. This is her instinct, that time
has played a role here in blunting the man—somehow.
Something has changed him. Her mind is wandering now,
not wandering away but winding its way through this
problem's labyrinth. To capture each quality in equal mea-
sure or at least with an equal degree of acknowledgment—
this is her challenge now. *Dulled*. A process. There's a

contradiction she wants to display. Or maybe a conversation she wants to depict. The debate between who he appears to be and who he appears to have been.

It would be good to discuss all this with George.

She's written George two letters since his death. Two letters in seven weeks. The first was angry. *How could you leave me . . .* The second, contrite. *I know it isn't your fault . . .* As she works, she thinks she may write him another one, this evening. *Since your death, I am obsessed with time . . .* There's no one else with whom she wants to share any of this. No one else who will understand how important this business is of trying somehow to combat the static, still quality of her work. To *not* capture a particular moment in a life. To give up on that attempt. No; to fight it.

It does indeed sound sophomoric, she thinks as she draws. It sounds as though she is playing word games in the territory of third-rate philosophy. But then George would see past that. He would. He would recognize that underlying all these musings on time and death and portraiture, pretentious as they might seem, she is struggling.

The two hours quickly pass. It is a luxury indeed to work in silence, she decides.

. . .

HOWEVER IT BEGAN, it didn't go on for long. Not then.

George made his decision in early August of that year. August 1979. He would stay with Janet. He would end the affair.

Only six months in. That was it. No amount of time at all.

But long enough. Long enough to have given Clara Feinberg a glimpse of joy.

For the good of the children.

The phrase covered her heart like a shroud.

• • •

THAT AFTERNOON, heading home, Clara spots Harold in the bakery where she's stopped to buy bread. Harold, of all people. It shouldn't be a shock. He's lived fairly close for years. But it is a shock, and the sight of him brings on a kind of exhaustion. Here is something else to do, another piece of history to navigate.

She taps his arm, tugs gently at the navy cloth of his storm coat. He turns toward her, a look of confusion in his eyes; and then surprise, then something strangely like gladness.

"Clara!"

"Hello, Harold."

Leaning in, he kisses her on the cheek. Like an old acquaintance, she thinks. As though there had never been any passion, nor love, nor rage, nor anything much, just some traces of innocuous familiarity between them. Live long enough, it seems, and every fire can burn itself out.

His narrow, gaunt face looks thinner than ever. His cheekbones jut out under ruddy skin, mapped with purple capillaries. Drinker's skin. How long since they've seen each other? More than a year. Since the newest grandchild arrived, and they stood together, side by side, compatibly squeamish and tipsy at the bris.

"How are you, Harold?"

"Oh, you know. Not bad. I'm doing fine. Not bad at all. Given everything."

"That's good," she says. But she wonders. He looks like an old man, to her—every day of his seventy-four years. Much older than George ever did. His posture seems a bit crumpled. And his brows have grown so bushy that if she were still his wife, she decides, she would insist that he deal with them—somehow. If necessary, she would cut them herself, in his sleep. She finds it ridiculous the way they trail down over his eyes, so one has to look at him as though through an upside-down, overgrown hedge. She wouldn't be able to live with them, she's sure. For a moment, she is sure. But then something else occurs to her. Maybe she would love them, she thinks. If she still loved him. Maybe she would want him as he is.

It's a painful thought. The ravages of time rendered irrelevant by love. It's something she will never find again, she understands.

As she and Harold exchange fragments of information about their children, each buys a baguette—his sourdough, hers not. Did she hear that Ellie's youngest won a statewide spelling bee? Does he know that Daniel is considering a move back East? Yes. Yes. It seems they've been told the same things. This is their peculiar mix of intimacy and distance. In many ways, it is the opposite of the mix she shared with George, their families separate, themselves so intertwined.

In the bakery doorway, as they part, they chat a little more about the children before he mentions George. "Ter-

rible news about George, wasn't it? George Cooperman?
You heard, I assume?"

Clara nods. "Yes. I heard."

Her voice is steady, though she feels many kinds of un-
ease. Not only the opened wound; there is an ancient,
weary guilt at work here, too. Because Harold never knew
a thing. Not back then, and surely not when she and
George started up again. It was always Harold in disgrace,
Harold who had cheated, Harold who had skulked around
the outskirts of her life, hangdog for years and years. Clara
was the injured party. Always. Clara was deserving only of
sympathy and only Harold deserving of contempt. It's a
hook she's never let him off—in part because she's never
trusted him with the information, and in part because she's
never quite wanted to let him off that hook.

"Poor old George," Harold says.

"Poor old George," she echoes.

"I don't suppose you'd have dinner with me sometime?"

"What?" But she's heard him, of course. "Dinner?
When? What's the occasion?"

He frowns, and the eyebrows lower, threatening to ob-
scure his eyes entirely. "No occasion," he says. "Just feeling
a bit lonely. Everyone seems to be dying. Maybe that's the
occasion."

After a moment, she nods. "Yes. We could have dinner. I
suppose. I don't have my book with me, though."

He'll call, he says. Maybe they'll find a night next week.
And then, somewhat awkwardly—a peck on her cheek, a
few more mumbled words—they part at the doorway,
walking in opposite directions toward their homes.

The weather has turned, and freezing rain begins to fall,

stinging Clara's face. It's a typical November sensation, a time of disheartening weather, disheartening events. The month of her wedding, back in the dark, dark ages. And also of her miscarriage, between the children. And then of her divorce—not the final papers, but the true dramatic end, Harold's two suitcases stuffed with random underclothes and shirts, his MacArthur-like stance on their front porch. *I shall return!* Oh no. No, you will not.

As she turns onto Spruce, hurrying past the brownstones, she wonders what it would be like to tell him everything, finally. She could write him a letter now that she's taken up letter writing. *Dear Harold, There's a little something that you don't know . . .*

He would hate her, she decides. It might be the generous, right thing to do. It would even up the score in a way. She's no better than he. She and George both. Not just years ago, but then again, their shared secret life, for the past five years. Harold would hate her—not for the love affair, but for the smarminess with which she's treated him all this time. He would be entitled to. He might even tell the children. He might tell Janet, drinker that he is. He wouldn't be able to keep it to himself.

It would do more harm than good, she decides.

. . .

IT BEGAN AGAIN, the second time, with a chance encounter at the funeral of an old friend. Millie Davidson, a woman in the same set back in the suburbs all those years ago. Clara attended alone, but sat in the church beside Harold, and soon spotted the Coopermans a few pews away.

It was hardly the first time she'd seen them since the summer of '79. There had been years still to get through of living close by, of having their children sing in school concerts together, running into one another at the grocery store. There had been one high school graduation they had all attended—Ellie and the middle Cooperman boy.

The encounter, inevitable, took place in the vicinity of the receiving line. The four of them stood in a group—she and George, she and Harold, George and Janet—the four of them and the weights of history and secrets and judgments and of so, so many forms of love abandoned now, all crowded in together, in the cool of this church.

She didn't look at the others, not really, just in a fleeting, disconnected kind of way. She listened to the words that seemed to float among this uncomfortable quartet, and contributed a few. She engaged only enough to be attuned to the proper moment to say her goodbye, not so soon as to be rude, not long enough for ancient pains to surface. She made her excuses and walked alone outside, into the air and light.

But then he called her that night. More than two decades after the fact. He called to say he'd like to get together for lunch, that he expected her answer to be no, that he knew she would say no. But then look at poor old Millie, he said. Look at them all. How much time did any of them have? He'd decided it was a call he had to make. He had to try.

He said nothing about his emotions. The word *love* did not come up. And if it had, she might well have said no. That word would almost certainly have angered her—after twenty-one years. But he didn't say *love;* he said *lunch.* And she said yes.

• • •

JOHN PARKER IS wearing a soft gray suit and a pale blue tie. This is the outfit in which his wife wants him immortalized. She'll probably have him buried in it too, Clara thinks. It's the third session, the third week, and she's almost finished with the initial oil sketch.

She's asked him to look toward her, to stare directly at her as much as he can. It isn't often that Clara paints a subject with his eyes engaged like this. She's never been all that interested in the kind of portraiture that results in a viewer trying to read the expression, the *Wow, it really looks like he's looking at me* pictures, as she called them to George. This is part of what George found so characteristic of her, about her work, this slight sense of disengagement. "You see, they're always looking someplace else. Because Clara herself prefers to keep her distance from most of the world." But in this case, she early on decided that the only route through that dullness she detected in John Parker, back to whatever had preceded it, would be through his gaze.

Fifteen minutes or so into the session, his stare shifts away. "I'm sorry," she says. "Could you just look here again? It won't be long." And obediently, silently, he does.

She's become quite engaged in this portrait of John Parker. There's a challenge here that interests her, in large part because she's become convinced that there's something wrong with the man, something desperately wrong. He's lost, and growing more lost by the moment. That's what the eyes of her painting will show, she hopes, a man in the process of becoming lost.

Possibly, she thinks, this is just another portrait George would characterize as disengaged. The direct gaze there, but the response it will elicit not *It really looks like he's staring at me* but *Where has he gone?*

Alzheimer's, maybe. Some other form of dementia, perhaps. The wife has said nothing, though Clara suspects she knows. Or perhaps, she herself suspects and doesn't want to know. It explains the protectiveness, and also this late-in-the-day desire to capture him in oils.

He himself has spoken very little, silence remaining his dominant mode, and what he has said has had a fragmentary, illogical quality to it. The early comment about his wife, a couple of sentences about a case on which he worked when he practiced law God knows when.

Behind her easel, Clara is distinctly clinical in her response to him, her sympathies taking a distant second to her interest in capturing the image of someone so caught up in a process. To convey that sense of transition and not merely try to characterize the man seems to her to be an infinitely compelling task. She has had other subjects whose bodies and faces seemed defined by sadness, but this is something else. This has become, for her, a portrait of time itself. The past, represented in the identity he is losing. The present, there in the glimpses still of someone trying to remain. And the future, well, the future is all too evident in the man.

The desire to talk with George about this particular portrait has grown strong, strong enough to be painful. In these last two weeks, it has become the focus of her missing him. His absence is woven throughout her life. It is there, of course, in her bed, where they made love, and talked for hours on end. In her living room, as well. On certain streets where they would walk together. In the restaurants they frequented, to which she doubts she will return. But the pain of losing him, finally, this time, not in some way that can itself be fixed by time, has coalesced around her longing to talk to him about this.

John Parker's gaze shifts again, but Clara says nothing. She has had enough of it herself for today, enough of that unmoored stare of his.

. . .

WHEN IT BEGAN AGAIN, it was as though no time had passed. And yet, in some ways, those twenty-plus years had changed everything. He would leave Janet now, he said. He didn't like the thought of hurting her, but he would do it. He would marry Clara. Maybe too little, too late, he said. He would, though. He was serious.

But Clara said no. She listened, noted his sheepish demeanor as he spoke; a marriage proposal, after all these years, the articulation of her own fantasies from the past. And then she said no. She had no interest in getting married. She preferred to live alone. She had come to value her independence. She now needed more solitude than a marriage would allow. The whole discussion took less than ten minutes. How funny it was. The very thing that had broken her heart, now no longer wanted. A trick of time.

It was time too that made them able to justify all of it, to themselves. Time and death. Life so short, eternity so long.

That and the decision that what Janet didn't know, et cetera, et cetera. He had looked at Millie's coffin, that April day. He couldn't do it. Couldn't face eternity without this. Without her.

He was late getting there. But he wasn't too late. They could have something still.

• • •

HAROLD HAS CHOSEN a restaurant Clara doesn't know, somewhere dark and clubby, up near Market Street. He's a regular, it seems. The waiters call him Mr. Feinberg and suggest foods they claim to be certain he would like if he would only try something new.

She watches his banter with them, and she tries to imagine herself as his wife. It would be forty years. Forty years this very month. She tries to imagine that they are married and they have gone out to dinner, in this place where he is a regular. This is the life they had planned, after all. They took vows, swearing to live this life. So, they'll meet for this dinner and talk about their day apart. And then they'll leave and head together to their home, where they'll switch on the lights, read their mail, share a nightcap, perhaps, brush their teeth. Then they'll undress. They'll climb into bed. Their bed. Maybe they will make love, and if so, they will see each other forgivingly, as she and George did. Eyebrows and all.

Harold orders steak and the waiter smiles, teasing that someday they'll get him to change his predictable ways. Someday. She orders lamb. They'll both have Caesar salads, an afterthought. Each of them already has a hefty scotch on the rocks, not an afterthought at all.

"Health," Harold says, lifting his glass.

"Health," she responds, and they clink. It sounds a little bleak, she thinks. The bar has surely been lowered, if health is now the most for which one can ask.

"This last one was the worst," he says, and she has no idea what he means. She raises her own brows in a question. "George," he says, then takes another sip. "Jesus, I'm seventy-four years old. I should be used to people dying. But I'll miss him, that's all. And it was so fucking sudden. Now you see 'em, now you don't. Hell of a game we're in."

Clara looks down at her drink, and at her hand wrapped around it. There's a speck of light blue paint on the knuckle of her index finger, a trace of John Parker's tie. The ice cubes, hollow cylinders, are melting quickly, the whiskey near them at the top lighter in color than that below. "I had no idea that you and George were in touch," she says, as she shakes the glass gently, so the amber of the liquid evens out.

"George and I? Oh, yes. For some years now. We were close, I'd say. I suppose that after enough time, all that ancient business, well . . ."

She had kept the Coopermans in the divorce, but apparently something else happened after that. "And Janet?" she asks, looking up. "Are you and she also close?"

He shakes his head. "No. No. No, indeed. Janet would never have a thing to do with me. I attained permanent pariah status, there. Loyalty to you, I suppose. I was never welcomed back. Didn't even go to the funeral. Didn't think she'd want me there. You?"

"No," she says. "I didn't go. She and I haven't spoken in years."

The waiter has appeared with their salads. It takes some time for him to leave, as Harold decides on a glass of wine, and Clara declines one.

It's ridiculous for her to feel anger at George, she knows, to feel betrayed. But she does. How could he have rekindled a friendship with Harold, after what Harold had done to her? She wants to ask him—to ask George. How could he have said nothing to her? She wants to dial him up and have him explain this, have a fight about it, if it comes to that.

"They make a good Caesar here," Harold says. Lifting her fork, Clara forces herself to take a bite. "The thing about George," he says, "the thing I'll really miss, is that clarity of his. You remember? That way he had of just seeing a thing for what it was." He's chewing as he speaks, wipes a bit of dressing off his lip with the back of his hand. "Maybe I'm just a grouchy old man, but it seems to me there's even more bullshit around than there used to be. But not with George. Clear thinker. Straight shooter. It always surprised me, because in general I think of psychoanalysts as slippery characters. But not George."

It is unbearable.

"Harold," she says, putting down her fork. "There are things you don't know." He is looking directly at her. "Things about George." she says. "He and I were . . ."

We were lovers. Twenty-six years ago, after I threw you out. And then, again, for the past five years. He was, he is, the love of my life. He was, he is, the only possible reason a woman of my cynical nature would ever think to use a phrase like that.

"He was a good man, Clara. Wasn't he?" Harold lifts his wineglass. "To George Cooperman."

"We were lovers."

And so. It is done. She sees that Harold's face has stilled. He is as still as a portrait, as though she has painted him with this news. Seconds pass.

"When?" he finally asks.

When? It is always about time, she thinks. Why does it matter when?

Because sometimes it does. "After you and I separated."

"You and George?" he asks. "Right after? Back then?"

"Back then. Briefly. And then again. For the past five years."

His face is mobile now, but in small, twitchy ways, the mouth twisting and shifting, the eyes looking down, then off to somewhere else, closed for a moment, open wide, looking at her, not looking at her. He is struggling to absorb what she has said.

It's revenge, in part. She knows that. He revealed his renewed friendship with George, and she has rendered that disclosure piddling. But she has also given him a gift. He's off the hook now. She is no better than he. George too. Look at what they both did to Janet. Just another pair of sinners. Harold can stop feeling inferior. After how many years? She has finally given him that.

"I don't know what to say, Clara. I should ask questions. Or I shouldn't. I don't know what to say. You and George?"

"Yes, me and . . . yes. But please, no questions." What other memories of her own might be revealed as illusions?

Might be taken from her as casually as Harold has just
taken from her a part of George she thought she held? As
effortlessly as she has just rewritten decades of Harold's
own life for him? At this table, with this man—her husband once, father of her children, her future at one time—
she feels her own history sliding away from her.

"Clara, I don't know what to say."

"We don't have to talk, right now, you know," she says.
"We can just eat our food. It's entirely possible that we've
both already said enough."

He looks at her for a moment, as though he might be
ready for a fight, but then he nods.

· · ·

A MONTH IN, and she's on to the real canvas now.
An art student has primed it for her, and Clara's done a little preliminary work on her own, using only the sketch, but
now John Parker is sitting there, and he's staring at her.
She's told him he doesn't have to, she's only blocking things
out, just broad strokes. But still he stares, and for the first
time in all these weeks, she finds herself unnerved. The
other times, she had insisted he look at her, but this time he
seems to be looking for himself. Clara is her eyes, she is
what she observes. She doesn't like being looked at. Before,
his eyes had seemed sightless; today she feels exposed.

She avoids his gaze, stepping all the way behind her canvas. She works a bit on the area below his jaw. George used
to say she had a therapist's instinct for invisibility. "I am
often whoever my patients need me to be," he said.
"Which is rarely me."

"I'm not even that," she replied. "I'm not even in the room."

She is absorbed in the canvas, actual brushstrokes, the movement of paint, when she's startled by a sound and looks over. John Parker is sobbing. His head is down, his body heaving. He is consumed by sobs.

"What?" she asks. "What?"

He doesn't respond. There's no sign that he has heard.

She puts the brush down and walks toward him, only a few feet, only a few seconds. He's still turned toward the easel, his elbows on the one arm of the chair, his head lowered into his hands, so all she can see is the yellowed skin of his scalp, the brown spots, the veins, the few strands of remaining hair. She kneels beside him, not knowing what she should do, or what she can bring herself to do, and, kneeling there, is filled with something new, something like guilt. She reaches out and wraps her arms around his body. *Shhhhhh.* She says it many times, each time she exhales. *Shhhh,* with every breath.

His head is heavy on her shoulder. He bleats against the cotton of her shirt. He trembles against her flesh. As she holds him, it comes to her, gradually. She knows why he is crying, and she knows why she feels guilty.

John Parker knows. He sees himself leaving, understands about time—as she does. What it is doing to him. And he is grieving, for himself.

She moves her hand up and down his back, feeling the knobs of his spine poking through the shirt, through the wool jacket. She presses her palms firmly onto his body. But she isn't calming him at all. It isn't her touch he needs, it seems.

What does he need?

"Shhhhh," she says.

He had been calm, she remembers, while staring at her. Before she stepped away, hiding from him, leaving him alone. Perhaps it is now unbearable for him to be alone.

She shifts her hands to his face, tries to lift his head.

"Look at me," she says. "Look at me." It takes her a moment to remember his name. "Look at me, John. John. Look at me."

He does, only inches from her eyes. He looks at her, and she is startled by the gaze that she has learned so well, startled to find a living man there, a feeling man. "I know," she says. "I know."

He stares at her, still, and it is hard not to read his sorrow as a wisdom of a kind, in this era of loss when knowledge and pain seem intrinsically linked. She thinks that maybe here is someone to whom she can speak all those thoughts, explain what she has been trying to do, what has upset her so, about her work, since George's death. What stillness means. What time itself means, how it rules us, how it flows away, away. How unkind, how dispassionate it can be. How in the end, for all we are given, we are all robbed blind. Of everything. John Parker understands, she's sure. He won't think her sophomoric or pretentious. He'll recognize her struggles. He'll know that she, like he, is at war.

But his gaze belies her thoughts. He is too dulled already, too absent to hear her out. John Parker is as unreachable as George. But he is still alive, still needs the comfort he cannot give. His face is drenched with tears and snot, his lips quivering still. She pulls the cuff of her sleeve over her hand and rolls it into her fist as she used to when the children were small. She wipes him clean, careful not to drop her gaze from his for long. "I know," she says again. "I know."

Time, she thinks. Both foe and friend. It will destroy John Parker, but it will also soon relieve him of the knowledge that he is destroyed.

It isn't long before she stands, reaches for his hand, gentles him up, and walks him out into the small sitting area, where they sit, still holding hands, silent, on the couch where he and his wife sat weeks before.

An hour or so later when Katherine Parker walks in carrying a few small shopping bags, Clara says only, "Your husband isn't well," and after a moment, the other woman nods.

"I know," she says, and she too sits, in Clara's usual chair. "I shouldn't have done this." She touches her forehead with one hand, her pale polished nails brushing against the fringe of short white hair. "I've upset him. It was too much. I should have known."

"It can be difficult to know what's right."

"I wanted . . ." Her voice is now quivering, threatening to break.

"You wanted to immortalize him," Clara says. "You told me that."

The other woman looks over, blinks, and nods. "That's right," she says. "As a present, for myself."

It can't be done, you know. Not with any of us. It's a false hope. A parlor trick. You'll think you've done it, you'll think you can hold on, but it's always just a trick. She doesn't say it, though. "You've had him for fifty-one years." She's thinking of George, of course, of the twenty-one years they didn't have, of the miracle of the five they found, of all the pictures of him she never drew, of her attempt to hold him entirely within herself, to preserve him that way, of how Harold proved that impossible, of the legacy of mystery every person leaves behind.

"I was seventeen when we met," Katherine Parker says.

"It's your whole life, then."

It isn't right, Clara knows, to tell her how lucky she has been, not at this moment, as her husband quivers beside Clara on the couch. It would be unsympathetic to call her blessed, to rush her through grief and insist on the silver lining. Clara won't do it. But she does envy her. Despite it all, she envies her. It doesn't matter about the many reasons, good, bad, and indifferent, that one might have stayed married for half a century. Right now, she can see only all the years.

"I should take him home." Katherine Parker is sitting straighter now. Clara notices again that veil etched into her skin, over her eyelids, her lips. Beside her, John Parker sighs an almost musical tone.

"If you like," she says, "I could try finishing it. Without him, I mean. I have enough sketches—I think. I could do it. Not the same way, but something."

Katherine Parker frowns. "But it's ridiculous, isn't it?" she asks. "It's too late. Isn't it?"

Clara thinks about the stark clarity with which she has been depicting John Parker's decline. Is it too late? Yes. It is. Of course it is. But arguably, it is always too late.

"No," she says. "It's not too late."

"Oh, it's terrible. I feel like such a fool."

"Time makes fools of us all," Clara says. "Every single one of us. It's possible we need to ignore that fact. And get on with our lives."

It is another moment before Katherine Parker nods. "Yes," she says. "I would like it, still. I would."

"It will take a week, maybe two. I'm not sure how long."

It won't be the same picture, of course, not the one that so interested her. She'll have to give up on the notion of depicting time itself—as a kindness. She'll have to pick a point along the continuum of John Parker's life and stop the clock there, search the evidence of her own observations and try to re-create him, as he was—as though that man were more real than the man he is now, as though there's a moment in anyone's life that is the truest one. As a kindness, she will pretend to this belief. A death mask? Perhaps. But also a token thrown to weigh in on the side of love.

Katherine rises, takes a few unhurried steps, then reaches for her husband's hand, and Clara, who has forgotten that her fingers and his are still interlaced, misses a moment before she thinks to let it go. Then she watches their hands clasp together, loose skin, knobby knuckles. She sees him respond to the familiar, gentle tug, rising easily, as though sensing safety in the air around his wife. The couch cushion exhales; the dent from his weight disappears.

"Let's go home, John. Let's take you home."

They begin to walk away. She will never see John Parker again, she knows.

When Katherine glances back, Clara gives her an encouraging look, a look that promises her the portrait she wants. Clara will do it. She will turn back the hands of time.

Katherine Parker smiles at her, seems almost to laugh, then turns away. The couple moves as one through the glass-paned door, their images visible only briefly, a bit distorted. Gone.

Harriet
Elliot

SHE WAS THE NEW GIRL in our fifth grade. Harriet Elliot. And when she told us that, she told it to us whole, the necessary pause between first and last name, that hard, repeated stop at the end of each, adding to the strangely adult air she carried with her, and signaling her separateness from us.

We were ten and eleven years old. Our parents, all of them friends, our fathers all professors, had started this school, an experiment in learning. We knew nothing of desks. Nothing of mimeographed sheets of paper with empty lines or boxes to be filled. We roamed the large classroom and Expressed Ourselves. We lounged, with books we chose, in beanbag chairs and on the shag rug, which smelled like the dog our teacher brought with her each day, and also like us. We played recorders and African drums. We learned our times tables with dried lima beans. We wore jeans or we wore blue-and-white-striped OshKosh overalls. Sometimes we wore Levi's cords, though they always

faded quickly at the knees, the ridges dissolving into trans-
lucent fabric, soft and grubby, like a loose second skin.

Harriet Elliot wore dresses, always clean, and white
tights that reached an abrupt conclusion at the start of her
black patent shoes. We wore shit-kicker boots and sneaks.
When we took them off, our socks rarely matched. Some of
us were tall—Freddy Steinberg, Peter Walker, Annabelle
Grant. Harriet Elliot was taller. Our hair was shaggy, un-
brushed, wild, long. Infrequently washed. Her hair was
pulled into a ponytail so tight that, though it sprang from
the elastic in a surprising mass of curls, it lined her head
without a single ridge, smooth and shiny as a mirror.

We were supposed to know better than to tease. We were
taught tolerance by our Quaker teacher at every chance.
There was God in each of us—even in those of us, like me,
who had been raised to believe there was no God. This puzzle, which puzzled me into contortions, never seemed to ruf-
fle my parents, in their own jeans and overalls, flannel shirts
and faded cords. My mother, a philosophy student, cooking
our dinner of beans, brown rice, carrot soup, holding the
phone head to shoulder, arguing in her quiet, even voice with
the other end of the line in favor of Nothingness, an argument she seemed increasingly certain she had won. My father,
an archaeologist, shaggily handsome, with a beard he kept
well-trimmed, shoulder-length hair he continually touched,
and the knack of being central to every situation he was in.
Our home, half a brownstone, the division clumsily built, an
illogical wall running through our front hall. Our shelves and
our tabletops crowded with my father's Mayan figures of
squat, clay women with pendulous, thick-nippled breasts to
which I, a ten-year-old girl, was supposed to be blind.

And of course we did tease. We were children, after all.

On the day Harriet Elliot joined our ranks, we set out, as if on the kind of formal assignment that we never were assigned, to make her defend her difference from us. Not in the large classroom, where we first mumbled our greetings as Teacher Margie encouraged us to do and then pretty much ignored her. But during morning break, our daily outing to Rittenhouse Square, where we would run up and down the pavement pathways cutting diagonals across the grass and climb the statuary and draw pink-chalk hopscotch boards on the cement.

Ben Granger began, asking her where she was from, as if the answer might be Oz. She told us that she was from New York. "Manhattan," she said, hardening the *t*'s in that, as well. Harrie*t* Ellio*t*, from Manha*tt*an. She clicked when she spoke. And she wore a white, furry coat, though the rest of us wore only long-sleeved shirts.

"Philadelphia's better," Peter Walker said. "New York's full of murderers." We all nodded. We all believed the same things. Mary Hudson, a kind-natured child, said that maybe they dress different in New York. I looked at Harriet Elliot and thought maybe that was true. Maybe she would come back the next day in real clothes.

"This is probably just your first-day outfit," Mary said, with a hopeful smile.

Harriet Elliot's white coat hung longer than her dress. Her white tights stuck out beneath. I thought her black feet looked like hooves on a sheep.

"No. I always dress like this," she said. "My father tells me I'm a princess."

And that was that. Of course.

We whispered the word *princess* daily among ourselves, careful so Teacher Margie wouldn't hear. We hissed it when we passed Harriet Elliot in the classroom and when we saw her alone in the small lav down the hall. We wrote it anonymously in the corners of her drawings, which were of castles, of unicorns. Which didn't look like ours.

When our parents asked us how the new girl was fitting in, we shrugged, knowing better than to share our unanimous judgment. We said she seemed okay. We tried to make our faces look as though we had found a glimpse of God inside of her.

As there was God in each of us. Sometimes I would try to find him there. At night, in my room, my eyes closed, escaping the unmistakable tones of an unending parental argument forcing its way up the stairwell through my door, I would stare inside myself. Lying in the dark, in the nebulous shadow of my mother's beloved Nothingness and in the quandary of my own curiosities, I would look until I slept for the God I had been told did not exist. Or sometimes at school I would peer at a classmate, at Freddy, who had an eye that always ran with yellow ooze, and who couldn't keep his lima beans from falling on the floor. And I would search, without success, for signs of God.

. . .

IN THE MIDDLE of October came Self-Expression Day. Other schools called it show-and-tell. I only knew this from my sister, who had missed out on the co-op. At thirteen, she was old enough and at odds enough already with our parents to roll her mascara-fringed eyes at breakfast, wrinkle her freckled nose, and say *Self-Expression Day* with great contempt.

"Why can't you morons just call it show-and-tell?"

My father, leaning against a kitchen counter, in his jeans and wool jacket, his black turtleneck, suggested I take one of his Mayan women to school. "How about the goddess Ixchel?" He ground a cigarette butt on a plate. "She would be perfect."

My sister laughed out loud. "Oh yeah, that's a great idea. Why don't you do that?" she asked, her blond hair hanging like window curtains around her face.

I said I thought I'd rather bring the kimono my grandparents had bought me in Japan. I had already pulled it down from the back of my closet shelf.

"Are you sure?" my father asked. "I have a few minutes free. I could write a little something for you to read. What time are you doing it? I might even be able to come."

"It's *her* self-expression," my mother said, standing up. "*Her* self-expression," she repeated, the pronoun poking through like a thorn. "Not yours."

For a moment no one moved; then my father muttered, *"Jesus Christ,"* stomped from the room, slammed out of the house. In the silence he left, I heard his car, its old engine rattling down the block. My mother began shifting the breakfast dishes around the kitchen with no obvious purpose and a grasp so tight I thought one would shatter in her hand. For just a second, my sister looked at me as though doing so might help, as though we might be aligned in this. But not for long.

"Thanks a lot," she whispered across the table. "It's all your fault, you know. For being born."

The classroom that morning was cluttered with odd objects, many of them foreign like mine, many borrowed from our parents' professions, as I had chosen not to do. Since we had no desks, we lined our treasures up against the wall under our coats, which hung in a primary-colored row, broken only by the puff of white Harriet Elliot wore each day. Nobody commented on what anyone else had brought. Nobody seemed interested in anything much, except the empty space beneath her coat, about which we whispered among ourselves with glee.

Late in the morning, Teacher Margie clapped her hands twice, the signal for us to stop what we were doing and ready ourselves for something new.

"Today, as you know, is Self-Expression Day. It looks to me as though we have a wonderful array of special things. Why don't you each go get yours and come back to the circle, where we'll share."

I rose from my beanbag, took the folded kimono from the floor, and sat down on the shag rug next to Mary, who held a doll from Holland in her lap. Soon Ben, with a wooden zebra, joined us there, and before too long, the circle was formed.

First, we peered through Jenny Wilkerson's microscope at something her father had prepared. Shapeless, wobbling forms and speckles shifted slightly in our view. We all said it looked *cool,* in flat, uncommitted voices that resisted the admission that we'd failed somehow to recognize a wonder we'd been shown. She waited until everyone had their turn before she told us what it was.

"It's spit," she said. "It's my father's spit." And all of us said *ewww* in unison. "Your mouth is dirtier than a dog's," she told us. "It's the dirtiest thing in the world."

Then we stared without expression at the zebra Ben had brought.

"I think my uncle got it on safari," he said. "Anyway, I know it's real."

And I was just old enough to wonder what *real* meant—about a wooden zebra brought to school. My kimono was met with silence, except from Teacher Margie, who said it was lovely and that maybe I could bring it back in the spring, when we'd be studying Japan. I said I would.

When Harriet Elliot's turn rolled around, we all exchanged expectant looks. The Princess hadn't brought anything. Once again, she'd gotten it wrong. She stood, her hands hanging by her sides. For a moment, she looked downward at our laps, filled with statues, silken fabrics, elaborate tools.

"I didn't know we were supposed to bring in an object," she clicked. "I thought we were supposed to tell something about ourselves."

"That's fine, Harriet. That's perfectly fine." As Teacher Margie spoke, we sucked in our cheeks, rolled our eyes to the ceiling, then looked down, barely hiding smiles on our lips. "Anything that expresses who you are. That's what today is all about."

Harriet Elliot nodded, slowly, before she spoke.

"Well, when I was three years old," she began, "I was kidnapped by bandits. In Italy. My mother left my stroller outside a butcher shop, and when she came out, I was gone."

We looked at one another now, deciding whether to laugh. Or make some other kind of noise.

"She said it was the worst moment of her life, because she knew I was the only child she could have. Because she'd been sick after me and there couldn't be any more babies. Her inside parts were gone. And anyway, she loved me. And my father wasn't there to help. Or to watch me. She was all by herself. Then an old Italian man saw her crying on the sidewalk . . ."

We looked at *her* now. All of us. Her blue eyes seemed to stare past our heads, as though she were speaking to herself.

"They called the police, who blocked the whole street with motorcycles and cars. And after a while they found my father, so at least my mother wasn't alone. But nobody knew where I was."

She stopped then. Ending there. And began to sit down, her hands tucking the skirt of her dress under her behind.

"But what happened?" Teacher Margie asked. "How did they get you back?"

"Oh." She straightened up. "They didn't. Not for a very long time. It took three weeks. It was almost a month. And then my parents got a phone call asking for money. In Italy, everything is in billions. They wanted billions and billions of Italian money for me. My father left it in an empty house, and the next day I was returned."

There was silence.

"They never caught the bandits," she said. "The men who took me. They're still at large."

This time when she stopped, she didn't move. And after a moment, we all looked at each other, again. Because there was a decision we had to make. Ben's face, close to mine, looked doubtful; but Mary, with her deep, habitual kindness, looked concerned. It was our teacher, though, who asked, "Is this true, Harriet? Or is this just some kind of story?"

"Oh no," she said. "It's really true." And for the first time since we'd known her, she seemed upset. Even when we'd called her Princess to her face, she'd stayed implacable as a mannequin. Now her eyebrows drew together, her lips pulled into a thin line. Again she scanned the array of improbable objects tipping and folding in our laps. "I know it wasn't what we were supposed to do. But it is true," she said, looking out at Teacher Margie again. "I was taken. By bandits. I was. And they've never been found." And then she sat down.

In the square we were subdued. There was no running up and through the crisscrossing paths. No hopscotch. Just the low murmur of our voices trying to decide what we thought.

"Who would want her?" Freddy asked, rubbing at the ooze around his eye. "Who would steal her, even if they could?" We all looked over to the bench where she sat, the bench that had become her daily place. "Who would pay billions and billions to get her back?"

I thought about the father who had told her she was a princess.

"It was definitely a lie," Peter Walker said.

And by the time Teacher Margie clapped her hands, this was the opinion that we voiced.

But newly, unexpectedly, I wasn't sure that *I* agreed with *us*.

From bed that night, I heard my father yell. And then my mother in response. I rolled over, my back to the door, and took the pillow from under my face, rested it on my head. I felt the cool unyielding flatness of the sheet beneath my cheek, and I tried to escape from the space their voices filled. With the pillow pressed over my ears, I conjured the sensation of sitting on our couch between my parents, equal portions of warmth on either side. And then I attempted, once again, to conjure God, wondering whose fault it was that he was so utterly invisible in me. And when, as always, he failed to appear, I thought about Harriet Elliot. Her father's little princess. And how much I hated her for those clothes, and for her drawings of fairy-tale landscapes, and most of all for her disregard of our disregard of her.

As the voices of my parents burrowed through the darkness into me, I decided I should have told them what had happened. How she had been kidnapped, in Italy. I decided they should know. A sensation of danger was swelling, beneath my covers, beneath my pillow, a feeling so real and so polluting that suddenly anything bad seemed like it must be true; and I was certain that we had been wrong. She *had* been stolen by strangers. She had lived for three weeks in the company of bandits. I pictured her at first, just as I knew her only younger, but prim and clean and dressed in ruffles and lace. I imagined her captors as unshaven men in black masks and black leather coats. She must have cried for her mother and her father. She must have cried out her eyes. But then, at some point, she must have stopped—an even more frightening thought. And her tights must have faded from white to the pale gray of dirt, and maybe eventually to black. She couldn't have worn the same dress for three weeks. She must have had to change. Change her clothing. Change herself. She must have had to stop being a princess, if only for those days.

I rolled over. From my bed I could see out into the hallway. I could see the pine cabinet that had sat there all my life. And at that moment, my mother's voice from below sounded as though she were singing—singing something sad and worn; a memory that would come to me always with the notes of certain melancholy hymns. I could hear the dishes clattering, water running. But underneath, her voice. As I stared and I listened, I saw my sister cross the hallway from the bathroom to her room. I thought of calling out her name. But then I heard her door squeak closed.

. . .

HARRIET ELLIOT APPEARED the next morning in a blue satin dress. At her collar were rings of lace that matched her tights. She hung her coat in silence, made her way to the bookshelf, chose a book, and retreated to a corner, by herself. Throughout the morning, as I went about my tasks, I watched her there.

In the park, during break, she sat on her bench with a box of crayons and a pad. Mary had brought out a big thick piece of chalk and gone over the lines we'd drawn on the pavement two days earlier, faded during showers overnight.

A few of us climbed on the bronze statues dotting the square. A pair of boys tossed a Frisbee back and forth. Teacher Margie moved without pause from one group to the next, her little dog trailing just behind.

I skipped straight through the hopscotch board, two feet, one foot, one, then two, then one, then one. And done. And I kept on walking. When I reached Harriet Elliot, she looked up from the drawing in her lap, silent. For some moments we just stared into one another's eyes, hers blue, as if painted. China-doll blue, and powerfully uninterested in me. As though she could choose to blink and I'd be gone.

"It's true, isn't it?" I asked. "You really were kidnapped, weren't you?"

"Yes, I was. I said so."

"Nobody believes you," I told her—though I did. "Everyone thinks you're a liar."

She reached into the pocket of her coat and pulled out a piece of old newspaper. "Here," she said, holding it to my face. "This proves that I'm not."

The headline wasn't English, I couldn't read it, but there was a picture underneath, a tiny girl with a mop of curly hair, held aloft like a prize in a man's arms. "That's me, on the day they got me back. I was on Italian TV too." The child in the photograph wore rags, nothing more than a sack, her bare legs and bare feet sticking out. "And that's my father." The man was smiling, his mouth open wide. Not facing the camera; facing her.

"How do I know that's you?"

She ignored the question and put the picture back in her coat.

"Someday I'm going to find the men who took me," she said, "and make them pay."

"What?"

"I'm going to go back to Italy and hunt them down. And kill them for what they did."

In the background I heard Teacher Margie clap her hands.

Harriet began packing up her crayons, arranging them carefully in their big box. "We're supposed to go in," she said. "Look, they're all lining up."

"What do you mean you're going to kill them?"

She shrugged. "I just am," she said. "But first, I have to grow up. Go through all of this. That's the boring part."

I looked over at my classmates in their line.

"How're you going to find them?" I asked. Then: "That's just stupid."

She smiled. "I remember every second. I was there, wasn't I? I was there the whole time."

She walked away, toward our classmates, and I followed, just behind, so I had to take her place as last.

Soon after that day, my sister began treating me much more cruelly than she ever had. In the car, as our mother drove us to our schools, she would whisper to me that I was ugly. And fat. That I smelled like I never took a shower. At meals she would reach beneath the table, with arms that seemed to lengthen for the task, and pinch my legs until I cried. When I spoke, she mimicked me, anticipating each word as it formed, rendering all my expressions foolish, meaningless. At night, as I lay in the shoulder of the hallway light, she would walk over and pull my door shut tight, leaving me to lie there in the dark.

One night, uninvited in my room, she first told me that I was too old to sleep with all the stuffed animals I had, then swept them from my bed, onto the floor.

"You're just so stupid and babyish. I can't even believe it. You act like you don't know what's going on."

I said nothing.

"I can't wait to see what happens to you when you . . . when you have to . . ." But she didn't finish the sentence. Just threw my pillow to the ground, stood, and walked away. "God. You're such a spoiled brat. You and those other stupid co-op kids." She slammed the door so hard, it bounced open wide. "You're so fucking dumb!"

I told no one about Harriet's plan to seek revenge. I knew that they would laugh at her. And I knew that if they laughed at her, then I would too. And something in me didn't want to do that. So a new wall of privacy came up. A new realm of secrecy. And a new us began.

Some days I would join her on her bench and I would ask her not about the future, but about how it had felt to be there with those men. To be taken from her family, not knowing if she would ever be returned. She told me stories that I believed, stories in which she never shed a tear, and never spoke, but only stared at the people around her—not just the bandits, but the strange women who cooked her food, the other children there who pulled her hair and tore at her clothes.

"I wouldn't let them see me cry," she said. "They wanted me to. But I wouldn't do it."

I nodded, aware of my classmates' occasional looks our way.

"I was very brave," she said. "I still am. I have never been afraid."

I didn't tell her how very afraid I was, every day. Every night. I watched her, instead, wondering how to be brave like that. In profile, beside me on the bench, Harriet Elliot's chin stayed slightly raised, as though she were always on alert, her eyes seeming to see past whatever was in her path.

. . .

THE CO-OP WAS CLOSED for Veterans Day, though we called it Resolution Day and passed the week before constructing peace signs out of popsicle sticks and out of tiny pinecones and out of mismatched buttons and even out of the lima beans with which we learned our math.

It was Harriet's father who called that morning, inviting me over, and it was her father, the man from the newspaper, who came to the door and waved my mother away, who took my coat off my shoulders, hung it up, told me *my friend* was upstairs in her room, then asked if I would please take off my shoes.

"It's the carpet," he said, smiling broadly, as though he had never stopped smiling since his daughter was returned. "We try our best to keep it white."

His hair was short, like a soldier's, and mostly gray. I thought he looked too old to be anyone's father. I thought there was something vaguely wrong with a father who answered the door and took your coat, who spoke to you as though you were interesting. Like a mother would do. "Overalls, huh?" He picked my boots up off the floor, setting them on a small bench. "Maybe we should buy Harriet a pair of overalls. Though I don't think she'd wear them."

I didn't know what to say. Of course she wouldn't wear them. And by then I didn't think she should. "Probably not," I said.

"No. Probably not." Then he told me to run on upstairs. He said he would call when it was lunch.

My stocking feet were silent on the carpet. As I padded through their home, I wondered what it would be like to walk on such softness every day. The floors of my own house were wood, battered oak, and bare except for a few scattered rugs from my father's travels, all too often sliding underfoot. I wondered what it would be like never to hear footsteps, so never to listen for them.

"I have been making plans," she said.

We sat on pale yellow chairs, at a pale yellow table, in her fairy-tale room, a room in which all of the colors were pastel, all of the surfaces softened, all of the light bulbs shaded, the three tall windows covered with lace, the sun diffused. Even the canopy bed cushioned the air, as though the atmosphere itself might be too harsh.

Harriet's chin was slightly raised as always, her eyes focused just above my head, and she was dressed like herself. Only the shoes were gone, so the white legs below her green velvet hem dwindled unexpectedly, seeming to melt into the carpet. "I have been working on details," she said.

"What details?"

"You'll see. There are things I have never shown anyone. But I think I will show them to you. Today."

I didn't speak, afraid that if I did she would change her mind about whatever exceptional quality she thought she had detected in me. I only tried to look special.

Harriet stood and walked toward a closet door, then opened it, revealing a row of dresses pressed together so tightly I decided she *had* to wear one every day, because the closet couldn't hold any more. She reached into the middle and pulled out a filthy rag. It was the rag from the photograph. The rag she had worn. I knew at once.

"We'll need this. And a few other things," she said.

She moved around the room, collecting objects, arranging them in front of me. First, the tattered baby dress, and then a lock of hair. Then a diary, a ring, a piece of crackly paper rolled into a scroll and tied with string, and finally a miniature bottle of amber glass. Then she sat down.

"Do you know anything about killing people?" she asked.

I shook my head.

"There's a difference between how men kill and how ladies do."

"That doesn't make sense," I said. It was a phrase I used a lot with her, a phrase that asked her to go on without admitting how much I wanted to hear her words.

"Women use poison," she said. "And men use guns. My father says if he ever saw them, he would shoot them. But that's not what I'm going to do." She picked the ring up from the table. "This one doesn't work," she said. "It's just a toy. For practice. But there are rings in Italy that open up so you can pour poison in your enemy's food." She tapped the black stone with her thumb. "That's how women kill. Especially in Italy. They invite you for dinner, then they poison you. That's how I'm going to kill. Here," she said. "Try it on."

I straightened my fingers as she slid the ring down. Her face was closer to mine than it had ever been. Each blue iris, I saw, was ringed by black.

"It's heavy," I said.

She leaned away. "Do you want to smell what's in the bottle? It's a potion. But it's not the real thing," she said. "I have to wait for that till I'm grown. Like everything else. This is only flower petals and lemon peel."

I nodded. "Sure."

"I think it's important to practice," she said. "Even if it's just with toys. That's what professionals do. Professional killers. That's what *they* did. They practiced stealing babies. They practiced on dolls. I know they did. I saw them, all these dolls stuffed in a tiny closet. Hundreds of dolls they would grab from each other. Then they would run away with them."

"How do you remember so much? If you were only three?"

"Here." She stuck the bottle under my nose. The smell reminded me of the library near my house.

"*This* was all my parents had left," she said, picking up the lock of hair. "My mother never let it go. She slept clutching it every night."

The rolled-up paper was a map of Italy. "Here," she said, pointing to a star drawn in pencil. "That's where they are. That's the place where they took me."

"How do you know?"

She rolled it up, without a word.

From her diary, Harriet read me the names of boats that sailed the Atlantic. Then she told me about poisons that inflicted excruciating pain before they killed. She told me that one bandit had a scar that ran the length of his long, bumpy nose, another had hair that grew in perfect stripes of black and white. One of the women had no thumb on one hand, but two on the other. One of the babies had been so fat he had to be propped up with half a dozen pillows or he might just roll away. She listed the foods she would prepare for her captors' last meal. Caviar. Lobster. Strawberries. Chocolate éclairs. But, she told me, she would poison their first bite.

I still wanted to know more about the past. "You must have been afraid," I said. "When you saw the dolls, you must have been."

"I had to keep my wits about me," she said. Then, for once, she looked directly at my eyes. "You should too."

For lunch, Harriet's father served us clear soup in china bowls. We sat in the dining room, at a long, wooden table glossy with polish. When he left, telling us to call him if we needed anything, Harriet reached for my wrist.

"It's done like this, so no one knows," she said. "See? Just a little twist of your hand." She turned my arm a quarter turn. "And the poison comes out. You try."

I touched the toy ring, pretending to open it, then moved my wrist the way she had, as though poisoning my own soup.

"That's good," she said. "But you have to be less obvious. You have to not get caught."

"I wouldn't get caught." From the kitchen I heard a bell ring; a timer had run, and I realized the air was filled with something sweet. "Is your mom here?" I asked.

"Because if you do get caught murdering," Harriet said, "you'll rot in a jail for the rest of your life. Especially in Italy. They won't even remember to feed you and if they do, when they come with your bread and moldy cheese, because that's all you can have, not even water every day, they'll find just your bones one time, your rotten bones. Do you understand?"

I nodded.

"If it were France," she said, filling her spoon with soup, "they would chop off your head."

And I nodded again, slowly, as though letting these facts sink in, as though I too were plotting my revenge.

When Harriet's father came back, he was carrying a plate of cookies. She smiled at him, seemed almost to laugh; and I realized I had never before seen her smile.

"There must be something that you want," she said, back upstairs, after lunch, her door now locked. "Something important enough to make you brave."

I thought of my parents. I only shrugged.

"It has to be something you want so much that it hurts. So you feel like your arms and legs will fall off if you don't get it. And your head. Your head will roll away. And your backbone will crumble. So if you think about that, how bad that would be, you can't be scared. Not of other things."

I could feel my eyes begin to sting. I could picture my head rolling off and my backbone crumbling.

"There's something, isn't there?" she asked.

I shrugged again.

"Don't tell me what it is," she said. "I know a ritual you can do."

She told me that first I had to write my wish down. In red ink, for blood. She gave me paper and a red marker. "Start by writing: *This is the wish that is dearest to my heart.*"

I did. And then I wrote the thing I wanted so much it kept me up through every night.

"There's more," she said. She told me that I had to lick my words. "Make sure the paper's wet. All of it. It has to be."

When I had finished, my tongue pasty, thick in my mouth, I found those blue eyes narrow and appraising. "Is it wet?" she asked, and I nodded. She told me to take my overalls off. She told me I had to be naked for it to work. That the wish had to be able to touch all of me. "That's part of it," she said. "That's the part where your bravery starts to be in your veins. You need bravery to make a wish come true."

I stood and undid the buckles at my shoulders. I let the denim fall—trying to feel like it was normal. Just as though I was home, about to take my bath or go to sleep. I kicked the overalls from my feet, then pulled off my shirt, my underpants, my mismatched socks, certain as I did that she'd thought I'd chicken out, determined to pass every test she gave, and only when wholly naked, feeling the full bore of her gaze on my still skinny body, still flat chest, on the area between my legs my sister said was bald and vowed would always be.

Harriet's face was expressionless as she told me to rub the paper on myself. "Your wish has to cover you," she said. "All over. Every part of you. Even the parts you think you shouldn't touch. Especially those."

The red ink trailed across my skin, leaving markings like the openings of tiny wounds. I could picture the words I had written seeping in. I was certain I could feel them in my veins. I smoothed the paper over my front and through that arch between my legs, made sure to press it there, then down, away, to knees and feet. She watched until I stopped.

"It's almost finished," she said. "You're almost done." She told me to tear it into bits and swallow them as quickly as I could. "Think about how no one can ever hurt you. How no one can ever make you feel bad again."

The paper gummed in my mouth, but I forced it down, little bit after little bit. When it was gone, Harriet Elliot sprinkled my naked shoulders with her potion; then she brushed the lock of her baby hair across my face. And finally she declared me brave. Brave enough to make my wish come true.

And by then I believed every word.

· · ·

NOT LONG AFTER THAT, my father moved out. On the Sunday morning he left, my mother stayed upstairs in her room while my sister and I sat on the front step, watching him shift the last of his boxes from the house to his car. Snow from another day lay on the ground, still white in the center of our lawn, nearly black at the curb. The brick walk wasn't shoveled and the snow there had been pressed by our boots and our weight into ice. The sun was bright enough that I kept my eyes shielded with my hand while my sister puffed out cloud after cloud with her breath.

Every time he passed empty-handed, heading inside for another load, he would rub my hair, or he would rub hers.

The whole thing didn't take very long. After he slammed his trunk, he walked back to where we sat. And he told us he'd be by to visit any day. That we would see him all the time. Neither of us said anything, until we stood up on the front stoop side by side and waved toward his car, calling *Bye Daddy, bye Daddy* while he disappeared from view.

Back in the kitchen, we took off our coats and boots without a word. I sat on the coiled radiator for warmth, and when my sister walked toward me, I thought she wanted my spot. I thought she might shove me over with her usual insult. But then she smacked me so hard across my face my left eye swelled shut—as though she had closed another door. I tried not to move, hoping that the hit I'd taken was the end of something and not the start. But when she raised her hand again, the word *you* curling from her lips like something filthy, I grabbed those curtains of blond hair and pulled so hard that she just froze.

I was screaming as my knee slammed into her body. Screaming as my foot wrapped around her ankle, toppling her. My fingers gripped that hair as she fell, my hold on her pulling me down. "I hate you," I spat as we thrashed on the floor, our knees and feet all trying to deliver blows, her hands squeezing my wrists. "I hate you." I pulled as hard as I could, not letting go, not for a second, not until I had beaten down her years and years of practice torturing me, and I felt her give up.

"I really, really hate you," I said more softly as she began to cry. By then, her arms were dropped to her sides. Her neck had relaxed. I told her she was a crybaby. I told her she was the moron. I told her it was all her fault. Because she was so mean. I told her that our father hated her. That her evil was the reason he moved out. And then I heard my mother's footsteps overhead.

I left my sister crying on the floor. I walked as quietly as I could through the hall, along the peculiar wall that shaped our home, and into my father's ransacked study. There was little sign of him there. No books, no rugs, no cigarette packs, no round and naked women, thick-nippled, shameful, thrilling. Only sunlight pouring through the windows onto emptied surfaces, a few balls of rolled-up paper on the floor like tumbleweed.

My eye began to ache and throb.

From the kitchen, I heard my mother. *What is going on? What do you girls think you're doing? How am I supposed to handle one more thing?*

I slid to the floor and I waited to be found.

• • •

AFTER THAT, I stopped believing the things that Harriet said. I knew she had been wrong about my wish.

Just like I knew that when my father told us he would be visiting all the time it was a kind of lie, even though he meant it. Just like I knew that the God I had been looking for would never show himself to me. Just like I knew that Harriet Elliot would never ride a ship to Italy and kill those men.

I stayed away from her bench at recess. Most of the time, I sat alone. Occasionally I joined the others. But not very often. Sometimes, like Harriet, I would bring paper and a box of crayons outside. Or maybe a book. Sometimes I would play with Teacher Margie's little dog. None of my classmates ever said a word to me about my father, though I knew, even then, that their parents must have told them he had left.

My grandparents, the ones who had brought me the kimono from Japan, visited that Thanksgiving. The nights they were there, I heard voices floating up the stairwell to my room again. But no more arguments. No more chances for making up. After they left, my mother told us, very calmly, that we would be moving in with them, in Washington D.C. We would leave right before Christmas. "It's only until I find a teaching job," she said. But to me that sounded like just another wish that wasn't coming true. I mumbled something about it being okay with me, then glared at my sister until she did too.

"You're good girls," our mother said, and looked away.

On my last day at the co-op, I filled a brown paper bag with all the projects I had made, now peeled from the windows and the walls. I spent that recess watching my classmates try to build a snowman from the few fresh powdery inches on the ground.

Just before pickup time, Teacher Margie clapped her hands, calling us all to the circle. "We're having a Farewell Ceremony today," she said as we sat down. "We're creating a new ritual for ourselves. We've never had to say goodbye to one of us before."

She called their names, and one by one each of my classmates faced me where I sat, singled out, beside her feet; and each of them told me I was *cool*. Just as we had said about the slide of saliva that Jenny brought in and shared with the class. It had been great to be my friend, they said. It had been fun. And in the singsong of their voices I could hear the ease with which my absence would exist. A few handed me scraps of paper, their addresses written in an obviously adult hand. Mary Hudson unfurled a picture she had drawn of me in blue jeans and a sweatshirt, my hair a labyrinth of brown lines, my name written large, hers tiny in the corner.

When Harriet's turn rolled around, she stood as the others had all stood. But when she spoke, she stared out over our heads, as if alone. Her hands clasped in front of her, she said nothing at all about me. Not that I was cool. And not that we had been friends. She only said that the most important thing to remember was that wishes *made correctly* do come true. Always.

"Even when you think it's impossible," she said. "Even when you think that it's too late."

Then she looked at me. With those eyes that seemed so powerful they could will away anything in her path. She just stood there, motionless, staring into my eyes, conjuring with her gaze her own determination, those tales of her capture, the smell of crushed flowers and lemon juice, the feel of my words seeping through my skin, spreading out into my veins. The fantasy of putting things to rights. She looked at me until I could feel something like belief again take root. And then Harriet Elliot blinked; and I was gone.

Gaining
Ground

M<small>Y DAD DIED</small> on the night my bathwater ran
with an electric current in it. Or maybe it was the other
way around. My water ran electric on the night my father
died. In some ways that sounds better, more poetic, I guess.
For one thing, it scans. Ba-*duh* ba-*duh* ba-*duh* ba-*duh* ba-
duh ba-*duh* ba-*duh*. But it isn't truly accurate as to what it
felt like at the time. It felt more like the first way.

It was about a month ago, and you'd think I'd have figured out by now which way to put it. Harris says the whole
worry is stupid, the whole question of how to put it, because it makes it sound like I'm debating some point of
causality, as if the two events were in some way related.
Linked. Which they obviously were not. The water ran
electric because the house was not properly grounded. Because my electrician is an asshole. And always has been.
And ought to be shot. Or at the very least not be an electrician anymore. My father died because he walked in front of
a train. On purpose. Like in a movie. Like Anna Karenina.

Because he was a whack job. Mentally ill. And always had been. No connection. Unless you think having a lousy electrician you don't fire and a lousy father who offs himself is some kind of connection, which even I do not think. So in the end it's just timing. And timing is nothing, meaningless, a slim quality to build any conclusion around.

That's Harris's point, anyway. That timing isn't everything, like people say it is. It's bull. And that's Harris pretty much all around. Harris is a piece of work. Forty-seven years old, pretty fat now, he's got these lingering tufts of leftover hair sprouting all over him, any which way. He's got skin like badly mashed potatoes. He's got eyes like he knows perfectly well he's wrong. About everything. All the time. And couldn't care less. He works in quality control at the local paper plant. Which is a joke, since neither quality nor control, nor any imaginable combination of the two that does not involve adding the words "lack of" or "out of," can be applied to him. And he is just who you would expect to take you on about something like this. Just exactly who you would expect to pull the plug on trying to find meaning in anything. While he leans into my fridge, scrounging, foraging, investigating, making himself at home, taking it upon himself to debunk phenomena like coincidence. Like timing.

I used to be married to Harris and I know Harris well. Last year, just about halfway through realizing he had turned into a walking, talking laundry list of human decline, I threw him out. Harris. His cigarettes. His underpants. His poking through my food. His need to talk me out of things. Out he went. Still, he comes back around to see our daughter, Allison, who's four now. Or at least that's why he says he comes back. That is why Harris claims he is still always around. The fact is, though, that there is only so left he'll ever agree to be. Only so thrown out. Only so gone he ever gets.

"Don't you believe in anything?" I asked him, right while he walked suitcase number one out my front door.

"Nope," he answered me, standing there under a streetlight, his luggage kind of tilting him with its weight. "Nope." He shook his head. "Not a goddamned thing." And Harris, he just walked away, as they say, into the night.

He was the one I called. When it happened. My father. The water. All of that. About which fact I have nothing to say. Except that old habits die hard. And that if I could remember which part I told him first, I might have some idea about this whole how-to-put-it question. Either I told him my father was dead, and then that I had been bathing Allison when the bathwater shocked us both. Or I put it the other way around. I know that Allison was screaming bloody murder, dancing this awful naked wet jitterbug of fear around my bedroom. Wouldn't even let me towel her off, because she didn't want to be touched. By anything. Ever again. Ever. And I had this phone in my hand. This phone that had rung just as I was reaching for it, so I just answered it and said hello. And then a man asked me, some man on the phone asked me if I was my father's daughter, because if I was, there had been an accident. It was 911 calling me. If you can believe it. Them calling me.

"But I was just going to call you," I said. Then I heard what was being told to me, and I asked, "What kind of accident?" And then I took that in. The train, the dead, the my-father-is-over part. And then I called Harris. And told him something. I'm still just not sure exactly what. But I know I told him to come. I know I did that. So this one's on me, I guess.

Having a parent die who is crazy is different from having a parent die who isn't crazy. I know because I have had both kinds, and they have both died. My mother was just so normal you couldn't even be in the room with her and Dad both without losing all belief in God. In anything. In anything that made sense of anything. It just all seemed too impossible. Which, if you ask me, is why I married the king of nothingness in the first place. Why Harris's essentially unpleasant view of the world as a random and pointless sphere held some appeal. I mean, she was nice, my mom. She was pleasant. She was a mom. Picture a mom. Go ahead. You get the idea. Picture her cooking meals, coming to assemblies, chatting on the phone with her other mom friends. Walking the dog. Making your teacher smile at pickup at the end of the day. Making your teacher like you more. Nice. Normal. Smart enough. Pretty enough. But not too pretty. A real mom.

Now you explain my father to me. What he was doing in that house with her. When he was there. Or in those wedding pictures. Or on my birth certificate. You go ahead and make some sense of that, because I have pretty much given up. My earliest memory of my father was of visiting him in a linoleum room, little windows, bars on them, long tables, scattered with art supplies. Construction paper. Clay. Pipe cleaners. Glue. I must've been about Allison's age. Four, maybe three. I know I'd met him before that, because it wasn't like we were introduced or anything. That's just the first image I have of him. In the Art Room. At the Place. He had made a picture for Mom. A collage she admired like it was mine. Which it easily could have been. Red paper, shiny foil shit glued on it. It ended up on our fridge. And there was a woman there on a sofa who stared at me the whole time. That's all.

That's the whole thing. My first memory of my father. Except he isn't even in it. Not if you look carefully. He isn't there.

When I met Harris, in a bar about ten years ago, I was just twenties, young twenties, and he was the first person who ever said to me "So what?" when I told him about my dad. I was going on and on about how bad it's been, about this horror and that, how many times he was in the bin, how long he stayed, which birthdays Dad missed, and what graduations he ruined. And Harris, he just hoists a beer and shrugs: "So what?" I guess that was love. Not his saying it. Me hearing it. "So what?" I heard freedom in that. Like a great big chalkboard eraser getting rid of all that shit. So what. That won me over. Until I got sick of it. Then really sick of it. And then threw him out.

I mean, it's hard to build a whole life around someone saying "So what." Frankly, I think nine years was a pretty damned good stretch.

So I called Harris that night, and I called my same asshole electrician too. But the difference was that when I heard the electrician answer the phone, I just hung up. Then I pulled out the yellow pages and went for the biggest, glossiest, most expensive ad I could find. The kind of ad that has about sixteen phone numbers listed, according to time of day. Emergency and all. And that was the one I called. Because this was an emergency. I mean, for God's sake, if electric water isn't an emergency, what is? For one thing, not my father at that point. That much I had taken in. There was absolutely nothing I could do to help him. Which was actually not news; there had never been anything much I could do for him. But it was official now, in some way it had never been before.

"It won't kill you," the guy said who answered the phone, and right away I liked that I had never heard his voice before. I kind of trusted that quality in him. "You're not in any danger. The house isn't going to burn down. And you aren't going to be electrocuted if you need coffee or something. Water. Maybe wear rubber gloves. Wear rubber shoes. Sneakers, maybe. I'll come in the morning. By eight. I'll be there at eight."

"That's good," I said, hearing Harris let himself in downstairs. "That's great."

The whole father-daughter thing with Allison and Harris gets me down sometimes. Sometimes it's like I should have done better by her, gotten her a better dad. And sometimes it's just facing that there's Harris in her, Harris genes, Harris thoughts, Harris God knows what that's hard for me. Like her being upset when he moved out. Like her being so happy these days when he comes around to see her. Like him being able to reassure her that night, when everything I did just made her scream and dance around. It's like I spilled something on her. Harris juice. It's like she's stained. Like there's something that connects them, wherever I send him to live.

"You gotta go anywhere?" he asked when I came downstairs, those great big hopeless eyes of his staring right at me. And there she was wrapped in a towel, a towel Harris found who knows where, happy, happy, happy sitting on his lap. "You gotta deal with anything?" he asked, and I shrugged.

"Where is he?"

"Morgue. Hospital," I said. "Morgue, I guess. In the hospital. I don't know."

"They need you to identify him?"

"No one said. I have a number to call."

"You should call it then."

Allison had her head turned away from me, buried in Harris's big chest. Her hair was starting to dry, springing into its little curls. My curls. Her father. Harris. It's all just unbelievable sometimes.

"Yeah," I said. "I'll go call now."

My mother died just right. Which is to say, it was horrible. She got a terrible disease, had a series of unspeakable treatments, fought like hell, and lost. It took about a year, and it was just the worst thing ever. It was so miserable, it worked. It counted. It hurt like hell. Like death is supposed to do. My mother died and everything was sad. Ba-*buh* ba-*buh* ba-*buh* ba-*buh* ba-*buh*. Perfect. Her name was Alice, and I had Allison the next year.

This wasn't like that.

The man on the phone said that yeah, I was supposed to come identify my father, and I was supposed to tell them a funeral home to call too. To take him away after I gave the okay. While he talked, I flipped from *E* for *electrician* to *F* in the yellow pages. I went for the biggest ad again, and gave him the number.

"Yeah," he said. "I know those guys. They're good."

"Good," I said. "See you soon."

And then he said what I suppose I should be glad he said. He warned me about what I was going to see. "He's in pretty bad shape."

"Huh. Yeah." I kind of let that point in. That aspect of this night. "Yeah, I guess he would be," I think I said. And that was pretty much that.

One view is that Harris is too rational for me while my father was just the opposite. Completely irrational. The kind of guy who notices one day that the newspaper on the porch is lying at a funny angle, and then it's just counting backward from ten before he's back in the Place, doing Art. Just a matter of days before my own little masterpieces are crowded out by his creativity on the fridge. That's the view that says Harris was a reaction against my dad, but kind of an overreaction. And that's the view I take when I think that there has to be someone out there for me. A man. That Harris is too this, and my father too the other. And that what I need is a middle man. Not a pathological debunker. And not a lunatic. Just someone who thinks, Well, yeah, maybe things mean something but maybe they don't mean much more than that. And maybe sometimes nothing means much of anything at all. But maybe it does.

I want a man who thinks the way I do. It scans. It's short. But it does scan. Ba-*duh* ba-*duh* ba-*duh* ba-*duh* ba-*duh*.

I'm not going to talk about what I saw at the morgue. Not now. Not ever. But it was him. He was right there this time. And trust me, there were no art supplies. No glitter, no glue. Just my father. In this memory, he is there. They gave me his watch, his wallet, and the medical alert bracelet he had on, with my name and number engraved on it. A Timex, seven dollars, and my own I.D.

Harris had Allison all tucked in and dreaming away when I got home. He asked me if I wanted him to stay. I didn't, but I thanked him anyway. Because he had helped. And because he didn't ask me any other questions before he left. Part of me was thanking him for that. For just not going into it. Not being all that interested in the whole thing. His strongest, maybe his only, attribute. So what? His great attraction. At times like this, I still get the appeal. He grabbed an apple out of the bowl on my counter and let himself out, with the fattest part of the fruit headed toward his enormous mouth.

Marriage is a funny thing. Even when it's over. Maybe especially then.

In the morning, when Allison woke up, she came in to find me in my bed, just like every day, and climbed under the covers beside me. I wrapped my arm around her, at first just out of habit, but then I started kind of feeling her, feeling for the shock that had rippled through her the night before. I stroked her, I squeezed her, checking for some change in her skin, in her flesh, in her bones. Something left in her of the way that she had jumped and screamed. Something left of the current that had flashed through her. But nothing seemed different. Nothing at all. I tucked her little shoulders under my arm, and let her head relax onto my chest. She had screamed to me, "It stings, it stings," and I had snapped at her to stop complaining. "Oh quiet!" I'd said. "Stop being such a baby!" Yeah. Mother of the year. That's me. And then *bzzzzzz*, right through my own arm.

That morning I had her skip brushing her teeth. And I told her not to flush the toilet. Or wash her hands.

I thought I should call her doctor. I hadn't thought of that the night before. I had no idea if there was anything to worry about. Anything long-term. If getting shocked that way leaves a mark, does damage, hurts your heart, your brain. Makes you crazy. Makes you nuts.

I didn't say anything to Allison about my dad. The train. The whole being-dead thing. She'd never met him. I never talked about him to her. I never saw any reason to. The pediatrician told me not to worry. There wouldn't be any long-term effects.

And from that point on, it's pretty much all about dirt.

"The thing is," my new electrician said, "you have the pole where it should be, stuck in the ground. And it seems to be in pretty deep. But it's useless, because it doesn't attach to anything. You gotta have every wire in the house leading to this ground, every bit. And you've got nothing. No connection at all. Who did your electric work?"

I shrugged. "Some asshole," I said. "Can you fix it?"

"Sure," he said. "It'll run you, but there's really no choice. It's either that or frying chicken in the bathtub from now on."

The woman at the cemetery said the plot beside my mother was all in order and ready for use. "Just tell us the day, any day this week. We'll arrange it with the funeral home. We want this to be easy for you. We just need about two days' warning to prepare the ground."

"Let's do it in two days then," I said. "If that's what it takes."

I didn't ask anyone from the Place to come. They were just going to go on about how this really wasn't their fault, and how sorry they were. How they just can't understand how this could have happened. And I didn't feel like hearing that from them. Didn't feel like pretending that they had given a shit one way or another about some crazy old guy. Maybe they had. I just didn't care. I asked Harris to be there, of course, because at least with him I know where I stand. At least I know he just thinks it's all a great big meaningless mess. That nothing means anything. That none of this connects. Not in any significant way, anyway. It's all just timing, and timing is crap. That's Harris. That's Harris's big point, and now that I haven't got to be married to him, I am the first to admit that I need that perspective sometimes.

I need that perspective sometimes.

Ba-*buh* ba-ba-*buh* ba-ba-*buh*.

Yeah. Like that. Not all the time. Just like that. Just to keep me grounded.

Ha, ha.

The box went in the way it was supposed to do, right next to Mom. There's a blank space on her stone where they'll carve his name and dates in along with hers. I'll have to call someone to get that done. Back to the yellow pages, I guess. And I already know, even now, that every time I see that stone and those names linked together like that, I will lose all belief in God, just one more time. In anything. In anything that makes any sense. Of anything.

I just don't understand it. I never have. But this is pretty much the way they were supposed to end up, I guess.

While the diggers started filling in the dirt, Harris offered to go pick Allison up at school for me. Said he'd kind of enjoy the chance since he wasn't at work anyway. I said no, that I wanted to see her too. But he could tag along if he wanted. We could go together. Give her a treat. Take her out for ice cream or something. He is her father, after all. And she really does seem to like him. Strange as that may be. She even looks like him a bit. I do see that. Even though sometimes that's hard for me.

And I'll tell you something else that's hard for me, and that is that maybe Harris is right. About just this one thing. Just this one time. It costs me to say that, but maybe he is right about the root of this problem. Right, that I just can't believe these two events were unrelated. Just can't accept that it wasn't my father in that electric water, not him streaming through my daughter, not him burning down into me as he walked out onto those tracks and waited there to get killed. Not him hurting us, his flesh and blood, even as his life blew away.

I just don't believe it.

Because I see my father. I do see him there. I see him standing outside of that tunnel, in the dark. And I see myself at that moment dipping my beautiful naked child into her bath. I know exactly where they found him. I know the path he walked from the Place. And I know the ripples of water around her small body as she plays. I know the slight gray tinge of daily dirt that falls around her, and rings that bathtub. And I know how he got out. Which nurse had her back turned. Which orderly thought he knew that my father was tucked into bed. And I know the smell of my daughter's shampoo. The way her ears emerge as her hair rises into lather. I know what my father was wearing, his gray wool pants I mail-ordered him last month, a white T-shirt bought by my mother God knows when, no shoes. The last time I saw him, he'd lost so much weight. His food was all poisoned, he believed. I know that. The air was growing harder for him to breathe. The air that Allison breathes. I know that he couldn't breathe her air anymore. I know he was diminishing. I know that she is growing. The nurses were pouring toxins into his room with their words. I know the songs I sing to her as she bathes. The songs she begs me for. He wouldn't let anyone speak around him. He had forbidden even me to speak. Every word was deadly. Every breath was painful for him.

> There once was a man with a daughter,
> Whose electricity ran in her water.
> When his body was found,
> Her house had lost ground,
> But what was the lesson it taught her?

And that is why Harris is right about me. Why Harris, who is always wrong, is right. Because I just think there has to be some connection. I just think there has to be.

And Harris. I mean, just look at him. Examine him sometime. Look at Harris. Look into his eyes.

He just doesn't care.

"So what?" I can still hear him say, like when we first met. "So what?"

I just think there's an answer to that. Even if I haven't found it yet. I just think there has to be.

Tableau
Vivant

THERE SHOULDN'T HAVE BEEN MICE in late June. Not inside. It made no sense. Later, after the first frost, Jean wouldn't question their presence. The cottage was in the country after all, that was the point of the cottage, and in the country there are field mice, tiny, silken creatures seeking winter warmth, like everyone else. They weren't even so terrible then, not when expected. They were—an expression Jean's husband, Cliff, liked to use—part of the deal. If it weren't for the droppings and the general sense of God knows what on their feet, they would almost be amusing. One could flick on the light and watch them scurry through invisible exits in the seam of floor and wall, bumping into one another like Keystone Cops; though sometimes, a single mouse would stop, eyes so round and uniformly black, so like plastic toy eyes, it was a mystery to Jean how she knew the creature was gazing into hers—what exactly was that sense of connection?—and a mystery too why, when all the others fled, this one stayed.

But that was the winter, when there was snow on the ground and arthritis in her knuckles, and mice seeking shelter, understandably enough, and this was early summer, when they were supposed to be in the fields, where field mice belong.

Like so much else recently, this was wrong.

With her good hand, the right hand, Jean sprayed the evidence with bleach, then tore off a square of paper towel and wiped the butcher block, the specter of *filth* overpowering concerns about what was and wasn't good for the wood. At the sink she let the water run hot, washing both hands, the right caring for the left as it had learned to do in the seven weeks since her stroke.

Jean Kurek looked a bit like a field mouse herself, with her close-cut gray hair, in her shapeless gray dress—no zippers, no buttons. Stroke clothes. Her appearance was no more or less distinguished than it had been all her sixty-eight years, the most likely description of her a string of negatives. *Not really tall or short, you wouldn't say she's heavy but she isn't particularly thin, not ugly, not at all, but not pretty either, her hair is that color that isn't blond or brown.* Arguably, her most striking feature was the absence of any striking feature—though her hair had finally claimed a color, gray. She'd certainly never been considered beautiful, not by anyone other than Cliff, who had been adamant on the point for over forty years; but if she'd ever yearned for greater consensus, that yearning had been tempered by her knowledge of how she would loathe the attention it would bring. Jean had spent a lifetime trying to be inconspicuous, appreciating that nature had given her a head start. As she stepped out from the kitchen now and crunched her way over the garden's gravel pathways, even the briskness of her pace seemed designed to make her presence as little disruptive as possible, and the arm hanging loose by her side, like something she would soon remember to gather up. Which made it all the more peculiar that while she gave her garden this cursory once-over she was entirely preoccupied with trying to remember where she had stored a certain very long, very flamboyant, very turquoise scarf.

The move to the cottage, four years earlier, had come with old age—Cliff's, not Jean's. The fifteen years between them had opened up as if blossoming, fifteen full-petal roses, expanding beyond what she had ever imagined possible, so that she and he were no longer in anything like the same stage of life. "Your father turned eighty and became an old man," she told her children, "while I turned sixty-five and became a full-time caregiver."

It was Cliff who had wanted to move to the country. He announced this—as was his habit, to announce, pronounce, proclaim—on a particularly nasty January day, in Rochester. "I want to die somewhere beautiful," he told her by way of explanation, which was startling, if only because he had always seemed to be oblivious to his surroundings, at times enviably oblivious, given the places they had lived.

He didn't push her. Cliff Kurek was capable of pushing, but their history was such that he had every reason to count on her acquiescence before it came to that. And this time there was no doubt. Jean had lived in small cities all her life, third-tier cities like Wilmington, Delaware, and Richmond,

Virginia, Bridgeport, Connecticut, which was not third-tier at all but aspired to be. She had spent more than four decades accompanying—she dismissed the word *following,* when it popped into her thoughts—this restless but oddly unambitious man while he jumped from job to job, lateral jumps, long rather than high, because it turned out that an itch could be as powerful a motivator as a lofty aspiration.

"Running toward or running away?" her own mother had asked when they were still young.

"Toward," Jean had answered without pause. And then, with an uncharacteristic snap, "Don't be ridiculous." But she couldn't imagine what she'd have said if instead of just looking skeptical, her mother had asked, "Toward what?"

It had never occurred to Jean that there would be a final move, not one acknowledged as such before the fact. For all the time Cliff spent planning, there never appeared to be an actual plan. The endgame had always seemed likely to be one of musical chairs. When the music stops, you are where you are, wherever you happen to be.

The notion of a country cottage settled in her thoughts as a watercolor, red bricks, climbing roses, the house the most intelligent of the three little pigs built, but with some age on it now; and the place they found in western Massachusetts wasn't far off, solid enough to withstand huffs and puffs, small enough to feel manageable, large enough to hold visiting grandchildren, old enough to inspire optimism about what might, improbably, endure. They made an offer on the spot. Practiced at folding their tents, they moved with little trouble in just over a month, and country life soon began to seep into Jean's bones. She started going for long walks. She stopped wearing what little makeup she had worn. She took up gardening, literally put down roots. Her life became both more practical and more poetic. "Our cottage is nestled in the crook of three hills," she wrote on the change-of-address cards she sent, aware as she did of using words she had never used before. Though really, any description of this home seemed paltry. What was required was an explanation, the cottage having slipped in Jean's understanding from being a beautiful place to being something more like a mystical event; just as all the old cities blurred together into one cold, rainy day spent waiting for a bus running late.

She found the scarf in the closet of the large guest room where their daughter, Brooke, was to stay that night. Bright turquoise, covered in an extravagant pattern of pink feathers, it was one of those objects that no one in the family had ever claimed but that seemed unshakable, following them from place to place, never mind that Jean was certain she had given it to Goodwill at least three times. Five feet long, maybe a foot wide, it was the perfect shape. Though the puzzle, the paradox, was how to construct a sling with only one hand. There had been quite a bit of improvement since the stroke—*Any more signs of life?* her doctor would cheerfully ask—but she wasn't up to tying knots. She laid the scarf out on the bed, doubled it over, then stared at it for a bit, until she decided she could put it on the floor and use her knees to hold the fabric taut while she tied the ends together.

It took a few tries, and she felt ridiculous, as though she were playing Twister by herself, as though she were a bit demented, but eventually she managed to secure the ends together and wriggle her way into it, her left arm loosely cradled in a tropical neon blaze. It was a masterpiece of misdirection, she thought as she stood before the mirror and admired the effect.

Cliff laughed at the sight of her in the sling, great crags appearing on his droopy face. He hadn't always been so easily tickled, but in old age was prone to chuckles, as though he had finally gotten the joke.

She stood between him and the blaring television set, and turned all the way around, just once, a slow twirl made of many small steps. "Feast your eyes," she said. "The new me." She walked to the chair beside his. "I'm an awfully clumsy woman," she said, as she sat. "I'll be lucky if I don't break a hip next."

"Don't even think it," he said. "Goddesses don't break their hips."

A lung infection, she had told him seven weeks earlier, to explain her overnight hospital stay. A cold gone bad. The decision to lie had barely registered as a decision, just fallen in line with the deaths of friends he would never see again anyway and various other bits of unhappy, unnecessary news. His world had been winnowed down to conform to his dwindling capacities; if it couldn't be expanded to experience joy, she surely wasn't expanding it in order to worry him. And any trace of doubt she might have felt was dispelled by his failure to notice the arm drooping by her side. In the old days, in their young days, there was nothing about her body she could have hidden from him, not the smallest bump or bruise, much less an entire limb gone useless.

"Goddesses don't trip over trees," she said.

Brooke's early-morning email had read, in its entirety, *I'm going to be there around four,* very much as though it were the second email, the one after the one in which the visit was proposed and she explained whether she was coming alone or with Ian and the kids. It read like a second email, but it was not. It was the first and only mention of her plan, the whole thing feeling distinctly hasty, as Brooke's actions often did. Her mother thought of her as ramshackle by nature, seeming to move through life in great loops of forward and backward progress, trailing loose ends behind her like maypole ribbons.

It was close to six when she materialized in the living room.

"I knocked and knocked," she said, reaching for the remote control by Cliff's side, pressing Mute. "My knuckles are raw from knocking. How can you stand it?" She frowned toward Jean's sling, her head tilted in a question.

"I tripped," Jean said. "That's all. I tripped on a tree root this morning and stupidly broke my fall with my wrist. It's just a sprain, if even that." Brooke nodded, a single nod, a sympathetic grimace appearing but quickly gone, leaving Jean feeling a little stung. It was a bit painful having her lie so easily accepted.

She had been going to tell her children the truth—originally—but then she had felt this disinclination to have anyone, to have them in particular, interfere. That was what she told herself, the word *meddle* springing to mind. She didn't want them to meddle. There was this problem with the children, that they tended to waltz in and try to take over—briefly, for only as long as they chose to stay. They tended to give advice that sounded less like suggestions than demands on how Jean should manage the house, how she and Cliff should eat, what books on the aging body they should read—or, better yet, listen to on the devices they should buy. And then they went home. Initially, the lie had been to ward that off—or so Jean told herself. If there was also at work an intuition that the sympathies of others might somehow limit how sorry she could feel for herself, it was not a conscious one.

"You should fence off whatever trips you up," Brooke said. "Maybe you should have lights out there." Jean gave a noncommittal nod.

She thought her daughter looked well. At forty-three, Brooke kept her hair a brassy auburn that Jean hated when she thought about it, hated on principle, but admired face-to-face. It brightened her skin, nudged her eyes from hazel to green. Her body, no longer thin, no longer seemed striving to be thin and had acquired a relaxed, logical quality, as though the wide hips and general sense of plenty were the obvious right choice. She had an appealing aura of overflow to her. She was—a word Jean hadn't thought of in years—a bit blowsy, and it suited her.

"Did you see?" Cliff asked, chuckling again. "It's that same damned scarf. Good thing we never threw it out."

"Though truly, I did throw it out. Several times." Jean kissed her leaning daughter's cheek.

"Well, you look very exotic. I wish the kids could see their flamboyant grandmother. You look like you got tangled up in someone else's dance costume. Hello, Dad. How are you?" Brooke leaned into the pose of a hug, then quickly straightened. Jean recognized the tone, the question not really asked, the embrace not quite given, the legacy of a father so often preoccupied with planning his next move. Brooke turned back to her and smiled widely. "It's like Isadora Duncan's infamous scarf! Just be careful in the car."

"My secret life. You've found me out."

"It's always the quiet ones, isn't it?"

Brooke was still standing between Cliff and the TV, and though it had barely been a minute, Jean could see him growing, if not consciously impatient, physically twitchy. It was difficult for anyone else to understand how immersed he was in that world, to appreciate the degree to which caring about those flickers of color and light kept him from brooding on himself. It was one of the many features of their life that defined even the children as outsiders now. She was relieved when Brooke said it had been a hell of a drive, that she needed a shower, maybe even a nap if there was time.

"There's plenty of time," Jean said. "We can eat whenever you're ready."

Brooke pressed the Mute button again, and the TV blared on. "Is that better?" she boomed, much more loudly than necessary.

"We'll still be here," Cliff said, chortling a bit. "Until a better offer comes along."

The two of them resettled, one of Cliff's home shows on the TV. A family of five jumped up and down, squealing at the sight of their new family room. In the next half hour, a condo in South Beach went from sleek to unimaginably sleek. Cliff turned out to like design. He liked to talk about materials. He kept track of trends—stainless appliances, mission-style everything, bathroom vanities with double sinks. Granite counters. He could ballpark costs of renovations, costs of the homes themselves. He knew the names and little quirks of all the hosts, developed what Jean could only think of as relationships with them.

"I'm thinking we should put in . . . granite counters," said the beautiful young decorator—Lani De Rosso—as though it were a novel idea. "What do you think of that?" she asked the owners.

"I think it's obvious, Lani," Cliff said. "I think it's what you always say. I think you should consider something new."

They ate at the maple kitchen table, Cliff at one end, his wife and daughter on either side. Dinner was roasted chicken pieces, cooked and delivered by Nancy Lewis, a neighbor from down the road. She had long pitched in now and then, but had become a regular and a confidante since the stroke. Jean added a last-second can of baby peas, snatched from the back of the pantry. Brooke opened it. By themselves, they rarely ate side dishes, but that was one more expediency of old age best kept from the children.

Brooke cut Jean's chicken for her. "As long as I'm here, you might as well let me."

She gave no explanation for her sudden appearance. It wasn't Jean's way to push, and Cliff was long past knowing if her visit was sudden or if he'd just forgotten it was coming up. In a sense, everything was sudden for him.

They talked a little about Ian and the children, just details from the morning, email making it unnecessary to catch up on any real news. Hannah had been agitating to drive herself to school. Connor dreading the frog dissection on his schedule. Poor, sniffly Ian thinking he might be allergic to the cat—if one could develop allergies at forty-four. Brooke told a story about the pharmaceutical company where she worked, a ridiculous ad campaign scrapped, a proposed slogan that would have made them a laughingstock. Cliff talked about his shows.

"The new thing is to paint every wall brown. Jeanie, did we ever, in forty-plus years, paint a wall brown?" She shook her head. "Turns out, we were supposed to." He frowned, shook his head. "You never do know."

"You weren't supposed to then," Jean said, as though *then* covered their entire married life. "Brown was still ugly then."

As they spoke, Brooke picked at her nail polish, an old habit, though Jean hadn't seen her do it in years. As a girl, she used to leave little piles of tiny pink and red bits around the house, like fancy-dress pencil shavings.

When Brooke volunteered to do the dishes—"As long as I'm here, you might as well let me," she said again—Jean mentioned the mice.

"I know it's odd that they're inside in June," she said, almost as though apologizing. "It's possible I haven't been as tidy since . . ." She caught herself. "It's possible I'm slipping in my old age. Anyway, be sure to clean any crumbs."

"I will clean all crumbs," Brooke said. She brushed the pile of red polish shards into her palm. "They'll never know we were here."

The squeal and groan of the stairs woke Jean during the night, but the low gurgle of her daughter's laugh pinned her to her bed. Five hours later, bleaching the kitchen counters once again, she would wonder why she had been so certain there was another person there. It could have been a phone call, a middle-of-the-night exchange of anecdotes with Ian, one of the children doing something amusing, or even Brooke laughing at her parents and their tiny world of Mute buttons and home makeover reveals. But lying in the dark Jean had no doubt, no doubt that there was another person there, no doubt that this person and her daughter were lovers, no doubt at all—like glancing at the back cover of a book and inadvertently, irretrievably knowing too much.

Brooke appeared in the kitchen just before ten, wearing a light green sundress and shiny, strappy sandals, her hair still wet from the shower, her nails repolished smooth, and announced—when had she too become an announcer?—that she was walking the mile into town. She might see if there was a movie playing. She hadn't gone to a movie in months. They shouldn't keep lunch for her. They wouldn't,

Jean said, then told her daughter that the movie always started at one o'clock. "Around here," she said, "people like that kind of thing. A regular schedule, I mean."

"I'll keep that in mind." From the living room, the television blared. "I really don't know how you stand that," Brooke said, and in the moments after she left, Jean wondered exactly what choice her daughter thought she had.

In the old days, of course, she would have told Cliff. Parenting is a conspiracy. But these were other days, so she left him to his shows.

The wooden staircase, with its steep treads and its audible objections and the slight curve toward the top, had lain in wait for some years now, a sleeping serpent stretched in their home, ready to snap. It had been something like love, something like the myopia of romance that had blinded them to the inevitable collusion between a staircase and time. It was a miracle Cliff could still manage it.

One unexpected revelation of old age was the degree to which death solved certain logistical problems—a feeble justification for its heartlessness, but a notion oddly present in one's thoughts. Short of death, the plan was to convert the living room into a bedroom. "When my knees go," Cliff had said, speaking in euphemism, the language of the unthinkable.

Upstairs, the guest bedroom door was closed, and for a moment Jean paused as though she might knock, but then she turned the small brass doorknob.

She felt ridiculous the moment she did. For the second day running, she was doing something absurd in this room.

The bed was slept in, of course, though tidied. At its foot, a white nightgown draped over the milky-blue wooden chest. A red glass bottle, maybe perfume, sat on the windowsill. A battered pair of sneakers poked their toes out from under the dresser.

After only a very few moments, she closed the door, irritated with herself. What had she been planning to do in there? Sniff the sheets? She scurried downstairs, quickly, and then outside.

Late June, the garden was still more beautiful than demanding. By August, the weeds would win out. Heat and weeks of battling them would have beaten Jean. But now they were still almost courteous in their arrival, a weed here, a weed there. She could manage most of it on her feet, leaning over to yank one every couple of steps. In three weeks, she knew, she would be on her knees.

Jean had always been convinced that the price of the cottage had been for the structure itself, with the six acres of old farmland thrown in. It was Cliff's view that they were paying for the acreage, and the cottage had been more or less free. Either way, every year, Jean's cultivated garden encroached a tiny bit more on land long ago reclaimed by its own untended tendencies. Each April she hired a local boy to dig a new plot—as though the house were a tossed pebble and these long, curved beds the ripples that it caused. This spring it was roses, bare roots shipped up from Texas, tangled all together in a cardboard box.

She planted them at the end of April, six all the same variety, Winchester roses, white, double petals. It had seemed unimaginable that these thorn-speckled sticks might somehow—how?—explode into rosebushes. They would have to turn themselves inside out—a magician's trick.

April 27. The afternoon of her stroke. She'd been standing there with the boy, Nancy's son, Tyler Lewis from down the road, questioning him on whether the bushes seemed evenly spaced, and he'd been saying you couldn't really call them bushes, could you, when they looked so much like kindling. She was rubbing her left hand as they spoke, not thinking it through, just sensing that it had gone asleep while she'd been patting the topsoil over the roots. She was trying to get the blood flowing, waiting for the pins and needles to begin, when gradually her thoughts turned from the bushes to that heavy, numb sensation. She wanted to lift the hand, just to look at it, but realized she could not. It hung there limp, covered in dirt, as though it were already dead and had been dug from the ground.

Tyler drove her to the hospital in his tin can car. His mother stayed with Cliff, and then with them both, for many days, seeming to enjoy Jean's deception, giving Cliff and anyone else who called detailed, fictional accounts of her recovery from her bronchial woes.

The sticks suited Jean's mood those first few weeks. Having planted roses, she was reaping thorns, the perfect bouquet for her solitary martyrdom. But then even they seemed to stop caring, caught up as they were in themselves, sprouting red nubs like potato eyes, spinning out into green stems, five-leaf clusters, buds in a hurry to exist, in a hurry to bloom, pink-tinged white, blushing at their own exposure, insistently, ludicrously beautiful. Five of them anyway, a single one remaining bare—which looked peculiar, but turned out not to be.

They could be temperamental, she read online. It wasn't a sure thing they would wake from dormancy on command. What looked dead might actually be. After all, nature didn't make promises. On the other hand, mail-order plants were guaranteed. Shipping season was over for the year, the Texan supplier told her, but Jean's name would go on a list. First thing next spring, they would send her a new Winchester. Though the bushes did sometimes wake up, the woman said, even after taking twice as long as the others. "They're *jest* funny things. They have their moods. *Jest* like all the rest of us. Sometimes, they're *jest* playing dead."

And sure enough, right after Brooke left for town, a full seven weeks after Jean had planted them, she saw a tiny reddish bump, the unmistakable beginning of what would become unfurling leaves and bursting blooms—as though the last of her commiserating friends were moving on.

When Brooke returned just before dinner, she was as unruffled as her bedroom had been. All but her hair, which was a mess. She disappeared upstairs for a few minutes, returning with the whole auburn mass twisted into an elegant knot, for whose benefit Jean couldn't imagine.

As they sat again around the table, neither she nor Brooke spoke very much, leaving Cliff, always happier speaking than trying to catch others' words, to recount the many transformations he had witnessed that day.

The noises didn't wake her; she was awake when she heard Brooke's door open, then Brooke on the stairs, the front door, the distant hum of a car growing louder, the front door again, the stairs, the click of Brooke's door.

Distinctly irritated, she rolled onto her side.

When the children were teenagers, she had dealt with their sexual activities, those known to her at the time, by pretending ignorance. Some of it was her disinclination to have that conversation with them, and some of it was her sense that they were of reasonable ages, that if she wasn't going to object on principle, then she wasn't going to send them out of the house—or have Cliff send them, which is how it would have gone. No thinking parent was in a rush for their child to park out in the darkness somewhere. People had been known to get shot that way. Once in a while, some sound would escape from behind a closed door, a gasp or moan, a bawdy laugh, but those were somehow sanitized and neutralized as they registered in Jean's consciousness. Whatever sex her children were having was no more real sex to her than the stuff in their diapers had been real shit. Our children exist in some not quite human realm, she'd long before decided. They aren't exactly people to us.

So it wasn't parental squeamishness that made her turn the TV on now. And it wasn't a disinclination to hear evidence, further evidence, of her daughter's infidelity. Something else was producing this feeling, this pebble in her shoe, this grain of sand between her teeth. It was possibly, simply, the presence of sex in her home, when for several years she had tried to forget it existed at all. An absurd, impossible task, maybe. But what choice did she have? What choice but to pretend there was no such thing?

It hadn't been until their second spring at the cottage that Jean had let herself understand, could no longer prevent herself from understanding, how thoroughly what felt to her like her first home felt to Clifford like his last. How each room, each wall, each patch of grass, tree, pebble, shaft of light was defined for them in these ways. How this sensation of *not having to move* twisted and shifted in Cliff into the sensation of *not being able to move,* so what gave her joy hollowed him. These pleasures of hers, she knew, were indebted to his age, to the strength of his frailty, to the cessation of his restlessness. Finally, simply, to the proximity of his death.

They were in bed when she realized this or realized that she had known it all along. They were in bed together, with the television on, lying side by side, in a bedroom in which they had never made love, a bedroom in which, she had just admitted to herself, they never would.

If the idea that there would be an acknowledged final move had surprised her, the fact that there had been an unacknowledged last time making love was stunning. Some kind of bargain had been struck, somewhere, somehow. She had given things up to have other things. But she hadn't been consulted. She hadn't really bargained at all; life had preemptively done it for her, drawn up this deal.

So what choice did she have but to unbraid the different strands of love and learn devotion without desire again? Desire without devotion? Manage the business of sex as she had when a girl, by herself. Forget that she knew any other

way. What choice but to accept this cottage's chaste en-
chantment as being—as Cliff himself would say—part of
the deal?

As she lay there, once again rehearsing all of this, a chord
of two voices arced out into the air, over Cliff's regular,
raspy breaths, over the late-night banter of a television host
and his guest, through the wall Jean had built, was continually rebuilding, between her desires and her life as it must
be lived.

In the morning, agitated, resolute, Jean left Clifford sleeping on his side and frowned her way through the familiar
rituals. Teeth, face, toilet, clothes, performing any number
of two-handed tasks with one hand, only just remembering
to slip the sling on as she headed for the stairs.

She found her daughter in the garden, vibrant in a dark
purple dress, brassy hair blowing, staring out toward an ancient, long-abandoned row of apple trees. As they stood
side by side, the splash of color cradling Jean's arm looked
as though it belonged to the other woman, as though some
piece of Brooke had spilled onto Jean. They exchanged a
few words about how beautiful the setting was. Much more
so than anywhere they had ever lived as a family, Brooke
said; and Jean responded that the bar hadn't been set very
high, but yes, it was beautiful. For a moment, her mind
drifted toward thoughts of a connection between Cliff's
lifelong restlessness and Brooke's restless romance, affair,
whatever it was. It could be a causal link: they had moved
around so frequently, Brooke had never learned to stay
with something. Maybe a genetic one: she was her father's

daughter, after all; his restlessness might have taken this sexual turn in her. But none of it much mattered, Jean thought, spooling her musings back in. By and large, she had outlived her own interest in why things had happened the way they had, in cause, with its eternal backward glance. She put her right hand on her daughter's shoulder. She had decided she would use the word *company*. She would say, *Brooke, I know you've been having company.* But before she did, Brooke herself said, "We have company coming for dinner tonight. I hope that's okay. I'll cook, of course. A friend of mine turns out to be up here too, so I asked him over," and Jean, who had been knocked off script, found herself saying, "No. Of course. That's fine. Of course that's fine." And retreating to the house.

"You have to stand up to them," Cliff used to tell her. "Children need to know who's in charge."

But she had learned early on that she could not. She was incapable of battle, so if a child chose to fight, that child would win. Little things. Making them eat unfamiliar foods. Forcing them into clothes they had rejected. Ben had spat every ounce of medicine he was ever given across the room, if not directly into Jean's face. And Brooke would run away with both hands on her head, hiding in the empty cedar closet under the eaves when Jean tried to brush her hair. When Jean dangled bright metal butterflies and ladybugs, attached to elastics, and cooed about how pretty they were, how pretty they would look affixed to Brooke's curls, Brooke arranged her face into an expression of such haughty disbelief that Jean told Cliff that their five-year-old daughter looked like an old Frenchman. The one time she took her to have the curls sheared into some manageable form—like a topiary creature, she couldn't help thinking—Brooke threw the kind of tantrum Jean had only heard about from friends, her body seeming both stiff and capable of moving in ways the presence of bones and ligaments would argue against, her screams so piercing that Jean found herself glancing toward the large mirrors, as though to catch the moment of shattering. And needless to say, they had driven home, mop of hair still intact.

Looking down from her bedroom window, Jean can see that hair from behind, loose and windblown, the artificial hue without Brooke's face to testify to its worth, unsettling against the garden's greens and grays.

His name was Aaron. He was a great huge man a bit older than Brooke, maybe fifty, bald, and—Jean thought—remarkably ugly, dressed in blue jeans and a pale yellow shirt that looked recently ironed. His handshake was firm. His arms were enormous. His eyes were obscured by an unending squint. His lower lip hung just to the left of his upper, as though he were perpetually reeling from a punch. The sheer physicality of him took her aback, the size of him and the specificity of his oddness. He banged his head on the dining room doorway, the cottage itself making some none too subtle point.

Brooke had cooked all afternoon—*ruthlessly*, Jean had thought, walking into the kitchen at one point. Now, she shuttled dish after dish to the table, refusing help from both her mother and her, what? lover, it seemed. Her enormous, homely lover. No dish had fewer than five ingredients, or fewer than three layers. Chicken, plums, almonds, in pastry. White, purple, and yellow potatoes, sliced thin, stacked into little striped towers, sprinkled with cream, dusted with nutmeg.

He was an engineer, a structural engineer. He talked about the bridges he had built, about span and tension. He talked about what had failed in the ones across the country that had recently fallen down. With Brooke's encouragement, he also spoke about his three sons. Jean, who felt a bewildered form of curiosity, feigned genuine interest, while Cliff, who had been interested in the bridges, did not, but poked at the structures on his plate as though unsure of how to transform their architecture into food.

The oldest boy was an avid reader, he said, a real intellectual. He would be applying to college in the fall. The second, the middle one, was an athlete, he told Jean—as though between them the two boys might make one whole boy. How odd it was, she thought, that parents so often did that, handed out attributes to their children like sections of the same cherry pie.

"Aaron's youngest son is in a wheelchair, Mom. He was in a diving accident, two years ago."

"Oh," Jean said. "How terrible. I'm sorry." She thought she saw Aaron's eyes flutter open for just a second. She thought she saw his cheeks grow redder.

"Well," he said. "It's been very difficult. It is. For him, I mean. He was just nine when it happened."

"And for you," Brooke said. She turned to her mother. "It was a quarry. Kids diving off the rocks. You can't imagine what's involved now."

"It must be very hard for you," Jean said. "He's your child. I'm so sorry. It must almost be worse for you. In some ways."

Aaron shook his head, the lower lip, askew, now jutting out. "I used to think that." He picked up his fork and tapped it on the table, twice, then a third time. "I used to see children, like him, with something wrong. And I would always feel worse for the parents." He shook his head again. "Because I think, I think what you're really afraid of is how you'd feel. If it was your kid. But it isn't like that," he said. "Not really. You know—I know—it's worse for him."

Jean said nothing. Across the table, Cliff was wearing the face he had developed for times like this when he couldn't quite hear a conversation and didn't want to seem rude—a thoroughly noncommittal expression, poised to shift quickly should he suddenly catch some words. She hadn't been so ready, so poised, hadn't expected tragedy to join them at the table.

"He isn't an unhappy boy," Aaron said, as though reading her mind, banishing that word, probably practiced at doing so. "His mother has done an incredible job."

"She used to work as a lawyer," Brooke said. "But she stopped when the accident happened."

"He doesn't have a sad life," Aaron said. "When I'm with him, I'm not . . ." He was looking across the table at Brooke. "It's when we're apart that I sag. He's going to camp this summer," he told Jean. "It's a big deal for him. My wife did months of research to find this place. It's amazing when you see what these kids do."

"It must be," Jean said. What more could she say? "I hope it works out well."

"He's a great kid. He'll do great."

Jean was out of conversation.

Cliff, at his end of the table, was staring off now, a vaguely worried expression on his face. Maybe just unused to company, Jean thought, or maybe disturbed by some unformed intuition that there was more going on here than he had been told.

"You'll be pleased to hear that I bought traps, and Aaron has volunteered to set them," Brooke said, suddenly bright—though looking at Jean *diagnostically*, as though trying to determine how much she had guessed. "The mice," she said. "If you have peanut butter, we can use that. I'll do the dishes and he'll load the traps."

"In the pantry. No, in the refrigerator." Jean frowned. "It's the all-natural kind, half oil. I don't even know why we have it."

"Probably Ben." Brooke turned back to Aaron. "My brother's a granola type, a tree hugger. I think I've told you that."

"I thought your brother's name was Glen."

Brooke shot a look to her mother, tried a small, rueful smile.

"It's Ben," Jean said. "His name is Benjamin."

"It's just a family joke," Brooke said. "I should have told you. Because of Cliff and Brooke. Cliff, Brooke, Glen."

"We didn't do it on purpose," Jean said. "Brooke and Cliff, I mean. I wasn't trying to be clever. Or cute." That was what people had always said: *How cute*. It had embarrassed her then in a way it now seemed impossible to be embarrassed. The name Brooke had been a fancy of hers, a signal that the baby who had just emerged from her was special, a hope born of that moment's euphoria that with so unusual a name—this was 1965—her daughter would have no choice but to step into the world more confidently than she herself ever had. She had cried when the link between Cliff and Brooke was pointed out to her. Two years later, Benjamin was named after Jean's father, but also after her own retreat from flights of fancy. "I've always hated his being called Glen," she said.

"My oldest boy is named Wright, a family name, on his mother's side." Aaron was turned toward her, his eyes so squinted she couldn't see them. "So, his brother," he said, "the middle one, is always called Wrong." He frowned a bit. "I suppose that's obvious," he said. "He certainly hates it."

"That one's Edward," Brooke said. "The middle boy."

"He hates that too," Aaron said. "Somewhere along the way, he turned into Teddy. Ted now that he's a teenager, though we forget. I forget."

"What's your youngest named?" Jean asked.

"Jason."

"I love that name," Brooke said. "I think people grow into their names. Though I always loved mine." This was said for Jean—with a larger smile thrown in, to make up for Glen.

"I told the boys they could change whatever they liked once they were eighteen. Or maybe I said once they were paying for their own food."

"Funny," Brooke said. "I'm constantly telling mine everything they can do when they grow up too."

"Some days the list is pretty long." Aaron looked bleak.

"Yes," Brooke said, "and then you grow up and discover

how very short it really is." Jean watched them droop in unison, for just a moment, then recover. "Actually, I like Teddy for a girl, too," Brooke said. "Teddy and Sam. Alex."

"I like Alex a lot."

It had become an strange conversation, Jean thought. They sounded like a young couple broaching the subject of their future together. What to name the children? Except they didn't look excited. They looked, if anything, tense. They looked sad; and for the first time, it occurred to Jean to wonder at how deep their feelings ran. What they had done together, here, in the cottage, what they were doing, had loomed so large, like Aaron himself, taking up too much space, banging its head on the doorways. For just a moment, instead, Jean was aware of all they hadn't done, would never do.

Brooke stood; then Aaron did. "Let's go find that peanut butter," she said. "My brother only comes east twice a year, he and his lunatic wife, Cheryl. They smell of incense and leave the place full of food that no one else will eat." As Brooke spoke, she and Aaron began gathering plates. "But then, young Glenjamin doesn't worry a lot about other people," she said. Her voice had lowered, softening, taking on the tones of a private conversation. "That isn't his thing. Human beings, I mean." As she stood beside Aaron, she was practically whispering. He murmured something back. Then she murmured in response and back and forth it went, this indistinct exchange, these gentle vibrations of sound. It was like overhearing two tuning forks, Jean thought. Two whales.

It was like overhearing lovers.

When she looked over at Cliff, he peered at her expectantly, doubtless waiting for her to say it was time to go watch TV, as she did after dinner most nights. But she couldn't bring herself to shout, as she would have to do. She couldn't quite bear to signal so loudly that the soft pit-a-pat of their own intimate speech was a thing of their past. She smiled at him instead, just a little, and mouthed the words *Let's go*.

In bed that night, hearing what she thought were sobs from her daughter's room, unable to go check, lest she was wrong, lest Brooke wasn't alone, lest the heartbroken Aaron was there as well, their hearts breaking together, Jean sat up. There was a reckoning of some kind to come. There always seemed to be. It was something she had long understood. She could remember Brooke's very first few months, how she had been so little trouble, so docile really, that Jean had endured regular bouts of fear, not only that the baby wasn't normal—by which she then still meant exceptional—but also that so easy an infancy would be paid for one day, fear that it all evens out somehow, suspicious even then of the deals life might make on our behalf.

In the morning, Brooke came down the stairs just after eight and peered into the kitchen, her bags in hand. She was wearing the green dress from two days earlier, but the sandals were gone, replaced by the old sneakers that had poked out from under the bureau upstairs. "Driving shoes," she said, following her mother's gaze.

Jean walked her to her car, parked under the willow four

days earlier. The roof, sunroof, hood were all splattered with bird droppings. "Stupid," Brooke said. "Acres of open field, and I park under a tree. I was thinking shade, when I should have been thinking bird."

"Just watch out. It eats through the paint."

Brooke nodded, and mumbled something Jean didn't quite catch about a car wash on her way home. They hugged, and for a moment Jean thought she could feel the whole thing threaten to shudder its way out of wherever her daughter had tucked it, but when Brooke stepped back, a grim smile sealed her lips.

"Will you be okay?" Jean asked, not sure herself if she meant for the drive or for the next few days or for longer than that.

"I don't really know," Brooke said. "But I promise you, I'll be careful. More careful than I've been for months and months."

As Brooke opened the door, Jean had the impulse to ask her if she loved him, as though hearing her daughter say it out loud would make it any clearer than it was. As though she herself needed it stated, made official somehow, to justify all that had gone on.

She stopped herself. She watched as Brooke fastened her seat belt and slipped her dark glasses over her eyes. She stayed while the car made its way down the road, whispered *Safe travels* as it slipped from her sight.

It wasn't until much later, on an October visit with Ian and the kids, that Brooke told her mother she hadn't seen or spoken to Aaron since that night. She said it as though casually while the two women were alone cooking in the kitchen, Jean's hand enough improved that she could put the weakness off to bad arthritis, doubtless from the sprain.

"I just wanted you to know," Brooke said. "Since he was here. Since you met him."

And then at Thanksgiving, while they did the dishes together, Brooke wondered aloud where Aaron's son would be applying, what colleges. "He was so proud of him. Really of them all. He's so devoted to them."

"You're still not in touch?" Jean asked, and Brooke shook her head. For a moment, it seemed she might say more, but instead she shut the faucet, shook the water off her hands, and stepped outside.

Brooke wasn't there again until early in January, just after Cliff died, quietly, with no warning other than his age. The two families came, Brooke's and Ben's, crowding the cottage, bustle and noise descending where his quiet had been. Looking for an empty room, needing some solitude, Jean found Brooke in the guest bedroom, where there was no TV to draw an audience. They sat side by side on the bed, and it wasn't long before Brooke brought up that night, asking her mother if she remembered the silly discussion about names, if she remembered that he had set the traps, listing the dishes she had made, a litany. *Remember? Remember?* Looking excited as she described her efforts, looking bereft as she talked about the youngest son.

The next day she asked her mother if there had been any mice in the traps, if the peanut butter had worked. She had left for home so hurriedly, she had been so preoccupied. "One in every trap," Jean said; though in fact they had all been empty when she came down—to her relief—and she had sprung them with the end of her broom, tossed them in the trash behind the house.

"I've never seen anyone take such care with anything," Brooke said, smiling. "Leave it to an engineer."

She mentioned the dinner many more times over the next months, when she visited and also on the phone. She never told her mother the whole story, though whether because she understood that Jean already knew or because the story had an end it would always have to reach, Jean never decided. Brooke only wanted to hear this, over and over, like a child delaying sleep: He had been there. She had cooked for him. He had set traps. Remarkably effective traps. Jean had liked him, very much. And after a time, Jean could see them there, herself, the four of them. She hadn't earlier, not in the winter, when she had only listened as Brooke needed her to; but as weeks passed, she began to see them sitting there around the maple table, where Cliff was younger, much younger than he had been, those opened years between them back in their buds, closed tight; and though they were at the cottage, the scene seemed to crackle again with his restlessness and with their desires.

By April, when the newest bed was dug, it wasn't only when Brooke needed her mother to remember, needed the testimony of Jean's memory to confirm her own, that Jean's thoughts turned to that meal. Sometimes, by herself, she would mouth those words, *Let's go*, as though they just might, the four of them—all deals off, whatever bargains brokered, now dissolved. And every once in a while, by herself, she would touch the turquoise scarf, hanging now on the post of her bed, as though it were a souvenir of an important time, a talisman of what might lie ahead. *Let's go.*

And then, when a box of kindling and roots appeared like a foundling infant on the front porch, when she realized she had never had her name struck from that list, instead of sending them back, as she should, she asked Tyler to unpack them for her, so she could soak the roots overnight, softening and opening them, it not even occurring to her at the time that she had never before taken anything not rightfully hers.

Pine

HEIDI'S KITCHEN FLOOR is marble tile, a hard and unforgiving platform for her clumsy gait. If it were me, I think, watching her, I would have put down pine— soft, uneven planks of gentle pine to absorb the step-clump, step-clump sound of my own feet. My foot, and then the pause that would be seared into my soul, that sad and silent pause. And then my other foot.

If it were me, I would have built a smaller kitchen too, I'm sure, a room of easy reaches and rolling carts. But Heidi, with her latest-model leg—her fourth she told me, since losing the original—Heidi is more defiant than I, per-haps. More feisty. Or possibly just more in denial. And so her kitchen is bowling-alley large. Stadium large. Super-dome large. There are two cooktops, two dishwashers, two ovens, and a microwave. There are appliances so modern that their function is indiscernible, and these marvels are spread across three islands all in all, an archipelago of kitchen design, which Heidi navigates with great goodwill, cheerful as she clumps across each expanse.

Four of us, four women, are gathered here because Heidi wanted to bring together her friends who like to cook. She brightened, during chitchat at my daughter's soccer game, when she asked me if I do and I said yes. Yes, I enjoy it.

As we empty our shopping bags onto the largest of the countertops, I learn that the other two women here are Heidi's friends in a way that I am not. They know where she spent her vacation last August. They know where she keeps her coffee mugs. They know how she loves asparagus. They know that her husband, Roger, turned fifty last month, and they know why that fact is such a riot. *Hilarious.* They call her "Hei" and tease her about tendencies I cannot guess she has. "Well, you know Hei!" they say, smiling in the completely closed-circuit way of intimates. With their blond pageboy hair, their gray sweater sets, they look enough alike that I am forced to go for crude distinction at first just to remember which is which. One tall. One short.

"Well, that's exactly Roger, isn't it?" the short one says.

"Have you *met* Roger, Claire?" The tall one turns to me. "Don't you just *know* what we mean?" And I tell her that I have met him, but only at the girls' soccer games. Really just to say hello. Just as I met Heidi. My daughter, Alyssa, I explain, is on a team with their daughter, Katherine. I don't really know Roger, I admit; and as if I have disqualified myself somehow, the tall woman allows her eyes to drift off me as she states to no one in particular: "Well, anyway."

The thread of conversation is soon picked up, the story about Roger followed by a story about another husband, the husband of the short woman. He too has done something, or said something, worthy of their mirth. And so, it turns out, has the third. Every husband is comical, it seems, a figure of fun and yet also of obvious pride. A quirky, worthy companion for them each.

I try not to hear their stories in these terms, try not to be so entirely the widow here. I strain to hear the amusing yarns as only that, and not envy these women who are wives, not hate them, not fall into this familiar shadowed valley of self-pity and grief. But of course I do. I am going down. I feel my descent, as the words and the laughter fly, scattershot, unavoidable, catching me in the friendly fire. Still, I keep a smile frozen across my face.

From up the long granite countertop, Heidi rolls an onion to me and instructs me on how small the pieces should be. The tall woman hands me a short knife. Glad for an excuse to be occupied, I bisect the bulb and peel down the skin. As I begin to chop in earnest, tears swell in my eyes, threatening to burst and stream. They are only onion tears, but I fight them, feeling suddenly exposed. I blink, to no avail, as my cheeks grow wet.

It doesn't matter. The other women are oblivious to my tears. They chatter on. They laugh. I feel out of place and absurdly, embarrassingly hurt, angry that no one sees me cry, worried that anyone will, too obvious and too invisible all at once.

Heidi asks the tall one to reach for a mixing bowl tucked into a cabinet overhead. Obliging, she stretches impossibly far up, retrieving the enormous stainless steel container.

"It must be lovely to be so tall," the short one says. "Especially given who you're married to!" she adds, and they all laugh.

"You only went because she has a wooden leg," Kevin accuses me that night, over wine, wine, spaghetti, and more wine. He is over, keeping me company while Alyssa is out at a school dance. We are indulging in her absence now, playing Bowie too loudly and drinking too much. *How can you stand listening to him?* she would say if she were here. *He's so middle-aged.* And: *That much wine isn't good for you, you know.*

"It had nothing to do with her leg," I correct, though I think he may be right; and Kevin takes the accusation back. As I knew he would, because he has been my yes-man for years and I, his yes-woman—which for all this time has meant that we aren't allowed to disagree with each other. Not when it comes to things like why we did what we did, or whether we were right when arguing with someone else. Kevin has long been my best friend, and this unquestioning affirmation of each other has formed the central tenet of our best friendship. We met at work before Joe died, in the glory days of my marriage, when all I wanted from any man other than Joe was friendship, and all I wanted from friends was that they agree with me that life was good, that my choices were inspired and my future bright as anything can be.

After Joe died, while I was struggling within the tangled, matted mess that Once Upon a Time had been my life, I tried to take things somewhere else with Kevin, beyond friendship and into bed. But Kevin's inherently agreeable nature ruined the sex for me. At that point, I didn't want sex to be about concurrence anymore, about agreement,

about saying yes. That had been sex with Joe. That had
been the glorious synthesis of lovemaking and lust we'd
had. With Joe gone, I needed sex to be something more like
a knock-down drag-out fight, one I could only win by
fucking the living crap out of someone. And without having to think about making love. Or about love at all. Most
importantly, not about love. And I couldn't fuck the living
crap out of Kevin; he was just too nice. I fired him as a lover
after one tender, terrifying occasion on which, as I felt him
rocking just too gently back and forth in me, I lay beneath
him petrified he would declare himself in love. Horrified
that in fact we might be making love, creating love, where
love had not been before. Kevin came, I didn't, and I fired
him. Being my yes-man, he took the decision well enough.
At least he didn't abandon me, didn't stop being my friend.
And since then we've been pretty much okay. Not discussing what happened. Not discussing that we aren't discussing it. Not discussing that either. Just saying yes to each
other, and trying to be kind.

"It wasn't the leg." I shake my head. "Which, by the way,
isn't wood. It's like fiber flesh or cyberflesh. It has complex
circuitry. It's not like she's a pirate, Kev. I went because I
just couldn't come up with a good reason to say no. And
because, let's face it, next Saturday, there she's going to be at
Alyssa's game. It just felt expedient to go and get it over
with. And I left early, anyway. I didn't stay there long."

As I tell him this, I remember Heidi's face, round and
pretty, falling in disappointment at my hurried apologies.
Behind her stretched the long mahogany dining table set
with four place mats, four china plates, four sets of silver,
four long-stem crystal wineglasses. As I nodded my good-

bye, *yes, yes, I really have to go,* Heidi glanced over her shoulder at that perfect quartet, then turned back toward me with a mournful look.

"I'm so sorry. I just realized I have a conflict," I said. "I don't know where my brain is. I'm so sorry. This has been so much fun."

I don't tell Kevin that as I drove from Heidi's home, I imagined her making the long trek toward the table, unsetting my dishes, disrupting that perfect foursome she had created, laboring across the floor, every square of unrelenting tile a defiance of her amputated state. I don't tell him how I wondered if I, like more things than I can list—husbands and legs, to name but two—might demand a more difficult attention as an absence than I had ever required while there.

"That was a good call," Kevin says, which is exactly what I would have said to him. "That fancy food in the middle of the day would have made you sick as a dog. There's no doubt about that in my mind. Those women are all puking into their toilets right now. Does she sleep with it on?"

"Who? What?"

"The leg."

"I have no idea." I laugh a little. "I don't quite know her well enough to ask. Maybe when you come to Alyssa's game you can sneak that question in, you know, between penalties. Did I tell you this is her fourth leg? Her fifth, actually, if you count the first. The original limb." I reach across and pour us both more wine. "Do you suppose she keeps them all? Do you suppose she has them locked up somewhere? Like Bluebeard's wives?"

But Kevin is looking away from me now, leaning back

into his chair and staring at nothing much. Only away
from me. "What precisely is the line," he asks, his words
measured, slow, "between knowing someone well enough
for them to tell you they've had four or five legs and knowing them well enough to ask them if they sleep with any of
them on?" He lifts his glass and takes a long, steady drink.

"I don't exactly know. It's a good question, though," I
say, realizing that once again he and I have wandered to the
subject of intimacy, where it starts and where it stops. How
it is to be defined. This is the persistent unshakable hang-
over I can detect from those few nights of sex we shared.
This continual conversational drift we have. A current,
moving ever toward the question of how these lines are
drawn.

"I don't know precisely what the difference is," I say,
shifting in my own chair to meet his eye, holding his gaze,
pretending to us both there's no tension here. "But if I ever
know her well enough to ask, you'll be the next to hear." I
look at the empty bottle, wrap my hand around it, start to
stand. "We need more wine."

"It's a funny word."

"Wine?"

"Need."

"They're all funny words, Kev. If you think about it."

An hour later, as he leaves, he tells me to call him if I'm
sad. "Standing offer."

"I know. I'll be fine." I smile up into his gentle eyes, and
find them full of concern, full of offer: *Anything, anything,
anything at all.* "Don't worry about me," I say.

Not yet, I tell his eyes.

It hovers between us, increasingly. This other conversation. This critical discourse we never speak out loud. This dishonesty of ours, as we prop each other up, tell one another jokes, encourage each other to go out on dates and have some fun. It is the force of this pretense that pulls our words endlessly into those places of intimacy. With a sign, I believe, with just a whisper, I can have him still.

"Go home," I say and softly kiss his cheek.

After he's gone, I am grateful, in bed alone, for the fuzzy muting of all that wine. In general, I have become careful about drinking too much, too much of the time. There were months after Joe died, months that were a little drowned, a little blurred, in retrospect. Liquor certainly fueled some of the loveless loving my body sought and found with men I barely noticed, except to pummel them in bed. But I don't fool around like that anymore. And I watch it now, with alcohol. Every once in a while, though, that softening patina an extra glass of Chianti can give, that velvet cloth it lays over every jagged edge, evokes a kind of humble gratitude in me.

I can hear music humming still in Alyssa's room. She came in late, full of stories about her friends. I tried to listen with good humor to her tales of adventure at the dance, tried not to allow my resentment toward her companions seep in. But no doubt she senses how I feel about them all. Awkwardly emergent female forms, not children anymore, not adults yet, creatures of transition alone, they call my daughter *Ally* one day and then *Lyssa* the next, as though she were their property, to name and claim. As though she no longer belongs to me and only I have not figured that out. Deceptively clothed in bell-bottoms and horizontal stripes, outfits reinvented from my own youth, they are the trumpeters of my daughter's departure, the harbingers of yet another loss. They are the clock ticking forward with no concern for me. All of them. The one with bad skin. The one with enormous thighs. The one who dresses like a whore. The one who smells like dope. I have trouble telling them apart too—as I did the women in Heidi's kitchen. My tags on them are a mother's silent protest against their undeniable power over my own little girl, herself half woman now. Half already gone from my home.

It's not a level playing field. My foes do not play fair. Death and all of its traveling companions and close associates, all of those beings who sneaked into my house, camouflaged in the chaos that surrounded Joe's swift disease. Loss and grief. Reality itself. And always, with me since, this horrible heightened awareness of impending abandonment.

Booze is a necessary tiny kindness from time to time, I tell myself as I roll over on my side and try to sleep.

In the morning, Alyssa asks after Kevin as she pours herself some juice. "He's coming to the game, right?"

"He'll be there," I say.

Her eyes are large and brown, just like Joe's. I see them across the table, strangely highlighted with the traces of makeup she's started to wear. As though a part of him has been recently altered in her. Over her soccer clothes she has on his old Penn sweatshirt she found in my closet and claimed. Her long chestnut hair is falling, pooling, caught in the hood.

"So what do you guys do when I'm not here, anyway? Watch TV or something?" Her tone is casual, but I think that I hear worry underneath. I think I hear her fear that I have forgotten her father, that Kevin is replacing him. "Are you guys going out or anything?" she asks. "Are you a couple?"

"Of course not," I say. "We're just best friends. We talked and ate dinner—exactly what we do when you're here."

"Huh." She finishes her juice and stands to put the cup and cereal bowl in the sink to soak. "You certainly spend a lot of time together." Her back is to me, her voice raised above the running water. "If I were seeing one boy that much, there'd only be one reason."

"Alyssa, we're not . . ."

"Okay, okay," she says. "It just seems like you guys like each other a lot."

"We do," I answer. And I think about saying more to her than that. I think about reassuring her that no one could ever replace her father for me. I'm sure that is what she's really asking. "I just don't have those feelings for Kevin," I begin.

"Why not?" she asks, turning toward me. "Kevin's the best."

"I just don't." I'm surprised at her tone.

"Okay, but what about him?" she asks. "Why doesn't he have a girlfriend? Is he gay? You can tell me, you know. I'm not some ignorant kid."

She's pulling her hair into a high ponytail as she asks,

and memories of Kevin lying next to me, of his body moving in mine sweep through me.

"No, Alyssa. As far as I know, he isn't gay. And he does go out on dates. It isn't always so easy to find the right person, you know." I pick up my coffee cup and stand, as I see her shrug. "Life can be pretty complicated."

"I'll bet he's secretly pining over you," she says, leaning back against our kitchen counter. "If you ask me, that's why he doesn't have anyone else."

"Don't be ridiculous. And I didn't ask you."

"Really, Mom, I'm actually not kidding. Don't you ever wonder what he's doing? I mean, being here with you every Saturday night?"

"You know, Alyssa, Saturday night when you're forty isn't the same thing as when you're fifteen. And it isn't every Saturday night, anyway." I nudge her away from the sink and spill my coffee down the drain. "It's just possible that adults have things going on that are beyond your comprehension."

"Whatever, Mom." She pulls the zipper on Joe's sweatshirt up as far as it goes. "It's really no big deal. It's your life, not mine." She shrugs once more. "As long as he's coming to the game."

After she leaves the kitchen, I sit back down at the table and move the salt and pepper shakers around, fiddle with the napkin holder. I listen to her sounds from the other rooms, music, doors opening, closing, the toilet flushing, water running; but drowning them out is the silence that will replace my daughter, before many more years have passed.

Heidi and I are seated side by side on folding chairs, among the fallen leaves. I'm lower than she, in a banged-up old metal beach lounger, bright yellow canvas stripes. In the biting October air, under the solid-gray sky, bundled in sweaters and scarves, I look positioned to work on my tan. She is enthroned on something that must have been ordered from a glossy catalog, a black contraption with pockets for magazines, cell phones. God knows what else. I have already apologized again for leaving her gathering, already mumbled my made-up excuse one more time, and she has already shrugged the apology off.

We watch Alyssa score the team's first goal. Her thighs are raw red heat and muscle in the autumn sun as she plows past gaggle after gaggle of other girls. She slams the ball into the net, as though she is evening the score. The real score.

"Way to go, Al!"

"You rule, Lyssie!!"

She shrugs them off and jogs to her position. The girl discussing my love life in our kitchen is invisible on the field. She is all on and no downtime, here. She isn't playing to the crowd. Not playing to me. Not really playing at all. She is at work. Joe coached her all through grade school, every fall and spring weekend, kicked endless passes back and forth with her in the evenings, when he got home. The season after he died, she was twelve and talked about quitting her team. "It just makes me feel too unhappy to play," she said. But I talked her out of it, arguing how sad it would have made her father for her to give up, how nothing would make him happier than knowing she still loves doing what they had done together. Now she plays every game as though she believes he can see. I watch her dribbling the ball deftly down the field and think of how aware of him she is here; how unaware she seemed earlier, when talking to me about Kevin.

"She's really very good, you know," Heidi says.

"Her father was very athletic." As the words come out, I spot Kevin across the field, waving both arms over his head. "Excuse me. That's a friend of mine."

Pushing myself up from my low perch, I find Heidi's feet there beside me on the ground, and I notice for the first time that one foot is much larger than the other. Yet they are clad in identical shoes. As I straighten up and smile a bit at her—another goodbye, another time I am hastening to leave her—I realize she must have to buy two pairs of shoes, just to get one set she can wear.

Waving across to Kevin, motioning him to stay on that side of the field, I think about that other mismatched set, the pair that is left over. The wrong one too big. The other wrong one too small. And I wonder whether Heidi throws away that useless pair.

"She's pretty damned good, your girl," Kevin calls out as I approach. "I can see that sports scholarship beckoning her."

I hug him. "That's all Joe in her," I say. "No credit here. It's all Joe's genes." And for a moment I want to add: *Remember?* Because I know that Kevin does. He remembers Joe, in sweats heading out for a run. Joe playing tennis. Joe just walking through a room. He remembers that Joe's was a distinctly physical presence, that he had a body that demanded to be noticed as that, as muscle, bone, power. I want to say, *Remember?* and have the conversation; but I stop myself.

"So which one is she?" He nudges me with his shoulder. "Which one is old Long John Silver?"

I wave across the field at Heidi, who waves back to me. "That's her," I say. "But please don't be a jerk."

"A jerk? Me? What are the odds?" he asks, and looking at him I think: *Not very high.* "I'm disappointed," he says. "You can't tell anything from here."

"I think maybe the idea of the leg is a bigger deal than the leg itself. You joining us for dinner tonight?" But to my surprise, he shakes his head.

"Date," he answers, and cups his hands, bullhorn-style. "Go, Alyssa! You go! Go! Go! Actually, I may have to cut out a little early."

"Anyone real?"

"Real? You mean as opposed to prosthetic? She's okay," he says. "Better looking than interesting, if you know what I mean."

"Sex?" I ask, because this is what we do. We pretend that this is simple. We pretend that we don't mind.

"Female."

"Ha. Ha. Ha."

The action of the game is close to us now. A crowd of red-cheeked girls jog by. Kevin and I stand side by side, silent, as though we have lost track of which of us should speak. A whistle blows and Alyssa is pulled from the game, rotated out. She waves from the other side of the field. We both wave back.

"I haven't slept with her, if that's what you're asking," Kevin picks up. "I might, though. It isn't completely out of the question. If I were ten years younger, we'd have done it by now. I just don't know. That conversation afterward looms larger and larger with every passing year." He shoves his hands down into his pockets, and I touch him on the arm.

"Look. They aren't letting her stay out."

My daughter has taken her warrior stance again, poised to spring, her power covering an entire cosmos of conflict with the impossibility of loss. "I love how much this means to her," I say.

"She's lucky. To care so much about something."

"Oh, I can't stand the thought that she'll be gone so soon," I say, surprising myself with sudden, spilling tears. "Shit." Kevin reaches over, stretches his arm around my shoulders, squeezes me close as I smudge my hand on my cheeks. "Maybe in the end that's just what it comes down to," I say. "Oh, fuck. I miss her already. I'll probably miss you tonight. Jesus, look at me. I'm a mess."

"You don't have to miss her yet, Claire. She's still right here. Don't borrow trouble."

"I know." I burrow myself within his arm. "I know, Kev."

"Between the past and the future . . ." I hear him sigh. "You know, you're not leaving yourself very much."

I lean into the comfort of his chest. "Don't scold. Let me have my little cry, okay?"

And I feel him sigh again, his chest rising and falling against my back. "I'm just saying maybe you should try enjoying what you have," he says. "That's all. Maybe it's time for a little Buddhism or something. Try being in the moment."

Alyssa is pounding down the field now, her body a wall of force, her feet nimble as they move the ball along. Held by Kevin's arm, I glance across the way and find Heidi there. She motions toward the game and gives me an enthusiastic thumbs-up. I send one back to her. Her husband, Roger, has borrowed my chair, I see. He sits there beside her mismatched feet, and watching them I think to myself that I will tell Kevin about the different-size shoes. I think about making some joke to him about how what Heidi really needs is to meet a woman exactly her size who is missing the opposite leg; but as I open my mouth to speak, I see Roger across the field place his hand on Heidi's knee. It is a casual, marital gesture, except that it's her senseless, artificial leg he touches. He rests his palm on her as though she can feel him. Or as though that bloodless leg cannot disrupt any aspect of their bond. And Heidi sees the caress she cannot feel. She turns a little, smiles at him, and lays her hand over his. I look away and say nothing to Kevin. I make no jokes, no smart comments about Heidi and her feet.

"I almost envy Heidi," I say instead.

"What?" he asks. "Why?"

I only shake my head. The halftime whistle blows. My lips sealed against more tears, I see Heidi rise. She moves slowly toward the girls who have gathered for water and snacks.

The first time we met, I just happened to pull my beach chair up next to hers. There was an empty stretch of lawn beside her. We introduced ourselves. It was the second or third game of the season, and Alyssa was already the team superstar. I pointed her out to Heidi as mine, and she was impressed. She pointed her daughter out to me, and I said something nice about her as well. Something like *Oh, she's been great*. Soccer-mom etiquette. We watched our girls play, cheered when we should, made asides about the ref, the other team, the weather, the practice schedule. At half-time, as both of us stood and began to walk toward the girls, I noticed Heidi's clumsy gait, the drag of that second step of hers.

"I lost my leg to cancer, when I was sixteen," she said, catching me stare.

I lost my husband to cancer when I was thirty-six.

"I'm very sorry," I replied without a pause.

"I'm lucky to be alive, I know."

I just nodded my head. *Yes. Yes, you are.*

"Listen, Claire," Kevin now begins, his breath grazing me with his words, the warmth of him all around me. This soccer field is ringed, I know, with couples who care about each other less.

"Uh-huh," I say.

"There's no good way to put this . . ."

"What?"

His arm tightens, squeezing me.

"Honey, I don't think I can do this anymore."

"Can't do what?" But I already know what he means. I know right away. I try to move from him, but he pulls me in. "Can't do what?" I ask again.

"Come on." I feel him turning me away from the field. "Let's take a walk." His hand on my shoulder is pressing more powerfully now. Everyone around us has started moving the other way. "Come with me, Claire," he says. "Just for a minute."

"I don't know . . ." I begin. "I should go talk to Alyssa."

"Don't. This is important." He stops and draws his arm away. We're facing one another, far enough from the others that their voices are muted and seemingly abstract. "We need to talk," he says. On each of his cheeks is a patch of red. His nose is runny. He wipes it on his sleeve. "Maybe it's just me that needs to talk," he says. "Sometimes I think you could just go on like this forever. You could, couldn't you? Just you and me, bobbing along like this, on the surface?" Stepping back, he looks up to the sky, and all I want is for him to stop talking. "God knows," he says, still looking up, "God knows, I have tried to be patient. I have tried to be the perfect friend. But I just can't be this . . . I can't be your person like this." His eyes move straight to mine. "Your guy. But not really your guy. Your pal. Who used to be your guy. Or, at any rate, *a* guy." He wipes his nose again. "You know, sometimes I think I've made this way too easy for you."

"Easy?" There's an anger in my voice, that I hear before I feel it. "Just what's been easy for me, Kev? Widowhood? Grief? Being alone? Single parenthood? None of it feels easy to me."

"*Easy* may be the wrong word," he says. "I just wonder if I haven't held you back somehow. Given you a way to skip over having feelings . . ."

"Oh come on, Kevin—all I do is have feelings."

"New feelings, Claire. For once, I'm actually not talking about what happened three years ago. Believe it or not, this isn't about Joe. That's yesterday's news, Claire. It's three fucking years!" His voice is suddenly loud, our postures shifting into those of people in a fight. I look to the field to see if we're being watched, but the small crowd is distant and unconcerned. Kevin's face is only inches from my own. "You tell me, Claire. When do I get to stop being your husband's eunuch substitute? Is there an end plan for that? Or do we just keep on like this for the rest of our lives? Because I don't think I can do it anymore."

"God." I take a step back, but he moves with me.

"I can't just be his stand-in anymore. I can't pretend that I've died too. If it's not me, Claire, if I'm not the guy for you, if I'm not it, then let me get out of the way—and you go find him. Go have a life with someone. Honestly, don't you ever think it's time to put the widow's weeds away? Stop raising that girl in a mausoleum?"

"Jesus, Kevin." The tears that were threatening disappear. "Isn't that a little harsh? I never asked you to—"

"Three years, Claire. It's more than three years. When are you planning to come back from the dead?" He takes a step toward me and reaches for my shoulders—like a parent about to shake a child. His fingers press into me, hard. His teeth are clenched so hard his chin is trembling. Then suddenly he lets me go. "You know what?" He shakes his head. "I think it's time for me to find people who want to be happy. A woman who wants to be happy. I need . . ."

I look up into those soft, gentle eyes of his. *Anything, anything, anything at all.* It's all still there, I'm sure. It has to be. That love I was so afraid was inside him, when he was inside of me. I only have to give the smallest sign. Just tell him I can try.

"Oh fuck," I say, and watch his face fall, slack.

"That's all I needed, Claire." He shoves his hands back into his coat pockets. "I'm gonna head home now." He glances back toward the field. "Tell Alyssa I said, Good game."

"Kevin, this isn't like you. Please don't be angry."

"Angry? Why not, Claire?" He isn't looking at me as he speaks. "Think about it. Really. Think about it. Think about everything you and I have been through." He squints a little and then faces me again. "You don't owe Joe being miserable. And neither do I."

A hand comes out from his coat pocket; and I think he's going to reach for me. I think he's going to touch my cheek. But he just shakes his head one more time instead. I see his car keys glistening in his fist. And I watch then as my yes-man walks away. First one step and then another. I watch and I wait, as though at any moment he might come to me again, retracting his withdrawal. But first his light brown jacket fades from view. Then a minute or so later I hear the distant sound of a starting car. And I realize that I've been fired.

"Just be grateful it isn't Alyssa," Joe would say, forcing me to nod, to look into his deep brown eyes and agree to see some future hope. "We're so lucky it isn't either of you. Just be grateful that it isn't one of you. I can handle dying; I couldn't handle it if it were you or her."

But I can't handle this, I'd thought, helpless as the man I loved dissolved before my eyes. *I can't handle you leaving me.*

Kevin had resisted at first. "It's not even a year. I don't think you're ready to start something new."

"Nothing in the world can hurt our friendship," I said. "And this is only sex."

I find a clump of trees, a little apart from the playing field, away from Alyssa and away from Heidi, away from the other parents that I know. Away from having to talk to anyone or look anyone in the eyes. A few times I see Alyssa glance my way, questioning, as though she knows that something's wrong, but the whistle blows and the game resumes with its hustle and bustle, my daughter streaking up and down the field.

There are cheers and exclamations in the air, but a quiet hovers where I stand. It seems to have its roots deep inside of me, as though I am immersed again in the same unnatural silence I remember from the six weeks between Joe's diagnosis and his death. The minutes pass through me and the branches above lose their colors in the swarming dusk, darkening into black silhouettes against the sky. Under them, I struggle to stay here, in the present, as Kevin said. To resist those terrible, tempting days that have somehow become my refuge now. Only weeks for Joe to live and not a goddamned thing to do except stay by his bedside and watch him disappear. And disappear myself.

Across the way, Heidi is alone again, but Roger is close by, standing near the snack boxes, talking to another of the fathers. Before she ever introduced me to him, I saw them together coming across this same stretch of field, and I knew then that he had to be her husband. Just from watching how they moved, how they walked at the identical halting and gradual pace—as though that pause between her steps had become his pause too, as though the absent leg was gone equally, eternally from them both. A perfect, imperfect, made-for-each-other gait.

Kevin would do that for me, I know. Kevin would walk with a hitch in his own step, with a step-clump-step to match my own.

The end whistle blows—too soon, I think—startling me, and I see all the girls on Alyssa's team run together, hear them holler a whooping yell. The two teams line up to shake each other's hands. Muttering, *Good game, good game, good game,* their voices are flat and indistinguishable, but the undeniable facts of victory and loss are spread across each face.

"Congratulations," I say when Alyssa comes running to me. "Good job."

"Thanks, Mom. It was a good game." She frowns. "Where'd Kevin go? Did he get bored?"

"No, not bored at all. Just busy. Hurry up and get your stuff. I'll buy you a burger."

I reach to brush a wisp of hair off her damp forehead. Her lips are slack, open from breathing hard, and her cheeks are flushed red—except where the mascara she painted around her father's eyes stains her skin in gray, sweaty circles. There's a question lingering on her face, an unanswered question still about the man who walked away. She is only wondering how to ask me, I know, wondering if she has the right, wondering if I will tell her the truth. I touch one of the streaky patches on her cheek.

"I was right, wasn't I?" she asks. "About Kevin? How he feels?"

"Yes," I say, looking into her eyes, so like the ones I lost. "You were right."

"What happened, Mom?"

It's a good question. I look away from her. From him.

Around us, the families are all saying goodbye. The playing field itself is empty, silent, still. Soon there will be only hints that we were here at all; a couple of forgotten water bottles lying on the ground, somebody's jacket crumpled beneath a tree. No traces of the cheers or the names called out loud. No lingering tension over who will win or lose.

"What happened, Mom?" she asks again.

"Come on," I say, my hand on her back. "It's time to go home."

As we walk together, neither of us speaks. I cannot find the right words. She is asking for answers and I am as filled with questions as she could ever be, as filled with a sense of standing on an edge as my daughter whose childhood is loosing its hold, whose life is daily widening its embrace. At the curb, before we cross to the car, I turn around, toward the field, half expecting to see Heidi sitting there, as though she alone might still be waiting for me. But she has gone, and so has her canvas throne. Only my old yellow beach chair remains beside that empty space, out of season and left behind, improbably vivid, improbably bright, against the autumn hues, against the failing day.

A
Country
Where
You
Once
Lived

IT ISN'T EVEN a two-hour train ride out from London to the village where Jeremy's daughter and her husband—a man Jeremy has never met—have lived for the past three years, but it's one of those trips that seems to carry you much farther than the time might imply. By around the halfway point the scenery has shaken off all evidence of the city, all evidence, really, of the past century or two. Or so it seems to Jeremy as long as he blurs his eyes to the occasional black line of motorway snaking through it all, to the dots of color speeding along the line. Otherwise, it's pretty much all mild shades of green and milling cows, sheep clustered at copses, church steeples appearing at regular intervals in a gentle, reassuring rhythm. It's a fantasy landscape, he thinks. The kind that encourages belief in the myth of uncomplicated lives.

Jeremy is riding backward so is watching it all recede, and the sensation is oddly saddening. Or maybe not so oddly saddening. A scientist, a cancer researcher, he passes his days in the flux and flow between the minute facts of molecular composition and our comparatively clunky selves. He knows well that for all the brain's cellular elegance, it has too this kind of simple, simplistic aspect to it. Leaving is sad. Even just the illusion of leaving is sad. As each view recedes, his eyes are tricked and in turn trick his brain: he is *leaving . . . leaving . . . leaving . . .* Of course he feels sad.

That's what he tells himself anyway as he rides along, that his settling melancholy is at least in part the mechanical product of a cause-and-effect process of sensory input and reflexive response.

Maybe it will wear off as the day goes on, he tells himself.

The reason Jeremy Piper has never met his son-in-law is that he hasn't seen his daughter, Zoe, in just over four years. The reason he hasn't seen his daughter in all that time is a bit harder to determine, some lethal blend of ancient angers and the seductive ease of separation three thousand miles granted them thirteen years earlier. In the early days, back in Boston by himself, Jeremy was capable of working himself into a strangely personal anger at the Atlantic

Ocean, as though it were some kind of bully standing between him and his family, as though he were overmatched.
But increasingly he's aware of how much blame belongs to
him.

The fulcrum of his life, the fateful before-and-after line,
was the year they all spent in London, starting June 1996.
"Our very own annus horribilis," his wife called it at the
time.

They went to England, he, Cathleen, and Zoe, so he
could begin the work for which he has since garnered much
acclaim, a study of the potential cancer-fighting properties
of an enzyme found in a particularly deadly mushroom
growing only in Britain—or, as Cathleen began saying
some months in: *on the potential cancer-fighting properties of
an enzyme found in blah, blah, blah.* Neither Cathleen nor
Zoe, sixteen at the time, wanted to make the move, until
Jeremy won Cathleen over with the argument that taking
Zoe away from her thoroughly dislikable, probably criminal friends could only be a good idea. But then just about
one month into the stay, Zoe ran away from home with a
Boston boy, a school friend backpacking the Lake District
over his summer break. And she didn't just run away; she
left no word about where she had gone, no sign that she
had gone under her own steam.

Jeremy could only ever remember bits and moments
from those two weeks, the ones when she was gone. Merciful amnesia, a friend once called it—except it wasn't very
merciful, because only the worst of it stuck with him. Or so
he assumed. Like the first shock at her absence, as too
many hours passed for it to be benign teenage tardiness;
like walking the streets of London, night after night, as

though she might have become a nocturnal creature waiting to reveal herself in the dark; like the dawning nightmarish realization that he himself was a suspect in her disappearance. "We're not making any accusations. You wouldn't want us to leave any stone unturned." He imagined himself on trial, wrongly convicted, locked away, the headlines, clever if obvious plays on his name: *Tried Piper Lured Own Daughter* . . . That was a uniquely vivid memory. But still, there were long stretches from those days during which, for all he could ever remember, he might as well have been dead.

That wasn't true of what followed her return. The difficulty was never remembering that period but letting it go. Particularly his own trouble accepting that she hadn't been abducted, she had left of her own free will. And that she hadn't been unable to contact them, she had chosen not to. His own disbelief at the disappearance of the villain he had conjured and blamed for it all, the man who had been the target of his rage while she was gone, the object of revenge fantasies so violent and so vile Jeremy had barely admitted them to himself. The man who had doubtless killed his daughter, doubtless done God knew what else to her and in the process—minor collateral damage, Jeremy understood—destroyed her father.

Except there was no man. There was only his Zoe, sixteen years old and sorry, really, really sorry, for what she had done.

Or so she said.

At home, he would watch her. He would study his daughter the way he studied the animals in his lab, as though doing so might provide some kind of solution. She

had returned rail thin, all eyes and bone. Her honey hair
was jet black. Her lips were perpetually chapped, as though
she'd been drained of some essential human moisture. She
looked like a wraith, otherworldly, but she did normal
things. That was what kept him mesmerized. The way
she sat at the kitchen table eating yogurt. The fact that she
spoke on the phone. That she listened to music. That she
walked through the doorways of their elegant rented town
house without falling to her knees at every threshold to reflect on what she had done.

For reasons he never understood, Cathleen had escaped
official suspicion. And she had also resisted the idea that
there was a villain to the piece—so she hadn't learned to
hate as elaborately as he. That was his theory anyway, the
foundation on which he built his resentment: that it had all
been much easier on her. So he envied her, and he was
angry at her, and about six weeks after Zoe's return, Jeremy
embarked on a standard-issue, utterly predictable affair
with a colleague at the lab, despite the fact that he didn't
like the woman very much. Liking her or not liking her
seemed oddly irrelevant to the decision to have sex with her
a few times a week. The truth was, he wasn't a bit sure he
would ever like anyone again. He seemed to have lost the
thread of how affections worked.

Ultimately, the smug satisfaction of doing something behind Cathleen's back lost out to the impulse to hurt her, so
one night toward the end of the year, motivated more by
spite than by anything like remorse, he confessed. She
looked momentarily confused—shock at his disclosure, he
assumed—then confessed her own affair right back at him.
Under different circumstances, that might have signaled a

chance to start over, one betrayal canceling out the other, the slate wiped clean; but as it went, they were like the dueling pair that shoots simultaneously, so both end up dead.

There were never any fights after that, not even much open acrimony, just an overwhelming atmosphere of defeat in the house. With all the predictable unkindness of irony, as the family broke apart it turned out that Cathleen and Zoe had both grown to feel at home in England and they decided to stay on. It was while driving Jeremy to Heathrow for his miserable, solo flight back to the States that Cathleen borrowed the queen's phrase.

"Our very own annus horribilis," she said. "I feel positively royal."

It's Cathleen, unmistakably Cathleen, waving from the platform of the Thomas the Tank Engine station when Jeremy's train comes to its stop.

"Hello, you!" she calls out as he steps down.

He wasn't expecting her there. He waves—a small waist-level gesture, one arm pulling a bag, the other weighted with his computer. "Hello, you," he echoes, too quietly to be heard.

He's a bit numb as he walks toward her. It's been fully five years. He used to see her quite often at family events when she would jet over, sometimes with Zoe, sometimes alone, moving across the ocean with an ease he never thought about too clearly when cursing the Atlantic's role in his life. Over time, they progressed from avoiding each other at those events to seeking each other out as people with whom they could at least be themselves. They even once drunkenly stumbled into a sexual encounter that they tacitly agreed neither to repeat nor ever mention again; and the next few times they saw each other after that, he noticed they'd adopted an oddly jocular, teasing style of conversation that reminded Jeremy of the way his brother Jonathan and his old high school football teammates spoke to one another in middle age. But that was all years ago, as ancient in its way as their wedded days.

"I wasn't expecting you," he says as they embrace. "I didn't know you'd be here."

"Well." She says it with a slight shrug, as though to convey that it should be obvious why Zoe thought her presence necessary. "I hope it's at least an okay surprise. Can I help you carry anything?"

"It is. No, I'm fine."

He's startled by how entirely *known* she is to him. Not just familiar or even evocative but inevitable in some way, as though she were the mama duck and he the little one on whom she long ago imprinted her heart-shaped face and her dark blue eyes, the straight lines of her posture, the angle at which she held her head, a certain sighing sound she would make before she spoke.

As they walk toward a small lot filled with cars, he feels her settle over him like a climate in which he used to live.

Driving through the village in Zoe's ancient black cockroach of a sub-subcompact, Cathleen points out what she calls the big sights: a tea shop, a pub, a bank, an unlikely-looking hotel covered with a profusion of ivy that Jeremy remarks appears more spooky than quaint.

"There's always a fine line between the two," she says. "Isn't there?"

Conversation for conversation's sake. It doesn't have to make much sense.

Once they've left the village and are onto country roads, she asks him if he's seeing anyone. He isn't surprised by the question. It's always been a point of honor with Cathleen to show no discomfort discussing such things. So he says that yes, he supposes he is, that yes, he is seeing someone, you could call it that; but he doesn't volunteer much more. Not that her name is Rose—a syllable he loves for sounding more like an endearment than a real name. And not that she is thirty-four years old. Nor that he met her when she rented the third floor of the house he and Cathleen moved into the year after Rose was born. And not that he is in love with her, marrying her in four months. He isn't planning to tell Zoe any of these things during this visit, and Cathleen has always been a bad liar.

"She works in the university library," he says.

"Interesting." But her tone doesn't quite match the word, as though having proved that the idea doesn't disturb her, she's lost interest. Or maybe it does disturb her, and a brief display of equanimity is the best she can do. Either way, after a pause, she volunteers that she's recently ended a longish relationship with a Russian pianist; and Jeremy recognizes one of her words: *longish*. Along with *shortish, noonish, Fridayish*. A deep vein of imprecision has always run through Cathleen.

"I spent the whole last few months with Uri trying to decide if he was more of a *boooor* or a bore. Until I realized it wouldn't much matter if he were out of my life."

They drive in silence for a bit after that.

"What about Colin?" he eventually asks. "What's he like? Will I like him?"

"Well, if you don't, you'll be the first. But you will. He's one of those people who doesn't ask the world to worship him, so of course everyone does. And he's very good to her."

Jeremy would have given low odds on any husband of Zoe's lacking a little wash of saintliness. "She seems much happier. In emails, I mean. As far as I can tell, anyway."

"As happy as any of us," she says.

"As happy as any of us," he echoes a moment after that, struck, as he says it, by how happy he's been of late. Happier than most. Happier than Cathleen, it seems.

"She's very changed, Jeremy. You'll see." There aren't any intersections in sight when she flicks her turn signal, only property entrances, so he realizes they must be very close. "She's grown up a lot, you know."

But of course he doesn't know. "I'm glad," he says. "By nearly thirty, that's the idea. We were parents by her age."

"That hardly means we'd grown up." Cathleen turns at a gap between high, thick hedges, onto a long dirt drive. Its ruts and ridges bear witness to a persistent cycle of rain and heat. On either side, anywhere Jeremy looks, vast fields stretch, acres and acres of fields blanketing gentle hills. There are at least three barns in sight and a large half-timbered house right ahead. It is as though they've gone through one of those magical gates in children's stories, into a universe that couldn't possibly fit into the space concealing it.

"It's huge," he says. "It's enormous. I hadn't expected anything on this scale."

"Oh, that's right." She beeps the horn with three sharp hits of her fist. "I keep forgetting. You haven't been here before."

And Jeremy doesn't say anything to that. No response comes to mind.

It wasn't Rose's idea that he write Zoe and ask about a visit, but it was on her account that he did. Jeremy had long been ashamed of this aspect of his life, this glaring lapse of his, this daughter across the water, but he had never before cared so much about having done something shameful.

It was excruciating telling Rose. They were walking. They liked to take walks together in the neighborhood, commenting on the houses he had lived among for three decades but of course never quite seen before. They were just a few blocks from the house when she asked a question that had clearly been on her mind for some time. How often did he see his daughter?

Even before hating the answer he had to give, he hated the tone in which she asked. A reluctant, eggshell-walking tone. As though she knew she was in danger of learning something about him she wouldn't like. Her voice, always low, both deep and quiet, seemed to emanate from somewhere close to the ground. Her hand tightened its grip on his—as though defiant against the impulse to unclasp it.

He told her the whole story. But what did it amount to? He had let his daughter go. Like a kite that requires too much attention, too much sensitivity to its ways. Too much care.

Rose listened, quietly, and her grip on him never loosened, but she didn't pretend it was a matter of indifference to her. In the end, though, Jeremy didn't write to his daughter because he was ashamed of himself or wanted Rose to think better of him but because something about loving Rose, about Rose loving him, made him believe that it might not be too late.

The reality of his reunion with Zoe isn't a bit as he's imagined it. For one thing, he wouldn't have recognized her if he'd passed her on the street. Ever since the year in London—or *since London,* as he thinks of it—she stayed a collection of jagged surfaces, bones poking out at her collar, on her wrists, her knees, her ribs. Her shoulder blades, jutting straight out from her back, had seemed like vestigial wings, reminders of her flight. But now she's grown plump, round and soft, as though nature reversed a sculptor's work, encasing her true form in this obscuring one. Her hair is back to its honey tones. The heavy Goth makeup is gone. She looks like the woman he pictured her becoming when she was a child, not like the woman he believed she had become.

He'd also thought there might be a moment, a few words spoken by them both, something to mark this as a new beginning. But the tentative hug they exchange in the drive and his first impressions of her become tiny details in what is quickly a bustling, comic scene that includes their reunion and also an errant cow wandering over as though she too wants to catch up; a large dog jumping onto Jeremy, leaving prints and long muddy streaks on his pants; an ancient man on a small tractor waving, calling something unintelligible as he passes; the husband, Colin, appearing from a barn, smiling and ginger-headed, shaking Jeremy's hand, taking his suitcase; a tabby cat circling them all; a sense of rush and hurry in the air, something about the vet having been there, about dinner being close to ready, all of it conspiring to carry them through those first few minutes and through the front door of the house with a lightness that doesn't allow for anything as potentially heavy as an acknowledged fresh start.

"You must be very respectful with Jeremy," Cathleen says as they sit at the round oak kitchen table—so large Jeremy has images of the house being built around it. "He's become quite famous, you know."

"Not really." He hasn't come to be admired. He has come to be forgiven. "Not outside the field."

"Well, I'm certainly outside the field," Colin says, with a smile. His face reminds Jeremy of a well-disposed marionette, the jutting chin, the cheekbones like hills, a seemingly simple good nature beaming through it all. "Most of the time, I'm outside *in* the field. But I'm very impressed, from what I've heard." Jeremy tries not to think about what this young man has heard about him. More bad than good, no doubt. "It must be rewarding to do work that helps people."

"Your work helps people," Cathleen says. "You're feeding the world."

"Oh, yes. Indeed we are. One head of designer lettuce at a time. We're not quite up to the cancer-research standard."

"We're not there yet." Zoe is peeling a potato—with a

knife—so rapidly Jeremy is fearful for her hands. "But we'll get there. We do have bills to pay, and designer veggies are like gold."

"I'm looking forward to hearing all about it," Jeremy says. His gaze is fixed on the course of her blade, on the flying strips of skin. "I'm looking forward to seeing it all."

"I'll give you a tour," Colin says. "The whole operation."

"Not today, though." Zoe's potato falls into a ceramic bowl; another takes its place in her hands. "Dinner's in just a little while. I hope everyone's hungry."

"I am," Jeremy says right away, though he isn't. Prodigal father and obliging guest—the roles overlap. "The whole house smells incredible," he says. "How could anyone not be hungry sitting here?"

After a few more such innocuous exchanges—the weather, a pregnant cow—Colin excuses himself to make quick rounds in the barns, calling back *No rest for the wicked* with all the good humor of a man who knows himself to be anything but; and for a time, no one speaks. It's as though a gust of tension passed him in the doorway. Zoe has grown more intent on her potatoes. Cathleen is staring off into space, the corners of her lips drawn down, as though she's gone somewhere troubling, as though a bomb could explode without her noticing.

The last time the three of them were alone together in a kitchen, a kind of bomb had gone off. It was the final morning of that awful year. Sitting there now, Jeremy feels a churning of shame, like nausea, as he remembers the profound ambivalence of his goodbye to Zoe that day. How insincere he must have sounded. How insincere he was as he asked her one last time if she was sure she didn't want to go back home with him. What relief he felt at her sullen certainty.

The only sound in the room is the rhythmic rasp of Zoe's knife. This is one of those moments, Jeremy knows, at which he can pierce the social membrane and acknowledge what they're all thinking about anyway. This is an opportunity to be direct.

"Are those your potatoes?" he asks instead. "From here, I mean."

It's too soon, he tells himself. He's just arrived.

"They are." She doesn't look up. For all he's seen of her face, she could be wearing a veil. This was a point of contention way back when. She seemed eternally to be avoiding meeting his eye. "I'm making potato salad for tomorrow," she says. "We thought we'd try a cookout if the rain holds off. Grilled chicken."

"It's their own chickens, you know." Cathleen is back in the conversation, woken from her trance.

"I'm very impressed."

"You don't know the half of it. She slaughters them herself. Killed two yesterday. Does it without batting an eye."

"You make it sound like I do it for pleasure, Mum." He has noticed her unmistakably British intonations, but the syllable startles him. Who is *Mum*? The characters have new names. "It's just that Colin can't bear to. He's quite soft about such things."

Apparently she isn't soft about such things. Of course not.

"They have an abattoir and everything. She goes in there and does murder most . . . well, fowl. F-o-w-l fowl. It's a little hard to imagine, isn't it?"

"It certainly is," he says—though in truth it isn't. Not at all. In truth, this is the first information he's received since arriving that makes sense to him, that connects this quiet, seemingly diffident woman to the razor-sharp girl he knew. *Why don't you just go fuck yourself, Dad? Why do I even make these fucking trips?* "I imagine it's all in a day's work, at some point," he says.

"It has to be done." She brushes her hair off her forehead with the back of her hand. "So I do it. I don't enjoy it."

"I've always felt that way about the lab animals. People assume you have to be callous, but I don't think that's it. It's not callousness. It's a kind of acceptance. I'm truly sorry about what we put them through."

"Like father, like daughter," Cathleen says. "I think I'm in the Colin camp."

"Someone has to do it," Zoe says. "If people want to eat." She drops another potato into the bowl. "Or cure diseases," she adds.

He feels as though she's handed him a bouquet. "I'm amazed by how you've taken to this life, Zee. I really am."

She puts down her knife and stands, gathering the big crockery bowl of stripped potatoes in her arms. Her hands, flat against the pale brown glaze, are red and chapped, he sees. Her nails, clipped down to the nubs. "Dinner's probably twenty minutes off," she says. "If you want to wash up or anything."

Cathleen has told Jeremy that there isn't much hope for a cell signal, though occasionally one decided to roll through. "Like a beneficent mist," she said. She told him there is Internet, wireless, inside the house; but his computer is still packed up and he can't quite bring himself to ask if he can use theirs. Better to roam the fields in search of the beneficent mist.

The day has cooled, a chill leaching into the mild air. It reminds Jeremy of New England—and the farm smells, too, take him there. Weekend escapes up to Vermont in the early fall. Apple picking, leaf peeping. And then, later in the season, the ever-earnest selection ritual in a pumpkin patch. They had been big on that sort of thing, he and Cathleen, when Zoe was small. They didn't want her to be one of those city girls who seemed to be made of plastic, to exist outside the natural world. It's a little jolting to him now to see Zoe so connected to nature, over her head, as she is, in crops and livestock. It's disorienting in a way. He's unused to the possibility that any aspects of his parenting, even minor ones, may have stood her in good stead.

As Jeremy kicks his way over the tangle of grass and weeds and brambles that run along the drive, past a barn and then around another, he checks his phone, then checks it again and again, but to no avail. When he passes a square little structure, white plaster, flat roof, strikingly unadorned, he has no doubt it's the abattoir. Its function is evident from the deliberate lack of evidence about what its function might be. He thinks he may see a glimmer of a bar on his phone right around there and begins taking one step at a time, forward, to the side, back again, as though chasing a shifting shadow; but it's gone.

He so wanted to hear Rose's voice. Now, he knows, it's too close on dinner to fuss with the computer, so he begins a text. *Here with Z,* he writes. He decides against mentioning Cathleen. It's too complex a circumstance for the form. He'll tell Rose when they speak. *Who knows,* he writes. *All polite chat so far. All very civil. Not awful except no cell. I love you more and more.*

He knows it can't go right away, but sends it even so, hoping that if the mist does roll in it will find the message waiting there and carry it to her. It's an act of faith of a kind.

As Jeremy walks back toward the house, he remembers for the first time in years and years that when Zoe was missing, even though he didn't believe in God, he would pray.

"She doesn't slaughter the cows," Colin says, as he passes around the plate of steak. "We send them off for that. Though I've seen her in moods when she might."

"He's joking." Cathleen has a frown of mock disapproval on her face. She's pulled her hair back for the meal and a line of silver shines at the roots. Jeremy wonders what similar details of decline she sees on him. "Not everyone here knows you're joking, Colin."

"Oh, I'm definitely joking. She's a little lamb herself."

"Well, it's delicious, whatever the process," Jeremy says. "Perfectly cooked, too."

"I always eat my best meals here," Cathleen says.

She might as well have planted a flag, he thinks as Colin launches into a long story about a supposedly famous chef of whom Jeremy has never heard—though he tries to look impressed—and how the man came to the farm armed with a list of bizarre requests. Colin turns out to be one of

those people who take on the heavy lifting when the conversation sags.

"He didn't quite ask that we hold séances over the cab-
bage, but it wasn't far off. There was certainly some mention of only harvesting with a full moon."

"What did you tell him?" Cathleen asks. "Did you tell
him to piss off?"

"We lied," Zoe says. "We lie to him every time he's
here."

"Right through our teeth." Colin taps his front tooth
with his finger. "We describe the rituals to him in detail,"
he says.

"Oh God! That must be hilarious. And they look so
trustworthy, don't they, Jeremy?"

"They do indeed," he says, a little shocked, despite his
own spotty record, about the apparent ease of it for them.
"I would never have guessed."

As the conversation moves on from there to other local
matters, Jeremy has the growing sense of being an outsider,
almost as though he is literally being pushed from the table.
It's unpleasant, but also inevitable—unless, of course,
they're going to discuss what lies behind his visit, which
they clearly are not. Not at the first meal. There are so
many people the three of them all know, Colin's family, the
neighbors, Cathleen's London set. As the cast of characters
swells, so too does the effort it takes to catch him up. *She's
Colin's aunt on his mother's side and the first time I met her,
she was about to get married but then just a year later . . .* It's
Cathleen, mostly, who tries, and occasionally Colin, who
seems particularly bothered when Jeremy can't appreciate a

good joke. Zoe, more animated than he's seen her yet—as though his exclusion has energized her—makes no effort at all. She doesn't even look his way, and as the minutes pass, he finds himself sinking into the conviction that at best what's possible between them at this point is a kind of truce, superficial and civil. That they'll stay in touch—though now that he's met Colin, his guess is that it will be he who keeps up any regular contact. But Jeremy and Zoe will at least be over the worst of it. At least and at most.

He is preoccupied enough with the demise of his hope that a three-day visit might do any more than that, that he almost misses it when Cathleen brings up the subject of his personal life.

"She's a university librarian, isn't that right, Jeremy?"

He tells her it is. "In the rare books library."

"How did you meet?"

One bedroom, lots of charm. She had seen it on Craigslist. "The usual. A cocktail party. That kind of thing."

"What's her name?" Cathleen asks.

"Rose."

"That's very English," Colin says. "I have at least two aunts named Rose."

"She was named for a grandmother, I think. Not English. They're Jewish."

"Is she observant?" Cathleen asks.

He frowns. "No. Not at all. She knows how to cook all the food, but that's about it."

"Uri was always hinting at being in the midst of a terrible religious crisis. But he never went into details. I'm not even sure what religion. Russian Orthodox, I suppose."

"He sounds like quite the character," Jeremy says. "Was

he actually a good pianist, or more of a dilettante?" He's uncomfortable discussing Rose and trusts that the abundant world of the others will assert itself again if given the least opportunity, as it quickly does. Colin and Zoe spent lots of time with Uri, it turns out. He was a regular visitor at the farm for a time. *Oh, God, remember when . . .*

He misses her terribly, sitting there. Saying her name has done it, tipped him over some kind of brink. He misses the soothing quality that first attracted him when they started talking on their shared front porch. He misses her skin, her smell, the daily walks, their funny domestic arrangement. He misses the comfort of sleeping in her little apartment on his third floor, an unexpected womb in the aging body of his home.

I never believed him about having trained horses in his Soviet youth . . .

It seems to be going on forever, the supply of Uri stories never-ending, the relationship Cathleen described as *longish* eternal in the recounting; but eventually Zoe pushes her chair back from the table and stands, saying she's tired and thinks she'll turn in early.

"Are you all right?" Cathleen asks. "You look pale."

"I'm fine. Just tired."

Jeremy tries not to take either her weariness or her early exit personally. Colin says he'll do the clearing up and turns down Jeremy's immediate offer to help.

"Mom, do you mind showing him his room?"

"No, of course I will."

It's unexpectedly painful to have become a pronoun. "I'm sure I can find it," he says. "Just point me the right way."

"I wanted to ask you . . ." Zoe turns toward him. "I was wondering. I'm giving a chicken to our neighbor for some work he did on our roof. Tomorrow, if you want to see how it's done . . . ?"

It's the first time she's really looked at him, the first time he can see that her eyes haven't changed, brown and almond shaped, sorrowful even when she isn't. A poignant camouflage, he'd always thought. "I'd like that very much," he says.

"We'll do it in the afternoon, then. After lunch."

"I'll be there. Thank you. For asking me."

"See you all in the morning," Zoe says and she walks out into the hall.

"Nothing says rapprochement like slaughtering a bird," Cathleen whispers to him a few minutes later, on the stairs.

The ceiling of Jeremy's bedroom slopes so drastically that he has to slide into his bed as though negotiating a limbo bar. He's brought his laptop with him, and in the magical way of these things it quickly finds the wireless network that then finds the universe that then brings him the woman he loves.

When Rose appears, alive and speaking, listening, smiling through the screen, it's as though some kind of angel were making a visitation to this small, simple room, carrying a message of comfort and hope. Rossetti's *Annunciation* comes to mind. As he watches her, he feels something akin to what he had on seeing Cathleen earlier, that same impression of inevitability, but he feels a kind of surprise as well. He's perpetually stunned that he hasn't made her up. Rose doesn't just make sense to him, she seems to make sense *of* him, and he can feel himself emerge from behind the stiff and frightened version of Jeremy Piper he's worn all day. A thaw spreads, loosening him up, allowing him to expand back into himself.

But then, as he tells her about the proposed visit to the abattoir, he grows aware of a certain shyness—even with her. Not because of the act itself but because of the significance he's beginning to attach to it. It's embarrassing to admit, but what Cathleen said in jest resonated with him. It's strangely appealing to imagine himself and his daughter slaughtering a bird, engaging together in so blessedly impolite and uncivil an act, making it impossible to keep the niceties so unremittingly nice after that, impossible to ignore life's darker, more difficult side. And it's more than that. They would be killing something. It's fitting somehow. He's hesitant to pin the symbolism down, to let the thoughts go very far, but he's aware of a longing in himself that he hadn't thought possible. The desire to solve a problem without working it through for once, the hope that a ritual might do all that labor for him.

"I don't want to make too much of it, though," he says. "The fact is, she barely said a word to me all day."

"Well, it's something that she wants to do this. That's the real meaning. Why would she invite you, if she didn't care?"

"I suppose that's right." He is amazingly stupid about

people sometimes—still. About his daughter, anyway. "Of course that's right," he says.

Later, after telling him this and that about her day, Rose leans toward her computer, toward Jeremy, a smile like mischief incarnate on her face, and she propositions him. They had joked about it before he left, about having every possible form of distance sex while he's away. Phone. Email. Skype. "We've lived together since before we were going out," she said. "We've never experienced the pleasures of absence."

And Jeremy, to whom absence had brought such great pain, signed on for the idea, only because it was hers, because it seemed just possible that she could make even that cruel quality beautiful.

But now, in this small, soft bed, his daughter down the hall, his former wife across the way, it's unimaginable. He tells Rose he's just too tired, too jet-lagged still to be of much use along those lines. He makes a joke about his age.

She says he should watch her then, just watch. "I need it," she says, in that straightforward way of hers. "You only have to watch."

As she moves, she dissolves into pixels—Seurat from too close—then reassembles; and unmoored as he feels, it's that process of dissolution and resolution that mesmerizes him. The way the tiny squares of cream and pink and red and brown and white fall apart into nothing, then emerge reorganized as a nipple, an eye, her hand between her legs, her smile. It's as though the computer screen is complicit in the tease of it all and complicit, too, in some greater, grander conspiracy of elusiveness. Finally, with a response he'd thought impossible, he joins her as she evaporates with each shudder of release, as she gasps from behind a curtain of shimmering color blocks.

It takes him some time in the morning, when he wakes, to pull the simple fact of where he is into his consciousness and once he has, he lies in bed for a while, staring up at the ceiling, its slope like a lid about to close on him. Eventually, though, he showers and dresses, then makes his way down to the kitchen, where he finds Cathleen sitting at the table, her elbows resting there, her hands folded together in front of her chin.

"Good morning," he says. "It's quiet today. The farmers off farming?"

"Zoe's not here." She frowns. "They're not here. Zoe had a miscarriage during the night." She looks up at him. "I'm sorry, Jer. I should have done that better. I'm not thinking well."

The wooden chair creaks ridiculously as he sits. "I didn't even know . . ."

"She didn't want anyone to know. Not yet. It's actually their third. Third miss. They're at the doctor now. Colin's calling as soon as there's anything to report." She lifts the cup in front of her, peers into it, then looks back at him. He didn't think one way or the other yesterday about whether she was wearing makeup, but can now see the difference. Her features aren't so clearly defined; her face is paler. He always preferred her this way. She stands—slowly. "You must need coffee," she says. Her back is to him as she opens a drawer and takes a paper filter out, opens the freezer and takes a bag of coffee out. "Fuck it, Jeremy. She was all the way through the first term. Fourteen weeks. We were all starting to relax."

He asks if they know what the problem is, and she says no, it's all a big mystery.

"Last time, at Christmas, she made a point of telling me she'd never had an abortion. That it wasn't that kind of damage. I felt awful because of course that's exactly what I'd been thinking. That she was probably paying for those crazy years she had. Okay," she says. "Coffee will be ready soon."

When the phone rings, Cathleen walks it out into the yard. Jeremy watches her through the window, her face drawn, her body somehow tiny, as though she's retreated into a smaller self.

"She's more or less okay," she says as she walks back in. "He says there was no great blood loss, which is the big concern. She has to have a D&C though. They'll be there for some time." She puts the phone back in its charger. "Jeremy, he's asked if we can clear out. Being Colin, he was very nice about it, but she's upset and they need some privacy. He's upset too, of course, though he's being the stoic one. There's a schedule here somewhere. The trains run every hourish, I know. He told me just to drive her car to the station. They have a friend who can bring it back. All I have to do is change the sheets on their bed before we go. Apparently they're a mess. I'd like to do the dishes too. Colin never finished them last night. The place should be clean when she gets home."

"I can help," Jeremy says, standing up. He walks over to

her, meaning just to put a hand on her back, but then she falls a little into him.

"Fucking children," she says, into his shoulder. "Fucking heartaches. All of them."

They move through the house together as though every task requires four hands. He washes the dishes; she dries them and puts them away. They strip the bed upstairs, then remake it, tugging at opposite corners of the fitted sheet.

"I'm just throwing these out," Cathleen says, bundling up the old, bloody ones. "I'll buy her new sheets. I don't want these waiting here when she gets home."

Jeremy notices a white pitcher filled with wilted flowers atop the chest of drawers. "These are depressing as hell," he says.

They decide to go out to the garden for new ones.

"I know nothing will cheer her up," Cathleen says. "But at least when she gets home it will look like someone cares."

It's the same phrase she used over and over thirteen years before, during those terrible two weeks. *When she gets home. When she gets home. When she gets home.*

"She isn't ever coming home, Cathleen," he finally said. "You have to stop saying that."

They assemble a bouquet of red dahlias and small purple flowers Jeremy doesn't recognize. Cathleen points to the ones she wants, while Jeremy cuts the stems, handing them to her, one at a time.

"Where's the minister?" she asks as she carries the bouquet just in front of her chest. "Honestly, if I weren't so miserable, I could laugh."

At the station, she parks the car in the same small lot.

"Should you be taking those?" Jeremy asks, seeing her put the keys into her bag.

She looks at him as though he's crazy; then the penny seems to drop. "Oh, their friend has a set. I'll bring these back next time I'm here."

Inside, Jeremy springs for two first-class tickets. "Why not?" he asks. "We could both use it."

"I'm not arguing," she says.

On the train, they sit across from one another. Jeremy thinks she looks as though the morning's news has literally taken the air out of her. Her skin seems to have drooped, her body to have crumpled, softened. She seems emptied, somehow—as though she's physically connected to Zoe still.

"You look tired," he says.

"Tired and sad." She adjusts her seat and leans back.

When the train starts to roll, Jeremy watches the same scenery he watched the day before. It's oncoming this time, but again he is filled with a terrible sense of leaving something behind. So much for optical stimuli tricking his brain. Apparently, it's just his fate to carry this sense of departure in himself.

They speak very little for the first hour, just a few passing comments about the passing scenery, how endlessly pretty, how English.

"Believe it or not, I miss the ugliness sometimes," she says. "There's nothing like the Jersey Turnpike over here. Hideous as it is, it was home."

"But you love it here."

"I do. I love it the way you love something that isn't ever going to be yours. Not really. I hate the idea of being buried here, you know. Funny, isn't it? Odds are I'll have lived here for decades by then, but I still hate the idea."

He almost asks what keeps her there, but catches himself. "It's good for Zoe that you're here," he says instead.

Cathleen shrugs. "I don't seem able to protect her," she says. "You know, I think it's all these pregnancies that made her . . . made her agree to you being here." He doesn't say anything. "I couldn't tell you this yesterday, but that's what I meant about her changing. She's a more sympathetic person now. More tender. I see her trying to take care of people now. And I'm sure it's because of all this heartache. I don't know if that makes sense."

It makes perfect sense. "It must be terrible for her," Jeremy says. "I can't imagine it."

"Terrible all around." Then, with a sigh of resignation to something greater than having to pee, Cathleen pushes herself up and goes to use the loo.

Alone, Jeremy stares out at the painterly landscape, thinking it all through, and it begins to be obvious to him that he's gone about this all wrong. All of it. Not just the shameful thirteen years during which he more or less abandoned her, but this visit too. This meekness. This civility. Why did it never seem real to him that time was a limited quantity? Only with Rose is he aware of moments flying by, of a strand of pain running continually through him because of that. What did he think he was doing? He should have taken Zoe aside and begged for her forgiveness right away. He should have asked outright how he could make amends. Or not taken her aside at all but begged in front of Colin and Cathleen and the wandering cow and the old man on the tractor and the cat and the dog.

What had he been waiting for? A slaughtered bird?

When Cathleen comes back, she trips over the handle of the little leather bag tucked beneath her chair and he steadies her with his arm.

"It's a wonder I didn't walk in front of the train," she says. "I'm barely in my own head."

She pushes the bag back under the seat. It isn't much more than a big pocketbook, he realizes, nothing possibly big enough for the many days she'd been planning to stay. He asks her if she's forgotten her things at the farm. "It would be understandable," he says. "Given what's going on."

She frowns, looks puzzled.

He points to the bag. "I just mean, that can't be enough luggage for all those days."

"Oh no, it isn't." She seems to hesitate. "I keep some clothes up there."

"Right." Of course she would.

The train comes to a halting stop at a dingy little station. The building's brick is practically black, the windows either boarded or shattered. As far as Jeremy can tell, no one gets on or off.

"She told me last time it's an impossible kind of grief," Cathleen says as they start up again. "That people are always hurrying you past it. Telling you just to go get pregnant again. I feel bad sometimes that it never happened to me. It was so easy for us. I feel guilty about it."

"I can't believe the doctors have no explanation."

"You know, she wasn't letting herself think about there being a real baby, this time. She told me that. Christ, it was just yesterday. Right before dinner. Not even wondering about the sex. She and Colin had a pact not to talk about it."

When the food cart comes through, they both shake their heads no.

At one point, his phone vibrates in his pocket. He lets it go, then checks. Rose. Just waking up, no doubt. "Not feeling very chatty," he says to Cathleen as he puts it back.

"No. Nor am I. Was that her?" she asks. "Rose?"

"Yes."

After a few seconds, she says, "I can't tell, Jeremy. Is this something serious?"

He thinks for a moment. "Not really," he says. "It's not frivolous, but it's not what you mean."

She nods, turns to the window.

This is where they failed, all those years back, he believes. In taking care of one another when tragedy struck. It broke them, broke them all. The truth about his life can wait for a better time.

"I suppose neither of us has had much luck along those lines," she says. "Finding true love."

"Not yet maybe," he says. "But there's still time."

It isn't romantic jealousy he's protecting her from now. It's something else. Not that he's found love with another but that he's found love first. That he's leaving this limbo they've shared for thirteen years.

The train makes another quick stop and this time a quartet of boys get on. To Jeremy's surprise they settle in first class. "I hope to God they're not too rowdy," he says.

"I can't believe anyone buys kids first-class tickets." Cathleen checks her watch. Then, just a couple of minutes later, she checks it again. He can't imagine her hurry.

"I was thinking we could have lunch somewhere," he says.

Little furrows appear in her brow. "I'm sorry, Jeremy," she says. "I should have told you. There's somewhere I need to go." One of the boys laughs raucously and another passenger shushes him. "I have to leave you at the station, I'm afraid. I'm heading the other way."

He almost asks, "The other way from what?" since he doesn't have a destination, no hotel room, nowhere he has said he needs to be, but he catches himself. It isn't a mistake, he realizes. It's a lie. "That's fine," he says. "I know my way around."

"Maybe another time." She's looking down the open, empty corridor. He watches as her brow's furrows begin to smooth, some knot of tension leaving her face. Gradually, the ridges vanish, the shadows disappear. A network of thin lines remains. Lines that weren't there a decade before.

When she catches him staring, he smiles without much conviction, then turns to the window once again.

It doesn't make any sense. There's no reason for her to lie. Though it's possible that she made an appointment, a rendezvous, while in the bathroom. It occurs to him that she may be protecting him in precisely the way he just protected her. The thought is an appealing one. Two lies told for kindness, a bookend to the parallel confessions they made years before.

Outside, the landscape begins to show unfortunate signs of civilization. Beige, concrete buildings spring up like the mushrooms he has studied all these years. Just as ugly, just as poisonous in their way.

"We're going to be late," Cathleen says, just as they enter a tunnel. "A little over fifteen minutes. Nothing to do about it, I suppose. Did you notice, Jeremy? I'm not afraid of tunnels anymore. Remember how bad I used to be?"

In the darkness, the glass has become a mirror. He watches her reflection as she checks her watch again, then begins to drum her fingers on the armrest. She's clearly impatient to meet whoever it is.

The train stops.

"Dammit," she says, looking toward the black window. "God dammit! We're already late."

"They'll get it moving," he says. He can't imagine what's gotten into her, the woman who normally would shrug and say *So, I guess we're running lateish.*

She sits back in her seat and closes her eyes. "I just don't believe it," she says. "This train is never late." She begins to take deep breaths, long and even. Labor breathing.

The train starts up.

"Oh, thank God!" she says—as though for salvation. "Oh, thank God."

When their eyes meet, her face falls slack. Her mouth opens then shuts. Caught. Unmistakably caught.

"You're going right back, aren't you?" he asks. "To Zoe?"

For a moment, his certainty fails, but then she nods. "Yes, Jeremy. That's right. I'm going back."

"You mustn't be angry," she says as they stand together in the chaos of the station, unsure and unfinished, a phantom version of lovers who don't want to part. "Not at her. She meant well. It's an impossibly personal time for her, but she didn't want you hurt."

"I'm not angry."

Cathleen looks at him, appraisingly. "I believe you. Though you do seem upset. But I suppose we're all upset." Then her eyes open wide. "You can't tell her you found out. Not ever. You know that, right?" She looks fierce, suddenly fierce—and he loves her for that. "She thinks she's spared you pain. I know her, Jeremy. She'll always be proud of this. There's nothing she can feel good about today. Except there's this—that she did something kind. For you. You can't ever let on."

"Don't worry," he says. "I won't."

And he doesn't say more, though there is more to say. But he wants her to go. He wants her to hurry to the next train so it can carry her back to where she's needed. He doesn't want to slow her down explaining how he feels. That he isn't angry. That he isn't insulted or hurt at being sent away. He is overwhelmed—by his daughter's kindness to him. By the kindness of them both. It's so much more than he deserves. It breaks his heart.

"I'm so sorry, Jeremy," Cathleen says, a hand on his arm.

"Me too." Small words to cover a lifetime of all they might be sorry for, symmetrical, like wedding vows, like confessions. *I do. I do. I did. I did.*

"Where are you going?" she asks. "Do you need any help?"

He shrugs, shakes his head. "No. I used to live here, remember? I'll figure it out. Just tell her . . . tell her I'm so sorry for her loss."

Cathleen kisses his cheek. "Thank you for not making this a thing." She hitches the little bag up onto her shoulder. "I'll let you know what's going on," she says. Then she turns and walks away, hurriedly, as though late.

Her path is lined by pigeons pecking crumbs off the vast marble floor and Jeremy watches as one by one they fly into the air at her approach, then one by one descend and settle just behind her, when she has passed. As he stands there, admiring this spontaneous choreography, Jeremy knows that he'll tell Rose about it when he gets home. He knows that she can help him understand why this seems so beautiful to him, why the sight brings tears to his eyes.

As soon as Cathleen is gone, he begins to walk himself, in no particular direction, no destination other than that one in mind.

. . . Divorced,
Beheaded,
Survived

Without question, Anne Boleyn was the plum role.

Day after day, dusk really, in the time between school and dinner, in the small, untended yard behind my childhood home, there were fights over who would get to play her. Even the boys loved everything about being the Lady Anne. The telltale pillow under your shirt, long before the elaborate royal marriage. "Henry dear, I have wonderful news!" The twigs you could tape to your hands, just next to your pinkies, to show those extra fingers that she had. The fact that we all knew there had been extra breasts as well. The simple, distant weirdness of it all. "Ooooh, I'm a witch. I'm a sexy pregnant witch. And I want to be queen of all England!!"

My older brother, Terry, was undoubtedly the most convincing. Once, he stole a dress from our mother's closet—a red-and-white Diane von Furstenberg wraparound so he could use the beltlike part to hold the couch-pillow baby, the future Queen Elizabeth, in place. "Oh, Hal," he cooed to Jeff Mandelbaum from next door. "You don't need that old Spanish cow of a wife of yours! With her sour little daughter. You just wait! I'll give you that son you want and deserve. Right here, my sire." With a pat to his lumpy middle.

Almost nothing beat watching him sidle up to Jeff, who was always our Henry, due to his heft, to the early growth of untended facial hair across his heavy jaw, and to the fact that he was the only one of the neighborhood boys who steadfastly refused to play a wife. "Oh, Harry, let's go frolic in the meadow and leave these nasty courtiers all behind!" Then Terry would bump his swollen front against the damask tablecloth Jeff wore draped across his back, knotted in a bow beneath his chin.

It was almost worth giving up the role yourself just to watch Terry give it his all, and it might have been, if it weren't for the execution scene. But the beheading was just too good not to fight over. Molly Denham, from the house behind ours, whose parents were both Jungian analysts, usually asked to be the anonymous executioner.

"Do you forgive me, My Grace?" she would intone from behind an old Batman Halloween mask, her voice as deep as she could make it, her straight yellow hair hanging to her waist.

"I do, sir. I do forgive you."

And when I was Anne, I would then offer her my hand, to kiss and to hold as I knelt. Looking up to the sky, I would press my palms together, as if in prayer—or as I imagined people praying might do. Raising my own long hair up above the nape of my neck, I'd lean my head down over the chopping block—a white enameled lobster pot, turned upside down—and await the mortal blow from the black rubber axe that Molly swung.

It was all Johnny Sanderson's idea. His father was a professor in the medical school and had started up at the university the same year my father joined the history department. Those were the days when there were still teas and formal dinner parties for new faculty, and my parents and the Sandersons had struck up a friendship of sorts.

Johnny was a year younger than Terry, a year older than me, and he was one of those kids who seemed to know a lot about himself before any of the rest of us had much of a clue of who we were. By that spring, when he was eleven, he knew for sure that he wanted to be a history professor, like my father. But instead of American history, his thing was Europe. He was a short, skinny boy who pretty much always wore brown corduroy pants and a gray sweatshirt. And he looked young for his age. People were always thinking he must be in my class—sometimes even younger than that.

I don't know exactly what satisfaction Johnny got from having us act the thing out in my backyard time and time again. I think it must have been something greater than what the rest of us enjoyed, hamming it up as we laid our heads down on the lobster pot or moaned while giving birth to another of Henry's brats. There was more to it than playacting for Johnny; a kind of intensity crept into his voice when we all gathered after school, had some juice and fruit or crackers, whatever my mother had around. A kind of edgy tension as he said, "Hey, anyone want to act out the thing again?" And he knew how to hook us all too, every time, rotating which kid would play Anne, having the good sense to hurry through the more boring wives—though he never let us wholly skip a single one.

"Off with her head!" Jeff Mandelbaum would shout at the afternoon's Jane Seymour. "Off with her head!"

"Divorced, beheaded, *died,*" Johnny would correct. "The third wife died. No beheading. Jane Seymour died a natural death."

He was the first of the many obsessive, bossy intellectuals I have loved and have lived to impress. Nothing pleased me more those afternoons than when, as Molly's axe head hit my neck, Johnny Sanderson would burst into spontaneous applause or even sometimes say, "Great, Sarah. Really, really great."

That was the spring of fourth grade for me, 1973—the last months before Terry got sick, and then sicker, and then got better for a little bit, but then died in '74, which shocked me when it happened, but now, thirty years later, it seems to have been as inevitable a conclusion as the strike of Molly's axe.

To my own children, that long-neglected backyard is only part of Grandma's and Grandpa's house, where we go for Thanksgiving, for the Christmases we don't spend with Lyle's folks in California, for occasional weekend escapes from Manhattan, into Massachusetts. To see the leaves changing color. To celebrate a birthday. My mother's seventy-fifth. My father's eightieth. Events that for me

carry an inevitably muted quality. My mother's eyes damp-
ening over her presents with what she swears are tears of
joy. My father softly talking to himself, after the candles
have been blown out, after his wish has been silently made,
all alone on the back-porch swing.

The children are too old now to play out there much
when we go up, though I used to watch them dart around
the wild, thorny rosebushes in games of tag, and try unsuccessfully to hide from one another behind the lean Japanese
maple. Sixteen and twelve now, Mark and Coco are four
years apart—we had been two apart, Terry and I. And
maybe it was superstition that made me wait that extra
stretch of time before getting pregnant again. I don't know.
Lyle would have liked our children to be closer in age:
"Keep the parenting years compressed." But I put our second child off, and so my boy and girl were always just a little different from the pair we used to be.

I've been thinking a lot lately about all the ways we try
to protect our children. And ourselves. Three weeks ago,
Mark's best friend, Peter, was killed on the Long Island Ex-
pressway. That Sunday morning, I was making a special
breakfast—French toast and bacon—because Coco had a
friend sleeping over. The girls were still in her room, and
Mark was lying on the living room couch, reading. Lyle
was grading papers at the kitchen table, complaining
about them as he did: "How can these children be in college and still be so close to functionally illiterate?" I had
just pulled the eggs out from the fridge and held the car-
ton in my hand when the telephone rang. It was close to
ten o'clock.

"Can I talk to Mark?"

The voice on the line was a kid, but not a voice I recognized.

"Who's calling?"

It turned out to be a boy I'd known for years.

"What's the matter, Nick? You sound terrible."

As he told me, I turned my back on Lyle, who was suddenly alert, watching me. I opened the fridge and put the eggs away. "There was this party . . ." I'd known about the party. Mark had thought of going, but had decided he had too much work. "I don't even think they were drinking or anything . . . or not much anyway . . . The way I heard it, the other guy, I don't know, I think someone said it was a truck, he might've been stoned or something. Nobody else was even hurt . . ."

The bacon on my stove crackled as Nick spoke. My back still to Lyle, I reached for a fork and turned over the strips. Lowered the heat.

"Are your parents there?" I asked.

They were.

"We'll call a little later, Nick. Let me talk to Mark first. We'll be back in touch."

"Who died?" Lyle asked, before I even hung up the phone. I told him.

"Jesus Christ."

"Car accident."

"Holy shit."

"Yeah. Holy shit."

I turned off the bacon. And kissed my husband's motionless head before going in to talk to Mark.

"This is the part where Anne learns for certain that she's going to die," Johnny Sanderson had coached us, every afternoon. "No more chances. She's doomed. You should show a little emotion at this point."

And Terry would hold his face in both his hands, his shoulders heaving in enormous, racking, make-believe sobs.

But in real life, it was all silent hours. Vacant stares.

As soon as we learned Terry was sick, my house stopped being the daily gathering place. Everyone but me seemed to know what was coming. He stopped being the boy who would throw himself into anything that seemed like fun. And one by one the other children began avoiding us. We had played together all our lives, and then it ended. There was no more ease between us. Not even between my brother and me. I didn't know how to speak to the quiet, solemn boy he had become. And he didn't seem to need me, anymore.

I sat next to my son where he lay stretched on the couch. "Hey, bud." I took the book from his hand as I spoke, and lay it open on the tabletop. "Something's happened, sweetheart. Something bad." His face was still sleepy, unwashed, his brown hair a little messy.

I don't know. Maybe Jeff Mandelbaum's mother saw a different side of her son after my brother died. Could detect a new thoughtfulness in his eyes. Maybe Molly Denham cried herself to sleep for weeks. Maybe Johnny Sanderson's heart was broken. I never knew. They never told me. Johnny did go on to be a history professor, like he always said he would. Made a name for himself at the same university where our fathers had taught. But maybe his life wasn't exactly the way he'd always imagined it, because of what happened to my brother when we were kids.

My son's face changed as he took in the news.

"He's *dead*?"

I nodded. He shook his head.

"No. That's impossible. Just yesterday . . ."

I nodded again; and he still shook his head. Coco had come into the room in her nightshirt. Just behind her, I could see her friend in pajamas holding a hairbrush to her head.

"What's going on?" Coco asked.

"Nothing," Mark said. "Go away."

"Dad's in the kitchen, hon. Go on—he'll talk to you." And grasping my urgency, she left; but for a moment her friend just stood there staring at us, the brush caught halfway through her hair. Then she too turned and walked away.

"Mom, he can't be dead."

I didn't speak.

Can't be. I know that feeling.

Can't be.

But is.

I don't think about Terry every day, anymore. And sometimes I'm stunned by that fact. It isn't only the discomfort of disloyalty I feel, it's the fact of utter disappearance after death. The idea that as loved as we may be, we may also be forgotten. If only for a day here and there.

More than a decade ago, as soon as I thought Mark was old enough to ask me questions, I made the decision to put away the picture of my brother that I had carried from my parents' home to college, in and out of my first brief marriage, in and out of the first apartment Lyle and I shared, and finally into our family home. I took it down off the bookshelf, where it sat between my old books—all the orange-spined Penguin classics, Shakespeare, Woolf, all that—and Lyle's many chemistry texts. It just seemed to me to be too hard on the children, too hard on Mark particularly to have that happy boy face smiling down, and to know what had happened to that other boy. The lines between him and my own son were too easily drawn. I was afraid my brother's face would become a fearful thing for them. And maybe for me as well, with kids of my own. So I put him in the dresser drawer I use for the few really fine scarves and gloves I possess, the softest place for storage I could find.

But of course the children have always known that I had a brother and that he died. A brother named Terrance, Terry. They know about him without my ever having had to tell either of them. Uncle Terry, he would have been. It's family information. The kind that travels in the air that children breathe.

At Peter's funeral, we lined up in a row, my husband, my two children, and I. Mark and Coco wore the dress clothes

I had bought for Thanksgiving, which is fast upon us now. Another drive to Massachusetts. A family visit home. I'll have to phone my parents, I know, and tell them what happened. I haven't done that yet.

We never did call Nick back, the morning that we heard. And I don't think Mark's spoken very much to any of his friends since then. Not about Peter. He goes off to school, and comes right home. Heads straight for his room and closes the door. Coco's asked me if he's going to be okay, and I tell her that he will. And I know that he will. It just takes time, I tell her. It's only been a few weeks. It'll take some more time.

I forced myself to go up to Peter's parents as they stood beside their son's casket, and to say the things you say. Lyle came too, of course, and shook their hands. Mumbled something. Bit his lip. Stepped away so another family friend could do the same. I didn't force the kids, but eventually Mark made his way over. The mother and father both hugged him, hard, and Peter's kid brother shook his hand, with an empty expression on his face. Mark didn't come back to us right away. He just wandered to a corner of the church and stood by himself for a while.

The truth is that sometimes even more than a day goes by before I remember to think of my brother. It's only natural, I've told myself, time and time again. It's human nature, I've thought—as though there's consolation to be found in that. And maybe there is. Maybe it's a gift to be able to let go of the remembering. Some times. Some things.

"What was it like, Mom?" Mark asked me for the first

time ever, yesterday. "What was it like when Uncle Terry died?"

I took my son by the hand, into my room. I opened the dresser drawer and there he was, smiling out from above the softly folded scarves, the empty fingers of my own gloves seeming to want to hold him there.

"It was hard," I said to Mark, as he lifted the picture toward his face. "There is no secret answer. It was terribly, terribly hard."

When I got to Henry VIII in high school—European history, tenth grade—Molly Denham and I were in the same section. She still had that long, straight hair to her waist, and she wore overalls most days. The rap on her was that she smoked a little dope, but not more than most kids. We weren't really friends, anymore. And neither of us said a word to the other, not a single word, as the wives were taught, one by one. It was as though we had never spent those hours together. As though she had never held and kissed my hand. Never asked for my forgiveness, which I so freely gave. And neither of us had watched my brother in that dress, pregnant and cooing seductively to his sire.

There are things that go on, I believe, important things that make only an intuitive kind of sense. Silences, agreed to. Intimacies, put away.

"Divorced, beheaded, died, divorced, beheaded, survived."

Miss Rafferty wrote the rhyme out on the board while Molly Denham and I dutifully copied it into our notebooks, as though we might otherwise forget.

Some
Women
Eat
Tar

WHEN ARTIE SUGGESTED to Nina that they should have a baby, he did so at first kind of softly, just letting the idea slip in between them every once in a while, playfully, like a private joke shared from time to time. But gradually, his tone grew more serious and before too long Nina realized that he meant it. This was no joke. This was something Artie wanted. Very much. Really. Now. And without a lot of thought, Nina said okay, sure. Sure, they could become parents. It wasn't an unpleasant prospect, for her. Not at the time. Having a baby just wasn't Nina's idea; that was all. This wasn't something they would be doing because of a burning need in her, but hey, that was no problem. She was happy to go along with him, to answer his need. She loved him so much, that was fine. Men did this all the time, she told herself, let themselves be convinced it was the right time.

Why shouldn't she?

But then, when her next period never arrived and the first test stick testified to the success of Artie's plan with a blue plus sign and the second stick (Artie wanted the kind of certainty only using two brands, neither generic, can give) backed it up with two pink lines, Nina was shocked. More than shocked; completely flipped out. Those alien hormone hues on the pee-soaked magic wands charted for her a route she hadn't truly understood would be traversed: the distance between Artie tickling her thigh, joking about children's names—*Uriah, Abednego, Job, Jezebel*—and this: herself with another person inside herself.

Her alternatives, she understood, were terror or denial. She chose denial.

And so it was Artie who bought the seven pregnancy books he stacked under the bed on his side, and it was Artie who asked around at work—only people whose opinions he respected, of course—about pediatricians they should consider. It was Artie who knew to investigate, when they trooped together on interviews, where the doctor stood on the overuse of antibiotics for ear infections (or was it underuse? Nina was confused: *How do you keep these things straight?*), when kids need surgery for that, how soon or late babies should be weaned, and hey, what about circumcision? What's being recommended these days? Foreskin on or off?

And it was Artie who had already determined, going in, the answers he wanted to hear: *Yes to antibiotics. Four ear infections in a season means the child needs tubes put in. There*

is no "should" about weaning, not from the breast, that is a
highly personal, near-sacred, decision—as long as you nurse for
at least six months. Before six months, it's not a personal decision; it is **The Only Right Thing To Do.** And babies should
be off bottles altogether by fourteen months and should never,
ever, ever have one in bed with them. Never. Not even once.
Or their teeth will grow in rotted and black. And then fall out.
Breast-fed infants should be given their first bottle at around
nine weeks, and then emphatically NOT by the mother and
only sparingly, so there is no Nipple Confusion. And finally,
these days, most doctors are pro-circumcision. Studies suggest it
cuts down on diseases later on, and since Artie and Nina aren't
Jewish so wouldn't use a mohel—because let's face it, those fel-
lows are the best, it's all they do all day—the other way to go is
a surgeon, which you have to request specially. And that can be
difficult, arranging for that, but is certainly worth doing because otherwise you get some bleary-eyed obstetrics resident cutting away, and who knows what can happen. Not often, but
still . . . it isn't worth the risk.

The doctor who got every answer right—the winner—
was a young, pretty woman who made Nina feel invisible
from the moment they met. Especially when she repeated
the phrase *Nipple Confusion* and Artie nodded knowingly.
For just a second there, Nina thought that she would rather
steal her own car, jump a plane, and take on a new identity
than hear her husband discuss her potentially confusing
nipples with this girl. (Nina herself had cast her quiet vote
for Dr. Brown, the sixtyish rumpled guy who had suffered
through Artie's questions, answering each with a shrug and
a "Who knows? We all make mistakes. We try to do our
best. Me. You. All of us. What more can we do?")

But Dr. Swenson, this Dr. Swenson with her perfect hair and makeup, her clean white coat, and the little sign on her desk that read "Because I'm the Pediatrician, That's Why" held no such views. There certainly was a right way to do this.

This: the baby.

This: the schedule.

This: the breast.

The breast? Nina could remember when Artie would moan to her about the sight and feel of her naked *tits,* begging to kiss them, stroke them, fall into them.

Oh well.

When the baby kicked, at about eighteen weeks, Nina thought she would explode. It wasn't a bad feeling, it was just more feeling than she could contain. She started going on long walks to distract herself. Into town and out again. She took on extra work from the greeting card company where she had freelanced for years, doubling the number of witty/touching/rhyming/not rhyming captions she produced for them each week. Her just-out-of-college editor at Rainwater Greetings thought it was way cool that pregnancy really did bring on creative bursts. Wow. He was seriously going to have to think about getting married someday, or at least having kids. He was so jealous. He wished he could get pregnant himself.

Yeah, Nina thought. Tell me about it. There ought to be a club.

She wrote a total of eighty-seven salutations/congratulations/condolences—an inordinate number of which ended with the phrase *Believe me, I understand*—between weeks eighteen and twenty-eight, when she felt her first contraction grip her, months too soon.

After a quick and cold exam, Nina's obstetrician sent her to bed, told her to stay there for six weeks, and prescribed drugs that made it impossible for her to sleep.

Stay in bed and never sleep. Let us know if you have more contractions. Let us know if you feel the baby stop kicking.

"Shouldn't that be if you no longer feel the baby kick?" Nina asked. "How do you feel someone stop kicking you?"

"What?"

"Never mind."

One morning, about a week into Nina's confinement, Artie pulled three baby-name books off his bedside table and tossed them over to her half of their bed, which was now a full two thirds. He said she really ought to come up with a short list. Maybe ten names. He had; and he thought they should both do that without consulting each other, and then compare. And then narrow the list to ones that they both had on their original lists. Ten boys and ten girls.

"It's a girl," Nina said.

"Yeah, right. How do you know?"

"I just do. I know. Give me some credit. The one thing I have always been sure of my whole adult life is whether or not I have a penis inside of me. And right now I don't. Ergo it's a girl. She's a girl."

Artie laughed out loud at that, and for the first time in weeks Nina thought that there was still some hope—though for what, she wasn't sure. Then Artie said, "Just make a list, okay? Just humor me, Nina, and make two lists of names."

At her thirty-six-week appointment the doctor told Nina her cervix was holding together, the baby was big enough, and she was officially off bed rest. She could do anything now. No restrictions. No limitations. Take walks. Have sex. And no more medicine.

Yanking her swollen feet out of the stirrups and donning her jeans with the enormous stretchy waist, Nina felt shadowed again by the confusion that had hovered over her for months.

"People say things to me that make no sense at all," she told her mother on the phone that afternoon. "No restrictions? You should see me. What does that even mean?"

"Your problem, Nina," her mother replied, "is that you are unable to contextualize discourse. Within the context of weighing six hundred pounds and being kicked brutally from within, you are free as a bird. Welcome to motherhood."

"Thanks, Mom." Nina paused. "Actually, I think I hear the other line ringing. I'll have to call you back."

That night in bed she scrunched up against Artie and asked him to make love to her. And he scrunched away, as far as possible.

Nina began to cry. "Don't you want me anymore?" she asked. "The doctor says it's fine. Don't you find me—?" But she couldn't bring herself to say the word.

Sexy? It was ridiculous.

"It's not that," Artie answered, moving just a little closer, then clearing his throat, as if to make an official proclamation of some kind. "You're sexier than even you have ever been," he proclaimed, gingerly reaching to touch her left breast.

"Don't," she said. "They hurt."

"Sorry."

"Are you afraid I'll crush you?" she asked. "Because there are about a thousand possible positions . . . I could just lower myself, very slowly . . . I could get on all fours . . ."

But Artie shook his head.

"It's not that," he said. "It's what you said about her being a girl. I guess I don't want my daughter . . ." He stopped.

"Yeah?"

"I don't really want my daughter to see me like that."

"Like . . . ?"

"That," Artie repeated, and Nina leaned back away from him.

"You understand," she finally said, "that we have both gone insane? This baby isn't even born yet and already we have both lost our minds."

Soon after that, she went back to taking one or two long walks a day. In an attempt to make some sense of it all, to clear the confusion, she would talk to her daughter as she marched along. *This is us turning left,* she told her child. *Left gets you into town. Well, it isn't really much of a town, it might be more of a village, but village sounds pretentious to me. So I'll just call it town. This house here, this white one, I usually see kids playing outside. The mother is always*

pregnant. Always. Perpetually. I'm sure she's pregnant now.
She's bound to be, so that'll be a friend for you someday. He
or she can be your friend. As long as you are happy. That's all
I'll ever want for you. I won't have many rules. As far as I'm
concerned, as long as you're happy, you can do anything at all.
Except take a bottle to bed with you. That is the one thing
that's out. Even if it makes you happy. Apparently that is the
only true taboo left to us all. And this is the florist shop, which
is where we turn in. . . .

It was one of those doors with jingle bells tacked onto the
frame. Their tinkle would signal the end to Nina's mono-
logue.

The florist was about her age, thirty, thirty-two, a tall
and gentle-seeming man with wavy brown hair and search-
ing, sexy eyes that made Nina sad. The first time she
walked in, he appeared out from nowhere at the sound of
the door and smiled without hesitation toward her enormous front.

"Hey, my wife is having a baby too," he said, grinning.
"Our second. It's the best." And he pointed toward a row of
pictures tacked up on the green velvet wall behind the
counter.

"That's Sam. Our girl," he said. "Samantha. Three years
old."

"She's beautiful," Nina answered, meaning that he was
beautiful. She hadn't really looked at the girl.

"Yeah. Well. Sure." He shrugged. "*I* think so. But, you
know."

And suddenly Nina wanted to say: *No. Actually, I do not*

know. What do you even mean? Is she beautiful or isn't she? Do you love her? Does your wife? Do you love your wife? Does she still love you? And by the way, did you have sex when she was enormous and sore? And if so, how did you survive? And if not, how did you survive? But instead she just grimaced and looked over toward the glass refrigerator full of flowers.

"Can I get you something?" the sexy man asked, and Nina nodded her head.

"Do you have anything particular in mind?"

Nina almost laughed out loud. Oh yeah. She had something particular in mind. Had he spent a handsome lifetime asking women that, and watching them blush? She took a breath and began, "I only like things that aren't orange. Or yellow. Or pastels. I like roses." She frowned as she peered into the cooler. "I think. But not red ones. Or pink, obviously. And I hate those ferny greens and baby's breath and all that extra filler stuff." She looked at him. "Is there anything left?" she asked. "Or have I excluded everything?"

To her delight, that made him laugh—showing lovely white teeth and dimpling cheeks. And so Nina laughed too. His eyes twinkled, and she tried to make hers twinkle back. She tilted her head a little to the side. And then she leaned just a fraction forward and banged her belly hard against the counter's edge.

"You know what you should do," he said. "You should just go over there and help yourself. Just let your hands guide you," he encouraged her. "Just follow your hands. Watch yourself reach for what you like. That's the way I learned. You'll see what you're drawn to. You'll figure out what you want. It's the most important thing, figuring out what you want. That's still what I do." He held his fingers up, spread. Long fingers. Short nails. Silver wedding band.

Oh God.

What makes a man decide to be a florist anyway?

Nina sighed, turned to grasp the fridge door handle and pulled on it hard. As she leaned inside, she felt the crisp air around her, and right away, amid the insipid pinks and peaches, she found a tub of ruby-colored tulips toward the back, a deep color, something that looked powerful to her. Nothing sweet. Or passive. Or indecisive. Or babyish. Crimson: the color of blood. Dark and meaningful. She wanted to reach for it, felt her arm raise, her body lean; but then her center of gravity betrayed her and she lost her balance, stumbling up against the glass.

"Never mind," the florist said, as he approached. "I think I know what you want."

When Artie asked her later that week what all the flowers were for Nina said, "I read that it's good for the baby, having beautiful things around." And when he told her he would be happy to buy them for her, though maybe not new ones every day like she was doing, and maybe she'd like some brighter colors to cheer her up, she just said no, she enjoyed choosing them. She and the baby both. They enjoyed the walk.

When her mother asked on the phone why she didn't sound so blue for once, Nina said it was because she had fallen crazy in love with her florist and, just as soon as she had lost these revolting fifty pounds, planned to run away with him. To France.

"These revolting fifty pounds?" her mother asked. "Is that my grandchild to whom you are referring?"

And Nina laughed. And laughed. And laughed. Until she started to pee. And then to cry. And then she said good-bye to her mother and hung up the phone. In a few minutes, though, she picked it up again and called Artie to tell him she was taking to bed for the rest of the day.

"I think I've had it," Nina said. "I just want to sleep."

That night, Artie came home carrying a three-foot-wide yellow mylar smiley-face balloon and a greeting card that told Nina that whatever the other elephants might think, he was just nuts about her. Or something like that. She didn't read it very closely—just checked to be sure it wasn't one she had written. One birthday, he had accidentally given her a card that she herself had composed and the experience of reading herself tell herself how much she loved herself had made her feel distinctly pathetic in ways she preferred not to repeat.

"That's really cute," she said, tossing the elephants onto the bed. "Thanks."

"I know something's bothering you, Nina. Why don't we talk?"

She pursed her lips a bit, and thought. She looked up at the huge balloon smiling down at her and at Artie's face beside it, saturated with such well-intentioned distress. Comedy. Tragedy.

"I think you have the right to know," she began, her arms crossed over her huge front, "that I have fallen in love with the florist and we're planning to run away together.

After . . ." She patted herself. "Well, after this. I wasn't going to tell you, but I've decided that you have the right to know."

Artie nodded, slowly, still frowning. The balloon smiled still.

"Why did you decide I had the right to know?"

"Beats me. Maybe because you bought me a big balloon."

Both faces nodded at her—as if her explanation made perfect sense.

"And when did you and the flower guy cook this up?"

Nina drew in a deep breath and squinted toward the enormous yellow face bobbing in the air. What was there to be so happy about, anyway? Nothing much. But still, wouldn't it be wonderful to be that face? Perpetually smiling, not a care in the world. Delighted with all the choices one had made.

"Nina? Hello . . . ? I asked you when you and this guy decided all this?"

She shook her head. "We haven't actually discussed it," she said. "It's just that I know that's what I want. No offense, but I don't think I want to be a wife and mother after all."

He took that in. A short sigh. "Okay. Fair enough. What do you want to be?"

"My florist's concubine," she replied. "My florist's concubine. In France."

Artie didn't nod this time, or sigh, just twisted his lips a bit, then turned to go. "You want dinner?" he asked.

"That'd be great. Thanks."

Watching him walk away, Nina felt immensely sad.

At the doorway, he stopped, looked back at her. "Do you still love me?" he asked.

She could feel her eyes begin to sting. "Of course I do. Please don't make this about you, Artie," she said. "Because it isn't about you. Not at all."

The balloon had drifted Artie's way and he tugged without much apparent purpose at its string. The big head bounced and knocked against the ceiling, smiling still without complaint. "Then what is this about?"

"I think it's mostly about having a baby." She watched the bumping balloon as though it might suddenly react. "And it might be a little bit about how the florist really is drop-dead sexy hot. But mostly it's about the baby thing."

"What makes him so hot?"

"I just think there's something wrong with me," she said, ignoring that. "I see the books, the TV, the neighbors. Everyone in the world is pregnant, having kids." She shook her head. "And they don't seem to feel like something weirdly wrong is happening to them. Only me. The whole human race thinks this is a normal thing to do, and I just can't seem to accept it. It strikes me as utterly bizarre. The whole experience. How is this okay? How am I okay? There is a human being in me. It will be born and have a life. You can't imagine it."

"Have you and the flower guy . . . ?"

"Don't be ridiculous."

"Some women eat dirt when they're pregnant," Artie volunteered. "It's called pica. Some women want to eat the tar off the street."

"Excuse me?"

"I'm just saying some women eat tar. And they go on to be good mothers after that."

"Lucky them."

"I'm just saying."

Nina nodded. After a moment, she asked, "So, what's for dinner?"

"Whatever you want." He stepped toward the bed, the balloon string in his hand. Nina watched as both faces leaned closer in. Arnie so earnest, so serious; and his companion, so absurdly, consistently joyful. "Honey, you can have anything you want," Artie said. "You can have tar. All you have to do is tell me."

But that was just it.

"Surprise me," she said. "It looks like it's going to have to be a surprise."

With a single nod, Artie released the string and left the room. Gently, the gigantic face drifted up, where it bounced against the ceiling and twirled around, its smile hidden. A game of peek-a-boo. Nina saw only a blank, silver expanse as she felt the first labor twinge—not even yet a pang. Something she barely noticed while she stared up at that glittering circle, empty, bright, as the balloon seemed to seek her, drifting closer, closer still, until it floated directly over, so she could see her reflection shimmer there. And there it stopped. It stopped, as if it knew, in all its merriment, that it belonged to her. And that if she could just be patient, then she too would understand.

The
History
of
the
World

I.

ADDING UP THE SILENCES would be an unkind thing to do.

Still, if Kate Rodgers *were* to add up all the pauses in her brother Arthur's speech, all of them, over the last nearly sixty years, it would make for several days at least, several days of her own life spent waiting for the creaky gears of his brain to locate the proper word. He's struggling now to find *tollbooth,* and Kate is again waiting, wanting to give him a chance. And, as she waits, she thinks about his brain in just those terms—like a watch that's been dropped and possibly stepped on, so the gears still move, but with a hitch. The kind of hitch in the works that makes you lose a few minutes every day.

"Tollbooth."

She's the one who says it first. This is an instinct in her as old as any she possesses: knowing when and when not to finish her twin brother's thought.

"Yes, right. So I was driving up to this tollbooth yesterday and the car in front of me is this enormous what are they called . . . minivan like everyone drives in the States. But I'd never seen one quite this big, or maybe it's just because in . . . in . . . Italy, in Italy what I'm used to seeing are those toy cars, speeding around. That and the . . . the . . ."

"*Motorinos.* Vespas."

"Motorcycles. But yes, *motorinos. Motorini?* Anyway, this thing was really strange."

"I've seen so many American cars this trip," Kate says. "Many more than ever before." But as she speaks, she isn't sure that's true. She doesn't actually remember noticing cars one way or the other since arriving the day before. She's had other things on her mind.

"I suppose that's right," Arthur says, though in fact he has noticed no more than she. "Blame it on the global economy and all. Cable television. American imperialism. All the usual suspects, right?" He lifts yesterday's *Herald Tribune* to his face. He's read through it once already on the plane, but it's better than nothing. "It feels," he says from behind his shield, "seeing that van, that minivan . . . it feels . . ."

Another pause begins its unmistakable stretch.

Peering over the paper, he finds her pale blue eyes, his own pale blue eyes, staring back. These seconds, the empty ones, move slowly for him. Knowing she has what he wants. Preferring to produce the word himself. It's funny how this, the language thing, has never bothered him as much with anyone else as with her. He squints as though he might find the words written on her face, and Kate, who has lived with this look, with its silent, insistent pressures for over six decades, begins suggesting possibilities to him.

"Wrong?" she asks. He shakes his head. "Not foreign enough?" No. Not that either.

"Sad," he pronounces—the cloud lifting this time. "It just feels sad."

"Oh, it is sad," she agrees, though she barely remembers now what the *it* in question is. So much is sad these days, Kate is willing simply to assent to the word and leave it there.

"So, we're off to Orvieto today?" he asks, back behind the *Trib.*

"I'd like that. I'm still feeling jet-lagged and not too ambitious. Unless you have work you need to do. I'd like to sit together in the square and watch the passersby. Maybe talk." She stands, tightening the belt on her travel robe, silk—not for its luxury, but for its negligible weight. "I'd like to talk."

"I think that sounds perfect," he says, and puts the paper down. "Work can wait. I didn't come on this trip to work. I came to be with you. Half an hour?"

"Yes. That sounds right."

"I'm looking forward to seeing the . . . the . . ."

But it's gone.

"Cathedral?"

He shakes his head and slowly moves his hands together in the air, as if signaling a tighter focus.

"The façade?"

"Yes. That's it. Thank you. The façade. I'm looking forward to seeing the famous façade."

As a child Kate suspected that it was her own umbilical cord, and not his, that had wrapped itself around Arthur's neck, depriving him of oxygen for just long enough. No one ever told her this. No one ever told her much of anything about why Arthur spoke the way he did, why his otherwise razor-sharp brain seemed to have these holes in it, lacunae into which words would disappear. Their parents chose silence on the subject of Arthur's odd silences as the kindest and maybe the easiest course, and left it to their daughter to glean what little she might from bits of private conversations slipping out from under closed doors, or from relatives who gossiped, neighbors who thought they knew. The cord had gone around him three full times. An older cousin whispered this when Kate was five, maybe six. And he had been completely blue at birth. As blue and as silent as a blueberry.

Kate pictured it, a single image of the rope, thick and twisted, the kind sailors use, uncoiling from out of her own infant stomach, twirling itself around, around, around his neck.

In the shower upstairs, she soaps her body, wishing she'd remembered the razor still in her suitcase, by the bed. Not for her legs. The hairs come in finer and sparser now; and anyway, she's quite sure no one is paying much attention to her solid, matronly legs or, for that matter, to the area between them, where the hair has grown strangely lush in the months since Stephen left. Untended. Unseen. But under her arms there are bristles, sharp among the pale, pouching skin, and standing there, in a just too cold shower, she cannot bear the thought of herself as a woman of a certain age, deserted by her husband, traveling with her brother, a woman whose underarms have grown visibly unkempt.

There is no way around it. It would have been so much less painful had she lost Stephen to death, rather than to Rita. It wouldn't have been a referendum on her, on her marriage, her sexual worth. It wouldn't have been fun or easy; but it would have been possible—in a way that this is not.

The pressure is low and it takes some chilly minutes to rid herself of suds, step out, towel off. Before she dresses, she slips the razor from her bag. Standing naked at the sink, Kate lifts first one, then the other hand above her head, and shaves. Her breasts, slack and neither practical nor pleasurable anymore, stare out at her from the mirror like uninvited guests.

Arthur prefers to drive and Kate lets him, though the rental car is in her name, as is the two-week lease on the small farmhouse. In the elaborate, sixty-five-year-long allocation of traits between them, she has long been acknowledged as the practical one, which at times strikes her as odd, since *he* has gone out into the world and made a good living doing whatever it is he does with stocks, while she has moved seamlessly through the decades, dependent first on her parents and then, without pause, on Stephen, and even now, even discarded, is still dependent on the monthly checks Stephen sends. Yet with Arthur, when they are together, she is the practical one, the roles of the nursery, early ascribed, early learned, proving immutable despite what other truths a greater world may have revealed.

The July day is hot and still. The dove-gray sky seems to be holding its breath, ready to exhale a storm. Arthur speeds and Kate tells him not to. Like a wife, he thinks, aware of his own unkindness. A nagging wife. The kind of wife who gets herself left. He denies speeding while slowing down, and then of course speeds up again.

"Just try not to kill anyone," she says as they pass the emptying buses just outside the town.

"I'll do my best."

He finds a parking space, though the lot appears to be full and Kate has told him it isn't worth a try. And now, he notices, Kate withholds all comment. She sits there beside him, frowning.

These are the moments at which it's hard not to feel some sympathy for old Stephen.

"Do we have enough gas to get back?" she asks.

"Yes. I think we do. If I am reading the . . . the . . . well, the thing, that thing." He points to the dashboard, but Kate's attention is now directed to her purse.

"I don't suppose you have change?" she asks.

"As a matter of fact, I do."

They are silent as she deciphers the mysteries of the parking meter. They are silent as they climb the outdoor steps from the lot to the cathedral, then continue their way alongside the vast white building, silent as they weave through groups of other tourists, silent until they reach the front.

"Jesus," Arthur says. "I never saw such a thing. It's . . . spectacular."

Kate says nothing, only looks. Bright gold and blue and red, it *is* spectacular. A part of her knows that he's right, though to her, on this day, it looks more improbable than beautiful, sparkling against the darkened sky as if lit from within. She thinks it looks *fake*. That's the word in her head, though she questions the thought even as it appears. What can it mean? The word makes no sense. Yet the cathedral seems like confection to her, spun sugar. Sprinkle water on it, and it will melt. Like a promise that can't possibly be kept.

"Does it still look the same?" Arthur asks.

"Yes. It does. Strangely so. Just the same."

Almost forty years ago, Stephen declared this structure his favorite in all of Italy, while Kate said it was a little gaudy for her taste. She felt more kinship with the dark weight of the cathedral in Siena. She could have hidden for hours in the twilight of that building. But this was an optimist's façade, and Stephen was an optimistic man.

"I could use a drink," she says.

"Go ahead. I'll just be a minute. Pick a café, any café. Somewhere around the square. I'll be right there."

"Take your time." And then, "Stephen loved this place."

"When you were here?" he asks, his gaze fixed ahead. "You and Stephen? When was that? Exactly? Was that your honeymoon?"

"No." She steps toward the cathedral, so he sees only her

back as she speaks. "The honeymoon was a long weekend in Maine. We were still poor. Italy was the year before Martha was born, our last hurrah before the children began to arrive."

She doesn't say any more than that. The word that occurs to her next is *happy*—but she can't bring herself to say what she might. That they had been happy then, and she had thought it would last. That's all. It doesn't need to be said.

When she turns around, her brother sees the sadness on her face, the eyes seeming only to stare backward, the trembling mouth, and he takes pity on his sister, throws his arm around her back. "Come on, lady," he says. "Let's go find ourselves a table and tie one on."

Arthur knew that Stephen was leaving long before Kate learned. For nearly a month he kept the secret, believing she should hear it from Stephen himself and trusting his brother-in-law of nearly forty years, a man he had always rather liked, to handle the thing as well as it could be handled.

"As much as I hate doing this to her, I just can't agree to being unhappy for the rest of my life," Stephen told him over lunch. "I have no desire to hurt her. But I haven't loved her, not in any real way, for many years. I've puzzled the thing through and through, but I just can't see what's to be gained by giving up on, well, on moving on."

And Arthur knew what his sister would want him to say. He could feel her words in his mouth—condemning

Stephen, urging for counseling, for second and third hon-
eymoons if that's what it would take. But his brother-in-
law's eyes, gray and narrow, were already devoid of any
hope. His voice was saturated with the rather cool direct-
ness that had always characterized him. Only when he
spoke about the new woman in his life did he exhibit any
animation. She was everything Kate was not—he never
said that, not in so many words, but the message was clear.
She was largehearted, loving, fun. Always on the lookout
for an excuse to be kind. She was admirable in her generous
spirit. And Arthur knew it had been years since his sister
had been anything of the sort.

"I thought if I told you first, you'd be better able to help
Kate when it happens," Stephen said. "She and I aren't
happy. She may not know that, but we're not. I'm not
denying that we were, but not for many, many years."

For most of the lunch, Arthur only listened. But before
the meal was over, he cleared his throat. Looked away. "You
know, Stephen," he said. "For what it's worth, I think
you're . . . given everything . . . I know I shouldn't say this,
but I think you're probably doing the right thing."

And as if Stephen understood that for this to be expressed, it must fade as rapidly as possible in the air, he only
quickly nodded and said nothing in response.

The girl who brings them their carafe of local wine takes
them for a married couple. "Will you and your wife like to
eat?" Neither sibling corrects her. It's a natural enough as-
sumption: a couple, not a pair. As children, they had un-

mistakably been twins, their matching blue eyes large on their faces, both with almost white-blond hair, often dressed in coordinating clothes. People always knew. But adulthood had soon distinguished them, blurring the likeness with more obvious contrasts. Kate, short and somewhat squat, took to dyeing her hair a reddish brown, while Arthur grew tall, very tall, took up tennis and squash, stayed lean. His hair turned silver early. They no longer matched; though now, on this trip, Kate has noticed odd similarities resurfacing. Arthur's older-man arms sport the same clusterings of moles and freckles as hers. Her hair, no longer colored, has emerged the same bright silver as his. His eyelids droop at the outer corners with an identical, sloping crease, exactly her own, as though time, which made them different, decided to change its course and erode those distinctions, revealing the ways in which their very textures are the same.

The waitress's English is good. Kate offers up her own guidebook Italian, but the girl seems to prefer the play of a foreign tongue. "No, no, I can do English. You will see." Something—maybe the sight of the cathedral, maybe the emergence of the word *happy*—has solidly soured Kate's mood, and she can feel the familiar tension, the *Arthur* tension, each time the waitress has to struggle for the right word or phrase; and indeed when Arthur himself can't come up with the word *bread* it seems almost like a pretense, a chivalrous gesture on his part to make the girl feel less self-conscious, the host dropping his own fork on the floor.

"Could you please bring us a basket of . . . of . . ."

"Bread?" the girl supplies. "Yes, yes. Of course."

"Bread. Yes, bread. That would be wonderful. Thank you for that."

"And would you and your wife like water, with the bubbles or do you want it . . . do you want it . . ."

"Still?" Arthur asks.

"Just the wine is fine," Kate says. "For us both. And two menus, please."

"Yes. Of course. I'm right back."

"She's very pretty, isn't she?" Arthur asks as she disappears into the café. It is a comment Kate has been expecting. Because she *is* very pretty, with dark, great brown eyes, and that expression of easy good humor on her face, and because Arthur considers himself a connoisseur. Over the years, he's regaled her, and Stephen too, with stories—some hilarious—of his exploits in that regard, and she's laughed at his conquests and misadventures, and Stephen laughed too; but then in private they had raised the possibility of feeling a little sorry for Arthur. Despite all the fun of it. It had to grow lonely sometimes, they had agreed, skipping from woman to woman like a skillfully tossed pebble over the surface of a stream.

"Yes," Kate says. "She's very pretty. Are there women in Italy who are not?"

"Not many."

The girl reappears with wine and menus, smiling still. "Just call me over when you know. I'm Anna." She leans over the table, more so than is necessary, Kate thinks, revealing dusky, rounding skin.

"Thank you. Anna?" Arthur says. "You're very . . ."

"Kind," Kate supplies. "You're very kind."

"Yes, you are. That's just what I was going to say."

The corners of his eyes, his lips too, have relaxed—as though he is lost in thought, planning his next move. Twice the girl's age, more than that, and he is contemplating an approach—and it isn't even absurd. That's the unfairness of it all. A man at sixty-five can still do these things. Sixty-five is nothing for the male.

As the girl disappears into the ancient, crumbling café building, his face seems to wake up, as though a hypnotist has snapped his fingers. "Too bad she thinks I'm . . . married," he says. "To my sister."

"That's easy enough to correct, if you're serious. I'm happy to clear the way. I have shopping I can do."

"One thing I'm *not* is serious. Even if I do decide to . . . to . . . to . . ."

"Make an ass of yourself over a girl a third your age?"

"Hah!" He tips his glass to her. "Very clever, Kate."

"It's a bit of a sore point these days."

She looks at him now, one eyebrow raised, and he says nothing—though he knows this is an opening, an opportunity to talk, to talk in the way Kate means when she says *I'd like to talk. We'll have a chance to talk. I think we should talk.* But he doesn't know what he can say. And it isn't the words he can't find—for once. It's the sentiment. What he really wants to tell his sister is to get over it, already. Pull herself together. Stop dragging her sorry self around, around such beautiful sights as this, too teary and bleary and just too bloody self-absorbed to see what's before her eyes. Life is short. Too short for this kind of extended misery. *Stop wasting your life,* he wants to say. But this isn't what she wants to hear, he knows, and he doesn't want to be cruel. This is

Kate after all, his twin, his other self, the girl who threw rocks at the children who made fun of him, sending his torturers scattering.

He raises his glass in a toast. "To your future," he says.

She takes a sip, then stares out toward the cathedral.

"You know, Kate, if you mean it about shopping, I'm happy to wait here. I read in the guidebook that there's a ceramic store on one of the back streets that's supposed to be a cut above the rest. Better even than the stores in . . . in . . ."

A pause begins.

Deruta, Kate thinks. She looks back at him and takes another sip of wine.

". . . in . . ." Arthur is staring at her now, brows lowered, eyes squinting. She can feel him bearing down. He wants what she knows. He wants something that she has.

Deruta, she thinks.

"Oh, come on, Kate. What's the name of that town all the ceramics come from? I know that you know it."

Deruta, she thinks. But she just shakes her head and shrugs.

Stephen was the only person to whom Kate ever confided her in utero crime—the strangulation of her twin. She was a sophomore at Wellesley when they met and fell in love. He was simply the most certain person she had ever known; and it turned out that certainty—of all things— was what she then craved. Maybe what she had always craved, growing up in the concentric rings of Arthur's endless hesitations; though in the end it turned around and bit her, hard. Stephen's certainty. But as a young woman, she thought him positive in every sense of the word, like a great strong building himself, a shelter she willingly sought. After a semester of serious dating, they spent a night at an inn in Vermont where her virginity was more given to him than it was lost, and after that she confessed, as though all her secrets, all she had been holding close for nineteen years could now safely be revealed. Stephen, then in medical school, assured her it couldn't possibly be true—with certainty. A twin *could not* become tangled in the other baby's cord. Not three times around the neck. It couldn't possibly ever happen, he said, and in his arms she had believed herself absolved.

On the way back down the A1, Kate drives. "You've had too much wine," she tells Arthur. "And anyway, you speed."

He resists arguing, but as he gets in on the passenger side he makes a big production out of trying to move back the seat, and as they wind down the hill of Orvieto, they are back in the silence that seems to shadow them. But then, within minutes, Arthur remarks on the selection of meats at the *salumeria* they'd both explored, then says that Orvieto was much more interesting than he had expected. She agrees that it was and says that before the week is out she'd like to go back, and he agrees that they should, and only a few minutes later they are both calling the rented farmhouse "home"—just a single day into the trip. He tells her it's good that they'll be home in well under an hour, and she says that she's happy to be spending the evening at home, cooking up some of the pasta that she bought.

How seductive domesticity is, she thinks as she drives. How seductively benign it all seems. How easy to fall into a routine with someone you know. So familiar. Even the bickering. And then the quiet, unacknowledged glide into making up. A well-traveled road. Arthur is reading bits and pieces from the guidebook out loud so they can piece together the coming days, and she wonders, as she has from time to time, why Arthur never settled down with anyone. There was only one serious contender, at least whom she ever knew. Her name was Sylvia, an heiress of the old New England variety—complete with farmhouse in Vermont, town house in Boston, place on the Vineyard, skin that had worn a little tough even in her twenties, and a long rope of inherited pearls Kate had coveted at the time. Much better than any Stephen could ever afford.

The speedometer begins to rise and Arthur ostentatiously cranes his head to see it. "Hmm," he says. "Who's speeding now?"

"I want to get home before this storm comes on. And I'm not close to as fast as you were. But you're right. I'll slow down."

"Don't do it for me. I like the speed. It's the Italian roads, Kate. It's Europe. See? Even you. You can't help but speed. It's part of the culture here. You shouldn't be such a . . . a . . ."

"Such a what, Arthur? Such a worrywart?"

"No." Though she has hit the nail on the head. Why,

when he never means to be unkind, does he feel himself continually on the verge?

"Stick-in-the-mud? Is that it?"

"No."

"What then?"

"Pessimist, Kate. That's all. You shouldn't be such a pessimist. It makes me worry about you. You only see what's wrong."

"That's not fair, Arthur. I've had a lot to deal with recently."

"I don't mean to be unfair." He doesn't. "I'm only trying to help you . . . move on."

And for a moment there's a pause, another pause, and Kate wants him to fill this one. She has wanted to fill this very silence since suggesting that they travel together to mark their sixty-fifth birthday, wanted him to express rage at what has happened to her life, outrage that her husband, certain as ever, has left her to be alone—when she can think of nothing she has done to earn that punishment. She wants her brother, her twin brother, to insist that she recount in detail how awful these last ten months have been. She wants him to call Stephen names, wants him to offer to call Stephen out. Wants him for once to find the right words, the ones powerful enough to carry her rage.

Rain starts to fall, hard.

"It's probably better," Arthur says, "if you do slow down a bit."

But the warning comes too late. The speeding Fiat skids on a slick patch of road, hits a truck whose own brakes have been slammed, and the passenger side of the car is crushed.

II.

When the children were little, Kate would sometimes wonder what strange hypotheses they were concocting within themselves. What guilts did they carry? Of what imaginary crimes might they hope future lovers could absolve them? Martha, Ellen, and Dave. Spaced at two-year intervals, their bonds to one another had always seemed oddly loose to Kate. Loose and unburdened. They were playmates at times, sworn enemies at others, and it all seemed to wash out by the end of any day.

On the day following the crash, all three call her several times in the hospital where she has been kept for observation overnight. Nuns shuffle in and out of her room, crossing themselves, taking her pulse. The sisters speak in whispers, but the children's voices on the phone are loud and insistent. They declare themselves frantic. They declare themselves disbelieving. Committed to their jobs, to their families, they declare themselves unable to come get her, and she catches a whiff of the neglect she felt from them in the aftermath of their father's betrayal. They won't be rushing to her aid. Nonetheless, she must come home. They declare themselves agreed.

That evening, her right arm bandaged, walking with a cane, she returns to the empty farmhouse—because she doesn't know where else to go—and the children call her there. They insist again that she leave Italy. They have had a day now to take all this in. They have spoken to one another, many times. They have compiled a list of available flights. She should not be alone. She thanks them all for their concern—it all feels so strange—but she doesn't tell any of them the truth, which is that she cannot go home. An investigation is under way and the police have asked her not to leave. Speaking to her own children, she thinks her voice sounds oddly resolute, when what she really feels is *caught*.

On the third day, her sixty-fifth birthday, they each call again, but not one of them mentions the occasion, and she is grateful to them for that. She drinks herself through the day, Chianti, and when that's gone some unearthed vermouth that tastes like lacquer but gets the job done. Dispensing with the cane, she moves haltingly from room to room, touching Arthur's belongings with her good hand. His battered leather suitcase. His smooth, steely laptop. His shirts. The large bed in which he slept, and which he left so carefully made, the pillows plumped up in a row.

The owner of the farmhouse, a stick-thin Italian woman, comes by with a stew and some bread, enough food for two days at least. She asks Kate what else she needs. But Kate can't think of a single thing.

Late that night, Martha, the eldest, the lawyer, the practical one from *their* nursery years, calls back to tell her mother that a decision must be made—about Arthur. The body can be flown home, preferably with Kate, or he can be cremated there. Either way, it can't be put off endlessly. Does she realize this? He's left no instructions. No will that anyone can find. Since Kate is his sister, it's all her decision. So Kate says she will decide. Soon. She's decidedly drunk as she answers—only sober enough to hope that she doesn't sound drunk.

"I think you must still be in shock," Martha says. "It

doesn't sound like this has hit. I can't imagine why you're still over there, Mom."

"No, it may not have hit. You may be right. But I do feel tired. I should go get some sleep."

On the fourth day, Stephen calls. The rental car company has notified him—she is still on his insurance. Or the children have. Or the police may have found his name still on the emergency card in her wallet. She has the sense that he may have called her right away that first night when she was still woozy, but she can't remember clearly. It feels oddly like trying to remember the pleasures of their early years together, distant and doubtful, called into question now. His concern for her is offered in unmistakable tones of detachment, a man phoning his own past to offer condolences. The iron cage of shock begins to fail. Tears flow freely now. Arthur is dead. She is at fault. And Stephen is unable to make it right. Little squeaking sounds escape her.

"It could happen to anyone, Kate," he says. "Accidents are accidents. The children tell me that there was a storm. It's terrible, but these things do happen. Don't beat up on yourself."

She doesn't tell him she had been drinking that day, that she was speeding, that she felt petty and annoyed with her brother for having reached their sixty-fifth birthday in so much better shape than she felt herself to be. That Arthur seemed to be purposely withholding from her the sympathy she craved. That she had been knocked down, winded, by visiting the cathedral Stephen had long before taken for his own. Wishing *him* dead. Not Arthur, but him. She only says that she thinks she's still in shock and none of it seems real. It's true enough. She forces the tears away and thanks him for calling. She says it will probably hit her soon. But it hasn't. Not yet.

When they hang up, she lays her head down on the sofa, and sobs and sobs.

On the fifth day, she makes arrangements for Arthur to be cremated.

On the sixth day, she is awakened by a rooster's cry. The wooden window shutters are half open, yellow light drizzling onto the whitewashed walls. As her feet touch the floor and she pads across the room, the chill of the terracotta streams up into her calves.

The landscape out the window spreads up and over small hills, patchworked into plots of olives, grapes, barley, wheat. The olive trees glimmer their silver green, the grapevines twist tortuously in short, even rows, strung together with black wire.

Italy.

"It's known as *promiscua*," Stephen called back to her from a similar view all those years earlier. "*Coltura promiscua*. As in 'promiscuous.' It means that they chop the land into small bits, don't cultivate just one crop. They shuffle it around. The Tuscans are not loyal but promiscuous in what they choose to cultivate. *Promiscua.*" He rolled the word on his tongue. "Leave it to the Italians! Promiscuity even in their agriculture. Can you see? Here? Olive trees. And here? What looks like a patch of wheat. But in a year it will all have been changed." From the bed, Kate couldn't see what he was pointing toward, so instead she admired his back, the sunburn on his neck giving way to smooth strong shoulders, leading over and down into powerful arms. His cotton pajama pants slung low around his narrow hips. "It's an ancient farming technique that prevents the land from exhausting itself," he said, turning back toward the bed, his eyes taking in her body there. "The land," he continued lecturing, untying the drawstring around his middle, "in its promiscuity . . ." He spoke slowly as she lay back, pushing the covers off herself, " . . . is never bored."

At the window, Kate draws in a deep breath of air singed with fire, stained with smoke. What has been pruned is now set ablaze. *Coltura promiscua.* How funny it all seemed back then. How very much like a joke at someone else's expense. She turns from the view and takes a towel for the shower.

Later, the landlady comes by with more food and to ask Kate if she will be staying the second week. There's an American couple interested in the house. She can have a full refund if she chooses to go home. Without saying that she *must* stay, Kate tells her that she *will* and the landlady looks disappointed—as though Kate is a bad omen she would prefer to have gone. Or maybe she has just quoted a high last-minute price to the other people and is missing the profit. With apologies for imposing, Kate asks her for a ride to the crematorium where Arthur's ashes now await.

"I don't have a car. I would be very, very grateful for the ride."

"And then?" the other woman asks.

"And then I don't really know." Kate looks down at her hand, no longer bandaged but still mottled purple. "I'd like to rent a car . . . but I don't know if I'm allowed."

Two phone calls later, it turns out the landlady has a

brother who will rent her a car—nothing fancy, mind you, but no paperwork, the equivalent of twenty dollars a day. Up front for the week.

She isn't surprised by the lightness of the ashes. Both her parents were cremated, and her shock at how little of a person can be left came two decades earlier when she was handed her mother, in a similar cardboard box.

"We're mostly water," Arthur said at the time. "Dry us out, and there isn't much there. Just . . . just . . ."

"Dust?"

"Yes, exactly. Only dust."

On the seventh day no one calls, and Kate feels herself to be alone in the world. She has never been alone—not a twin like herself. But now she is. She lies on the bed in Arthur's room, under the covers he used and left, the box of ashes by her side, and when she closes her eyes, she sees again the heavy, twisting cord she hasn't thought about in years.

III.

The sky over Orvieto has no threats to make. The blue looks as though it has been painted there, in one tint. At the café on the piazza, the same café, Kate sits heavily onto a chair and lets go of the bag in her hand as though it is of no interest to her.

The same waitress walks toward her, a smile on her face. "You were here before," she says. "With your husband, yes? A week ago or so?"

For a moment, Kate thinks the girl has her mixed up with someone else, but then she nods. "Yes. That's right. We were here last week."

"You drank white wine? The local wine? I can bring you some."

"Thank you. Yes. That would be nice. And a carafe. But only one glass."

"Your husband is not joining you?"

Kate considers her response. "No. My husband won't be joining me today."

"Okay. I'll be right back."

"Thank you," Kate says, and as the girl walks away she fans herself with the collar of her blouse.

Jack and Jill went up the hill, to fetch a pail of water.

The rhyme has been stuck in her head all day.

Was it first grade? Kindergarten? Since the accident, Kate has felt oddly submissive to ancient memories, each seeming to grasp her, tenacious for a time, then pass because another has taken its place. Whatever the year, they were cast as the ill-fated pair. Of course. The tow-headed twins. What teacher could resist them in those roles? Arthur chafed at wearing the green flannel hat their mother made. The water in the tin pail was made of soft strips of blue felt, cut from a moth-eaten blanket.

What odd details remain of one's life.

Jack fell down and broke his crown, and Jill came tumbling after.

And indeed, he fell with great gusto, Arthur did. Did he hurt himself? Not badly, but she thinks she can remember that he did. Maybe only a bruise or two, but something. Something to show off as an honorable wound. She was the more careful one, tumbling after, arranging herself horizontal on the small ramp set up in their school auditorium. Lying there, she rolled, not in a fall, always too cautious for a true fall, but with her arms tucked tightly by her sides. Dizzy at the end. Dizzy, and essentially unscathed.

The sun has dropped in the sky so the cathedral is ablaze, beautiful in its glow of impossible promise, its illusion of grace; and now its unchanging façade seems somehow victorious to Kate. So much for her fantasy that it might dissolve like so many sugar drops. It was *this* when she was happy here with Stephen. It was *this* when she was bickering here with Arthur. It will be *this* when she leaves. *This* if she returns. It stares at her steadily, like the child who can go longest without a blink.

It was probably a mistake coming back. This town has become a scavenger map of her life. Another child's game. Find the building your husband most loved when he still loved you most; find the table where your brother ate his last meal; find the waitress with whom your brother might be pursuing a holiday dalliance had he lived.

Is this what life eventually brings? The return of one childhood ritual and then another, all newly imbued with a cruel humor of a kind.

The young woman is laughing now with a table full of men. On her black tray sits a large carafe, no doubt meant for Kate; but the men have delayed her, with their jokes, their admiration. Their wives are all off shopping no doubt, as Arthur had suggested that she do. As she has done today, though with little success.

At the ceramics shop, she held first one piece of pottery and then another, certain they would break in her hands. This is what has brought her back to Orvieto, the thought that Arthur would like for her to buy an urn or even just a simple lidded jar at the store he had mentioned. But the first piece she saw was painted with giraffes. The second with snails. It all seemed absurd.

The woman who guided her through the store, the artist herself, was dressed in a lab coat—like a doctor, as though to attend to the aspect of this task having to do with the human body, as though her art might shift seamlessly into science. These animals were traditional to Siena, the animals of the Palio, the woman explained. But they were only a small portion of what she had. She held a slender paintbrush in her hand, waving it in the air as she spoke. She named all the patterns on display, showed Kate what seemed like hundreds of lidded jars. She offered to custom-design anything. She had long, straight black hair and thin, bright red lips, and as her hand moved, Kate, unable to concentrate on the task, the idea of her twin inside any jar repugnant, incomprehensible, pictured this young woman painting her own mouth with the brush. In the end, she bought a lidless vase for a small fortune. Not for Arthur. Just because she had been in the shop for nearly an hour.

"Here it is!" The waitress—Anna—is back with the wine. "The same you drank last week."

"*Grazie.*"

Before the girl even turns away, the glass is to Kate's lips. She drinks thirstily, as though the wine might cool her down, and pours herself another glass. An English family fills the table next to hers. After they order, they set about planning the next week. The parents want to see the sights of course, the children to find a pool.

She realizes she has to pee, and now the waitress is nowhere to be found, so Kate stands and begins to wend her way through the tables. The bathroom can't be hard to find. It can only be inside the small building. At the door-way, she crosses into darkness and into an unexpected chill. As she passes by the kitchen, she hears two voices, a woman and a man. The Italian is too rapid for her, but the anger in the man's voice is unmistakable.

In her own life, she muses—while using the toilet, wash-ing up—she has never had a voice raised to her that way. She has heard other people fight. She had an aunt and uncle who used to battle, roaring by the end of family meals, but she had been proud of the fact that she and Stephen never did anything like that. She couldn't remem-ber him raising his voice at her. At the children, yes, but not at her.

Catching herself in the mirror, she wonders now whether this detachment was something for which to feel gratitude or more like a sign of things to come.

It doesn't matter, though, she knows. It doesn't matter what warnings there were or were not, or whether she could somehow have averted his departure had she been more aware. That is the problem with the past, she thinks, as she flicks off the light. This illusion that revisiting it might somehow change what has occurred, the same illu-sion that brought her to Italy a week before, that brought her to Orvieto on this day.

Stepping outside, Kate almost bumps into Anna. There are smudges of wet mascara on the girl's cheeks, pale streaks down her cheeks. But the girl's mouth jumps into a smile as she asks Kate what more she needs.

"Wine," Kate says. "I would like another carafe of wine."

As the heat hits her again, she feels a bit faint, and sits gratefully at her table.

"Where is your husband today?" Anna asks, bringing the new carafe. "Will he meet you here?"

"My husband . . . the man you met . . ."

"Yes."

It's ridiculous, this confusion of a comedy braided into her tragedy, but impossible to clarify now. "No," Kate says. "He won't be picking me up. I'm here on my own."

"You can call him?"

"I can't call him. Why?"

"You should eat something. It's not good to drink with no food." She straightens the second chair at the table, wipes at something with her rag. She seems in no hurry to step away. "Where are you staying? At a hotel?"

"No."

The girl doesn't move, and with a sense of surrender, Kate explains that she has rented a farmhouse. She names the town and answers more questions about the location. Anna says she knows it, she knows the house. She went through school with the children of the spindly landlady. They were an unusual family, she says. All three left the area to study art. One became a very successful painter, living in Florence.

But there is a limit to how much interest Kate can feign. This young woman's childhood has so little to do with her, she barely believes in it. And the farmhouse can hold no history before the one night Arthur slept within its walls. Just as it will disappear when she goes home. She is relieved when the English family calls Anna over, and she makes quick work of the wine in her glass.

It's a good question, she thinks, as she pours herself more, whether she will ever make it home. A policeman was there at the house in the early morning, dressed in uniform, wearing what looked to Kate like an unusually large gun. A little man with a big gun. Still in her robe, she let him in and offered him coffee, which he refused. He then offered her his condolences, which she accepted, though with a sense of impatience.

They sat across from each other at the massive kitchen table—just where she and Arthur last sat—and he asked her to describe the accident again. Her answers the other night had not been completely coherent, he said, which was entirely understandable. She noticed a slightly British flavor in his speech. His circular face was bisected by an enormous mustache all but covering his mouth. His brown eyes seemed almost imploring as they looked at her. She had the strong impression that he wanted her case dismissed, that he wanted to send the poor, bereaved American lady home. He smiled as he spoke, prompting her.

"You were the one at the wheel?"

"Yes. Yes, I was."

"And you were driving within the speed limit?"

He nodded as he asked. It all felt like a formality, as though there was an implied response of *yes*. She could almost hear it, the next word he wanted her to say. The word that would make all of this disappear, as if it had never happened. She looked away from him, from his encouraging smile, down at her own bruised arm, her skin lined with small brown moles, galaxies of freckles. Her brother's skin, on her arm.

"No. No, I wasn't," she heard herself say.

"No? Do you understand? The question?"

She thought for a moment. "I don't know the exact speed limit, but I believe I was above it."

"You told us previously that you were not."

She could remember the scene. Her hospital room, the day after. The story she had told was that she had been driving carefully but the road had been terribly slick. Or maybe there had been something wrong with the car. Sitting at the kitchen table, she could clearly recall the sensation of *trying to get away with it,* and a chill ran across her flesh. The idea of trying to get away with it had become repugnant. If she killed him, let her pay.

"I misspoke the other night. I know I was speeding, or at least driving very fast. There was a storm coming on and I was . . ."

"Yes?"

"And I had been drinking."

"This is not what you said before." His features had settled into exasperation.

"It may not be," she said. "But it's the truth." As she spoke, she tried to shut out the voices of her children, urging her to retract. Retreat. Stop playing this game and just get the hell home. The image of Stephen, wild over his insurance bill, wondering what has happened to the wife he so confidently left. "It's as simple as that," she said. "I wasn't being adequately careful. And I probably shouldn't have driven at all." She frowned, as something obvious occurred to her for the first time. "I would much rather it had been me."

The captain scribbled notes. He would have to speak with his colleagues, he said. He would be back in touch soon. It would be better if she stayed in the country for a while.

And so she will stay.

The carafe is empty when Anna returns.

"I'll take the check," Kate says. "But first . . ." She gestures toward the building, the ladies room again. She stands, she tries to, but the world is lost, a black screen fluttering before her eyes.

"Here," the girl says. "Sit. Here. Here."

Somewhere far, somewhere else, the metal table is searing into Kate's cheek. A hand touches her. A motorcycle guns. There is a voice. Then nothing at all.

"Kate's heading out again," Arthur would say. "Hold steady, there . . . tim-ber!" It was a family joke. Even at her wedding, in the receiving line, she had needed to sit for fear that she would crumple to the floor. "Good thing you're marrying a . . ."

"Doctor," Stephen had supplied.

The waitress is holding a glass of water to Kate's lips. Kate shakes her head. No.

"You should," Anna says, now sitting. "You should drink."

Kate takes the glass in both her hands, then puts it down. "It's so silly . . ." she begins. "It's the heat. And I haven't eaten. But really, I'm fine."

Anna looks concerned. Gone is the professional smile. She touches the glass, moves it an inch toward Kate, repeating her entreaty to drink. She suggests that the husband should be called. Kate can't drive, she says. She shouldn't drive.

"I'm fine. I will be. In just a few minutes . . ."

"It isn't safe," Anna says.

"I have no choice." Kate can hear the sharp edge of her tone, but does nothing to soften it. "I'm all alone."

Anna nods, slowly, as though considering, and then she looks toward the café building. "Maybe you can help me," she says. "Maybe I can help you."

As Kate sips at the water, the girl tells her that she herself has no ride home at the end of her shift. She knows the house where Kate is staying, and she can drive her there. She has a cousin who can fetch her then. "My own ride has disappeared," she says.

The chill of the water spreads through Kate's body, waking her.

"It isn't only you," Anna says. "Or me. It isn't safe for others, to have you drive your car so . . ."

"Drunk?" The girl is silent. "Well, you're right," Kate says. "About the others. It's the others, isn't it, who always get hurt?" She puts down the glass. "Thank you. I accept your offer. I appreciate your help."

Anna tells her she only has to work a few more minutes. They will be gone very soon. Kate should use the ladies room, she should be ready to go home.

Fifteen minutes into the drive, the women pass the site of the crash. Anna slows down and points out the small road-side shrine someone built, a cross made of white-painted sticks, a basket of purple flowers, drooping, long dead now themselves. She tells Kate about the tourist who was killed. A man, she believes.

"This is why you have to be . . . to be . . ."

"Careful," Kate supplies. "Yes. This is why." She thinks of asking Anna to stop the car, but her mind is moving slowly and the shrine has been left far behind before the thought can leave her lips. She wonders if she will come back tomorrow, maybe bring fresh flowers. She wonders how long it will be there, once she is back home—assuming she doesn't land in an Italian jail instead.

Night is still some time off, but the sky has lost its brightness. Still, Kate can feel the heat of the air through the open window. She is just beginning to doze off when Anna asks if it's okay that they stop by her house. She may be needed to help with her brother, she says. It's on their way. It won't take very long. Kate agrees without thought. "Anything," she says, then realizes how very little she cares what happens now. Nothing feels real anymore. She is in a car she doesn't know, with a girl she doesn't know, and she has loosened the truths of her life with this girl, allowed reality, which has been supposed to hit her, like the slap on a newborn child, instead to fade and disappear.

Sitting up a bit, she asks Anna how old her brother is. He's seventeen, she says, but that isn't his true age. Not really. He's like a child in a grown body. Like a baby. He is mentally retarded, she says.

"He can be a problem for my mother. I only want to look at them and tell them I'm going to my cousin for the night. It won't take long. Then I can bring you home."

"Take your time," Kate says. "I'm in no hurry to be home."

Soon, Anna pulls the car up into a dirt patch—barely a driveway. On the lawn are terra-cotta pots, most of them empty, two or three holding scrubby shrubs. Anna repeats that they won't be here long.

"It doesn't matter," Kate says.

"You can come in, if you like. It isn't . . ." Anna pauses. "It isn't so nice," she says.

"It doesn't matter to me," Kate says again. "It doesn't matter to me at all."

It isn't clear to Kate what does matter now.

Inside the house, the air is dark in a way that night is not, a hazy dimness falling like gauze. A woman, younger than Kate and worn thin as a leaf, sits with a newspaper folded on her lap, where it looks more like a covering of some kind than something to be read. An enormous boy, his long hair pulled into a ponytail, sprawls on the couch. He wears jeans and an orange T-shirt. His feet are bare. As she steps closer, Kate can see filth on the balls and heels of his soles, only the high arches not black with grime. The sight holds her attention for several seconds, until she forces her gaze away.

Anna speaks rapidly, quietly to them both and Kate picks out the story—her own story. A customer. Wine. A husband. A home.

She looks back at the boy. His eyes are like one-way streets, taking in, taking in. Nothing revealed. Kate tries to smile and he looks away.

In one corner is a stove, something cooking. As Kate steps closer, the smells of lemon, of rosemary, something to long for, rise in the air, at odds with the squalor and sadness of the room. Anna throws her purse down on the long wooden table and pulls out a straight-backed chair. "Please," she says. "Please have this seat. I won't be long."

All around Kate are unfamiliar sounds and scents, unfamiliar sights, people she understands she cannot know. She closes her eyes, as though to limit this flood. She concentrates on the voices only, how they stop one another, then seem to spur each other on. The boy speaks only in answers. *Sì* and *no*. Anna's tone is the questioning one, the mother the hardest for Kate to understand. She says the most, all of it addressed to Anna, all of it in urgent whispers. Soon, Kate picks out a pattern: the mother speaks, a long string of words. Then Anna asks a question to the boy, who answers his sister, yes or no. The mother speaks again. There are no silences between them. None of the pauses Kate has spent a lifetime filling—or not.

She opens her eyes. Anna is by the stove, dishing food into a bowl.

"We won't be long," she says. "They'll be okay here, while I'm with my cousin. I just wanted to . . . to be sure."

Kate needs the bathroom, and Anna sends her up the stairs.

"Just a few minutes more," she says. She looks like a different girl from the one at the café. She looks a decade older. "I'll be ready to go when you're back down."

In the car again, Kate asks where the father is, and the girl tells her he left long ago. "I think it was the sadness. About Marco, about . . . life. Sadness. And maybe he is a . . ."

"Womanizer?" Kate asks. "A man who likes ladies too much?"

"No. Not that. A man . . . a man who is afraid. There's a word . . ."

"Coward."

"Yes, that's the word. My father is a coward. So he left."

"Many men do leave," Kate says. "Do you see him still?"

"No. I don't want to."

"I thought maybe the café, in the kitchen . . . ? I heard voices . . ."

"No. He is someone else."

Her tone bars further pushing, so Kate asks about the cousin, and Anna smiles, as if remembering a joke. He is her best friend, she says. He is the funniest person she knows. "We laugh whenever we are together."

"I don't have cousins like that," Kate says. "I'm not sure I have anyone like that."

"That's too bad. You have to have people for fun."

At the farmhouse, Anna parks and says she'll call now for her ride, but Kate has already realized she doesn't want the girl to leave.

"If you stay for dinner, for the night, I'll drive you back to Orvieto tomorrow. Or to your home."

Anna says she is going with the cousin to a festival in his town, a festival of flowers. They have plans for the day.

"I'll take you there, then. I'll be sober by tomorrow. I'm sober now." It's almost true. "I just don't want to be . . . to be . . ."

"Alone?"

"That's it," Kate says. "I don't want to be alone."

"But where is your husband?" Anna looks toward the dark house. "He isn't here?"

"My husband has left me. Like your father. He too is a coward. And he won't be coming back."

Kate's cell rings two times as together the women heat up the landlady's latest offering—a veal shank about which Anna has nothing good to say—and pour themselves more wine. She ignores it. It is the children calling, no doubt. Martha wanting to know when Kate will be home. Or possibly, just possibly, she thinks, it is Stephen again, with his doing-the-right-thing tone of voice. Checking in on her the way one checks in on an ancient, burdensome aunt.

Let them go to hell, she thinks. Let them all go to hell. Every single one of them.

Over the meal, she asks Anna about her brother. Has he always had problems? Or was there an accident? An illness? Anna tells her he has been like this since birth. There was something wrong with the pregnancy, she explains. Her face seems to slacken as she speaks. She tells Kate her mother had been sick with fever. "I'm six years older. And a girl. My mother is not good with him. So, he has always been my . . ."

"Responsibility?"

"Yes, like that. Like my job. My mother and my father, they are both people who . . . people who . . ." As Anna concentrates on pouring more wine, Kate allows the moment to extend, understanding with something like gratitude that this silence isn't hers to fill. "They are not strong with problems," Anna finally says. "And then they have a big problem in their life, so I have to be good with it. I know there are better doctors for him, in Rome. I did research on the computer at the library. There are people who can help. They can't fix him, but he can have a better life than this. There are things to do. But it's expensive. It's not just like a pill he would take."

"You're so young to be so responsible." It's true. She looks like a child.

"I don't feel like I'm young."

"I had a brother, too," Kate begins. "But I wasn't . . . I wasn't . . . We were twins." Kate thinks of the shrine. Of the ashes upstairs. "He died," she says. "He's dead."

"I'm sorry. Were you close? Were you friends?"

Kate considers. "Yes, we were. Most of the time. I don't think I was always a good sister, though. I was . . . I was impatient with him. Very often." In the car. Just before the crash. She had been so angry. She says nothing more.

"I am also impatient with Marco. It's very bad. All the time, I feel . . ."

"Guilty," Kate supplies. "You feel guilty. All the time."

"Yes. I think life is . . . hard."

"It's very difficult. It can be."

"But hardest for women. More difficult for us."

Kate frowns. Is that really it? It seems too simple; and she isn't sure. Was it not difficult for Arthur too? Difficult for Marco? For the cowardly husbands who have left? Was it not difficult even for the ones who have fled?

"I think it may be difficult for us all," she finally says. "For brothers and sisters, both."

It's decided that Anna will sleep in Arthur's room—which Kate calls the spare room—and use Arthur's bath—the spare bath. While Anna clears away the dishes, Kate straightens the bedclothes and strips the space of his things, bringing them into her own room, where they sit in a small, disordered heap. The laptop, the shaving kit, a pair of dress oxfords, the neatly folded shirts, and, atop the pile, the box of ashes. *Only things,* she tells herself, leaving them there. *Only things.*

On the landing, she hands Anna a gown and the women say good night. As Kate thanks Anna once again for the ride, for her kindness, for staying with her, she kisses her cheek and a smell of smoke, of meals, the smell of Kate's own hours in Orvieto, rises off the girl, then vanishes when she steps away.

For just a few minutes, Kate stays outside the door, listening to the noises of the house. The water running. The pipes creaking—complaining, as if making a great effort to perform the task they were crafted to perform. As if old. As if tired. Did she notice these sounds the night Arthur was here? She doesn't remember; it all seems new. She was another woman then. Kate closes her eyes, and the swing of the bathroom door sighs itself into her thoughts. She has been many women, she understands, has slipped surefooted through the years from one identity to the next. Daughter, sister, wife, mother. And now to be this—to be a woman without even the illusion of knowing herself. The sensation is like flight.

When she hears nothing more, she opens her eyes, knocks, and then opens the door. How strange the impulse is, but how strong. Anna is there, sitting up against the pillows, lost in Kate's own white ruffles, like a child waiting to be tucked in, or like a bride. Kate sits by her side on the bed.

"Are you comfortable?"

The girl says that she is. She nods her head.

It's hard for Kate to know how to begin. "Maybe this isn't my business," she says. "But I heard today . . . I want to ask you, Anna. I heard a man at the café. I was passing by the kitchen, and there was an argument. His voice . . ."

The girl nods. "Carlos. The owner."

"He sounded very angry." Kate moves her hand to Anna's cheek. Her fingers barely remember softness of this kind. "No man should ever talk to you that way."

"Carlos is mean. He's a terrible man. He owns the café, but thinks he owns me. Like I belong to him. When he touches me . . ."

"You shouldn't let him touch you."

"His hands . . ."

"What?" Kate has been touched by only one man in her life. Stephen, gentle, cool, loving at one time. "Is he rough with you?"

"His hands have no feeling. From the stove, from being burned. They are dead. He touches me, but cannot feel. I hate this. This not being felt. When he touches me, I feel myself disappear. Like I am not real." Her face seems to have grown paler, as though the white of the gown has soaked into her skin.

"Don't let him," Kate says. "Why should he touch you?"

Anna reaches for Kate's hand, and guides it to her own shoulder. Kate almost pulls it back, as though she might be burned. As though she is still herself. But she doesn't.

"Tell me," Anna says. "Tell me what my skin feels like."

Kate's hand lies motionless for a moment; then she begins very lightly to trace circles down Anna's arm.

"You feel me?" Anna asks. "You feel my skin?"

"Yes." Smooth as moonlight. "Yes, I do. You feel . . ."

"Tell me."

"You feel soft." It isn't right. It isn't enough. "You feel . . ." Kate watches her fingers, wrinkled at every joint, against the silken olive of Anna's skin. It is like touching a memory, reaching into the past and caressing what is gone. "You feel beautiful," she says.

Anna opens her eyes. She touches Kate's arm, barely grazing the bruises there. Her fingers on Kate's skin feel so strange. Being touched by anyone feels strange.

"Your husband . . ." Anna begins.

Kate looks up. "Yes?"

"I want to say this. I hope it doesn't make you angry. But maybe you are better now, better without him." She lifts her hand to Kate's head, pushes a silver lock off Kate's face. "I saw how he treated you that day, with so little respect. How he flirted with me, with you sitting there. And I see the bruises on your arm. A man who does that, maybe it's better for him to be gone. You need better . . . better . . ."

"Better treatment?" Kate supplies.

"No." Anna shakes her head, pulls her hand back from Kate's hair. "Not that word. My brother needs treatment. Because he isn't right. That's the word I see, the word I read for him. Treatment. You need . . . you need . . ."

The pause stretches out, but Kate has no further guess.

"Love," Anna says. "You need better love."

The old word surprises Kate. Love. Immediately, she thinks of Stephen, of the day he left; and all those cold, cold apologies of his, all that efficiency of emotion he displayed. What was it she had wanted of him? Something like loyalty. Something like honor. She had wanted him to stay. That was it. When had it last occurred to her to think of love? The girl's eyes, large and beautiful, are so serious. Her face is so sincere. Her advice is so sincere.

"You should sleep," Kate says. "Here." She moves closer to the bed's edge, so Anna can stretch out her legs, lie flat. The girl turns on her side, away from Kate. "Here," she says again, her hand on Anna's back. "Here. Go to sleep. Go to sleep."

"No more talking tonight," Anna says.

"No. It's time for quiet." In the darkness, she sees it like an ocean, the quiet around them, like all the waters of the earth, the silences of her life, larger, more powerful than what has ever been spoken, mapped, planned.

When she's sure the girl is deep asleep, she shifts away, then stands. Her body remembers the particular tread away from a sleeping child, the careful slowness, and then the hurry to be gone.

The heat and light have both fallen from the night air, leaving the scent of the rosemary bushes that hover along the stone patio, like motionless shadows. Kate cannot remember when she was last outside so late. The moon is a slim crescent that seems as though it might easily flicker out.

Only feet from the farmhouse it is so dark the surrounding hills and valleys could themselves be an ocean now; or could be nothing at all. But there are vipers in the grass, Arthur told her, black, poisonous snakes, so she stays on the patio, in the light, where she can see what is close to her.

In her hands she holds the box of ashes. She won't look for somewhere special, not try to do this well, not worry about the questions to come. She will just sprinkle them, a handful, another, a third, out into the darkness where they belong.

IV.

The entrance to Città della Pieve is through an enormous stone gate, built, no doubt, to keep some medieval army from devouring the town. Anna, at the wheel, is talkative, impatient to be done with the drive, impatient to show Kate the flower festival, but the central streets are closed to cars, flimsy barricades at all possible turns.

"I'll park anywhere," Anna says. "Here is fine." She pulls onto a grassy crescent where other cars have been left. "It's perfect," she says, handing Kate the keys. "We'll go look for my cousin now."

"Don't forget your jar."

Kate gave it to her, early that morning, in the kitchen. "Sell it," she said. "Or bring it back to the store. You can probably return it. Use the money, for your brother. It was very expensive. It might be of some help."

Her head is still throbbing from last night's wine.

"There's a meal today, outside, for the entire town," Anna says, beginning to walk away. "A town party. Come."

The music in the air is familiar, maybe a song that Kate learned as a child. She follows Anna into an open square and finds a small crowd gathered around a brass band of young people, in black shorts and white shirts. A nun, also in black and white, conducts.

"From the school," Anna calls back, walking fast. "This is their big day."

"Very nice," Kate says, but too quietly to be heard.

It is already a big day for her too. Captain Marconi called early to ask if she was sure of what she had told him. It was very difficult for them, he said. There was no way to know how much she had been drinking, how quickly she had driven. There was no proof. She might be misremembering. Such mistakes can occur. While he spoke, Kate walked outside, to the patio. The darkness and whatever it held had vanished, the landscape appeared again, the patches of olive trees, wheat, jostling one another on the hills. *Coltura promiscua.*

"I'm glad you called," she said. On the grass around her, dew had beaded, sparkling now, as though everything she had scattered the night before had been washed away by dawn. "Yesterday morning, I'm afraid I misspoke. I have been upset, and quick to blame myself. But I do not believe it was my fault."

A moment's silence passed. In that case, Marconi said, the office would like again to offer her their most sincere condolences. She is free to go home.

Anna is still in sight, but far ahead. In this tandem, they pass rows of closed shops, through a stream of people in festive clothes, until finally, at the mouth of a street, Anna stops. "Here," she says, gesturing into the road's opening. "Here you will see. The festival of the flowers. This is why we have come."

Kate makes her way to where Anna stands, but at first she sees nothing. Nothing at all. And then what she does see makes no sense. The road that falls before them has been painted, with many colors. It has been drenched with color, as far as Kate can see, as though an endless supply of paint has been spilled from this, the highest point.

"Is it always . . . ?" she asks Anna. "Is the street always painted?"

"Look closer," Anna says. "Go and look."

Kate takes a step, and then another, and she sees it isn't paint, not flat, but textured rough. It's a tapestry, she thinks. A massive, unfurled tapestry. She takes one more step as a tiny wind blows, just a breath, and the colors before her seem to exhale, in a sigh.

"But they're flower petals," she says. "All of them."

Anna's hands are clasped together, her face wide with a smile. "Don't look," she says. "Not yet. Don't start here. Come with me to the bottom of the hill." She guides Kate away from the petals lying there. "It's the history of Italy," she explains. "The history of the world. Going up the hill. Beginning with Adam and Eve, of course." It is an annual town project, she tells Kate, done for as long as anyone can remember. "Families, neighbors, they are in teams. By tradition. Something like Siena, like the Palio. Each group has a square, and a time in history to show. They draw the scene, before sunrise, on the street. They have all the petals. They dry them for months. The parents draw the picture, just the . . . the . . ."

"Outline?"

"Yes, the outline. The children are the painters. They paint with flowers. They fill in all the color on the street."

By now, they have reached the lowest point. Looking up, Kate can see the long banner, dozens of squares draped up the hill. Just before her, at her feet, is the first. A black *vipera* twines himself around a gray-barked tree, hung heavily with fruit. His split tongue slithers, long and pointed, blood-red from his mouth, as a naked Eve bends toward him, hand outstretched, while Adam's back is turned.

Kate stoops, leaning in, her eyes on the broken flowers, none of them much bigger than an inch. When she stands upright, they disappear, the whole picture emerging clear once again. It all seems impossible to Kate, impossible that these weightless wisps have conspired into this scene. Into Eve, so complete in her struggle, leaning eternally forward, reaching so fatefully for the fruit, aware and unaware of what she does. How can it be this moment is only sprinkled here? Scattered onto the ground, held by the slimmest gravity?

Looking uphill, she watches the children at the ready along the way, their hands brimming with endless petals, placing them down, filling in colors where the edges have loosened into ragged floral shards. Anna has moved ahead again, just several feet, studying a different scene, her hands on her hips. Suddenly Kate is afraid of a wind that might blow, afraid the colors will vanish as it all floats away.

"But what happens?" she calls. "At the end of the day? What happens to it then?"

"At the end? It only takes a broom," Anna answers with a smile and a shrug. "At dusk, you will see. One old woman with a broom sweeps it all down the hill." She wipes her hands together in a brisk gesture. "And that's that," she says. "It is done."

For a moment, Kate watches her climb to the next square. "Come with me, Kate," she hears Anna's voice say. "Come with me, now. Come see."

"I will. I'll catch up. I'll be right there."

But she has difficulty leaving this opening scene.

Kate turns back to see Eve surrender once again, knowing now how little time is left. Only hours before all of history is swept down on her.

A light breeze blows and from this distance Eve's flesh seems to quiver, as if alive.

Acknowledgments

I have been so fortunate throughout the long process of writing this book. I have been helped by so many people. My extraordinary agent, Henry Dunow, has steered me and my work far beyond any hopes I ever allowed myself to have and been a friend and wise adviser all the while. I'm immeasurably grateful to him and equally grateful to have him as my companion through this. My editor, the brilliant Kate Medina, has shown an understanding of my fiction that amazes me always and buoys me often. She, Laura Ford and Lindsey Schweori have made a mighty, mighty team. I'm so fortunate to have benefited from their insights, enthusiasm, and care, as well as from the extraordinary support that everyone at Random House has given to this book.

The earliest of these stories were written in the Rittenhouse Writers Group in Philadelphia, and I only wish that every anxious, hopeful writer who expects at any minute to be declared a fraud had such a place to be and to grow into their own words. Other stories emerged while I was in the

Warren Wilson College MFA Program for Writers, where I learned incalculable amounts from my work with C. J. Hribal and Kevin (Mc) McIlvoy, and also from the insights of Peter Turchi, director of the program at the time. I'm still trying to figure out how I got lucky enough to work with Steven Schwartz my first semester in the program. He was an extraordinary teacher then and has been a generous mentor and friend ever since.

Before these stories were ever in a book, they were in literary journals, where they benefited from the talents and the inadequately celebrated commitment of editors who work with devotion and artistry to ensure, quite simply, that good writing has a good home. Every one of those people has my gratitude and my admiration.

Since beginning this project, I have been honored to receive recognition from the Leeway Foundation, the Mac-Dowell Colony and the Pirate's Alley Faulkner-Wisdom Writing Competition, and I thank them all. A very special thank-you goes to Antonio and Carla Sirsale of the hotel Le Sirenuse for my Sirenland Conference Fellowship, and for their most generous hospitality to both me and my husband. Special thanks too to Jeffrey Levine and Grace Dane (Gretchen) Mazur of Tupelo Press for their invaluable role in the creation of this book. My deep gratitude as well to Kate Harvey at Picador, UK, for her acute insights, her good humor, and her friendship.

Shannon Cain, Erin Stalcup, and Jim Zervanos have been loyal and cherished readers. The fact that each happens to be a brilliant writer in his or her own right makes the gift of their attention to my work that much more precious—but still the gift of their friendship far outshines even that. More support, more entirely essential care, more extraordinary friendship has come from David Black, Gavin Black, Eleanor Bloch, Jane Cutler, Donald Goldberg, Amy Grimm, Stephanie G'Schwind, Allan Gurganus (my very first writing teacher), Laurie Schafer, Dani Shapiro, Alice Schell, Daniel Torday, Bettyruth Walter, Richard Wertime, Bonnie West, the extraordinary alumni of the Warren Wilson MFA program, and the amazing students I have had along the way who have allowed me to learn by their side.

I have been blessed with a mother, Barbara Aronstein Black, who understands that unless she tells me when my writing is problematic, I'll never believe her when she says it's great. She is one of the most astute readers I have and one of the best friends I will ever have. I think it's a toss-up which of us cared more about getting my work out into the world—and for it mattering so deeply to her, I am more grateful than she can know. Also, importantly, in ways too complex to describe, too precious to me to qualify, my father, the late Charles L. Black Jr., has been a constant partner in this project from the start.

As a writer, I have a lot of faith in the capacity of language to express anything really, but am unable to find words that fully express my gratitude to my children, Elizabeth Simins, David Simins, and Annie Goldberg. All I can say, E, D, & A, is that nothing you've done has been lost on me. I know what you have given and I know what you have given up. And I hope you know that you, my true first collection, are my heroines and my hero.

As for my husband, Richard Goldberg, no writer has ever had the obstacles cleared for her as surely as he has cleared those in my way, nor had her path illuminated as brightly as he has lit mine. I have been given a lot of amazing gifts by many, many people, but finally, truly, it is Richard who has given me this book.

It took me eight years to write the eleven stories here, and there is simply no way to acknowledge every person who helped in some way, whether with writing advice or kindness or childcare or faith or by authoring a story that amazed and inspired me. I hope I'll have the chance to thank you all in person. I surely mean to try.

If I Loved You,
I Would Tell You This

ROBIN BLACK

A Reader's Guide

A Conversation Between Karen Russell and Robin Black

Karen Russell is the author of the story collection *St. Lucy's Home for Girls Raised by Wolves* and the novel *Swamplandia!*, both published by Knopf. Recently she was selected by the National Book Foundation as one of their 5 under 35 and by *The New Yorker* as one of their twenty best American writers under forty. She is the Writer in Residence at Bard College.

Karen Russell: Robin, your writing career has had a really interesting, nontraditional trajectory. You had already raised three children when *If I Loved You, I Would Tell You This* was released. How did you come to writing? Did you always suspect that you would be a writer, or was it a vocation that you came to later?

Robin Black: I first started writing in college and then wrote off and on over the years, but when I was thirty-nine years old I decided to make a steady effort to make a career of it. A lot of things went into my ability to focus on it then, including that my youngest child of three had entered school.

KR: These stories are so rich, and fed by so many different streams of life experience—they may be "short," relative to, say, *The Brothers Karamazov,* but they have all the insight, heartbreak, and complexity of the best novels. In your acknowledgments, you mention that it took you eight years to write the eleven stories in the collection. Do you feel like the gestation period for the stories has something to do with their emotional depth?

RB: In part, I think the whole process took a long time because I never set out to write a story collection. I wrote each story as its own thing without focusing on how it would fit into a manuscript, so I didn't feel hurried to finish a book. And I am remarkably inefficient. I honestly think I throw out a good 80 percent of what I write. On a less logistical level, I think that some of what you call complexity and depth—thank you, Karen!—comes from a childhood spent trying to figure out the familial complexities into which I was born. So many of my stories deal with aftermath, years of history echoing down, and I can see now that I grew up with a sense of a household still trying to deal with its own history. Maybe this is true of all families, but in mine anyway, the stories from the past seemed to loom incredibly large and I was always aware that my parents and my grandmother, who lived with us, were carrying the legacies of these complex narratives within them. There had been deaths before my birth that were still being grieved, injuries and illnesses from which people had never recovered. I know that isn't unique and my preoccupation with those things is probably the strange part, but for better and worse, I have always been obsessed with the question of how personal history determines the present moment.

KR: So many of these stories deal with the biggest themes—love, loss, our thirst for meaning in a world that can often feel chaotic, impersonally cruel, and random. In "Gaining Ground," the narrator is deeply anxious about how our desire for meaning, for the events of our lives to cohere, and for the stuff of our lives to matter, might create patterns where there are none. Might fool us into projecting meaning onto the void, the "nothingness" as described by that cosmic sourpuss Harris, whose motto is "So what?"

By the story's finale, the narrator's choppy sentence fragments have stitched together into a glorious crescendo, one of the most stirring moments in the book. It's a paragraph that seems to rebuff Harris's view by suggesting that there may in fact be an answer to the "So what?" question, even if the narrator doesn't know it yet. When you were writing "Gaining Ground," did you intend it to answer its own question? Do you see the "So what?" challenge as being in some way connected to the aim of fiction—to make sense of our lives, to make meaning?

RB: "Gaining Ground" is the oldest story in the book and for a long time I have thought that I wrote it as a kind of unintentional manifesto. I wasn't conscious of this at the time, but I think that the subtext there is me saying: *I am* *going to try to make sense of the world and of my own existence by telling stories.* I'm not sure this jumps out at people, but it's a tremendously optimistic piece, very much about the human capacity to look at tragedy and insist that there is some purpose to it. In my conscious, thinking life I have a complicated relationship with that capacity. I can't look at children who die—to name but one terrible tragedy—and believe there's any kind of hidden sense to it. But I am certain that the unconscious *drive* to make sense of such things is in all of us, including me. How else do we get through life except by continually trying to see something redemptive in its brief, often harsh nature? By telling story after story about people navigating the rough waters of grief, I am absolutely rehearsing for myself, again and again, the notion that there is a purpose of some kind to it all. And that the redemption lies somewhere in how we help one another through.

KR: Your characters felt very real to me, some more real than many people I know, as though they had a secret life beyond the page. I got the sense that every one of them casts a shadow, has a past, and will have a future. How much do you know about your characters when you sit down to begin a draft? Do you draft out biographies for them? Or do their histories, quirks, and preoccupations become clearer to you as you write?

RB: My characters definitely reveal themselves to me in process. Going into a story, I know almost nothing about the people, the events, the reason it feels urgent to me. And I like that. Characters develop in a kind of conversation that takes place between actions or plot elements that occur to me as I go along and the responses the characters have to those, which then in turn spark on more plot developments. When I first wrote "Immortalizing John Parker," Clara Feinberg wasn't even a portrait painter. It was a story about a woman whose lover of much earlier in her life and then more recently had just died. It's almost impossible to imagine that now because the story is so very much about the portrait painting aspects, but she only became a portraitist when I started thinking about what other plot line I could develop that would complement and dovetail with her grieving process. In the sort of stories I write, the story grows out of character, meaning the people do things because it makes some kind of psychological sense to me that they would, but the characters also evolve to serve the story. Like so much of fiction writing it's a messy and inexact process.

KR: Antonya Nelson says that "all stories are coming-of-age stories." I think most people associate the phrase "coming of age" with the pimply, hellacious adolescent and teenage years—the Judy Blume terrain, the transition from childhood into adulthood. But the stories in *If I Loved You, I Would Tell You This* are gorgeous and wrenching examinations of what it means to "come of age" at sixty, and fifty-four, and forty-two—at many different life stages. I almost think that the final story, "The History of the World," could be read as a cosmic coming-of-age allegory, where the festival of the flowers stands in for the chaotic slide of world history into silence, a rosy cascade of being into nothingness.

What draws you to the thresholds in your fiction such as burying a spouse, moving into your last home, confronting an infidelity, watching your children suffer as adults? Would you agree that they are also coming-of-age stories, and if so, how does the traditional rite-of-passage story change in middle and later age? What exactly is in flux for these characters?

RB: I think of coming-of-age stories as narratives in which the balance between innocence and experience shifts, and I absolutely believe my stories fit that definition. Just recently I was having a loss-of-innocence reflection of my own when I realized that as a child I had assumed that there is a finite amount of complexity to life and that as we age we gain more and more mastery over it. Of course, what adult life reveals is that our capacity to perceive complexity always outpaces our ability to understand it, so life never actually seems simpler. If anything, quite the opposite. And it's that process that I am drawn to as I write—the business of life becoming more and more complicated and all of us working to keep up with that. So I am drawn to the points in life at which that process is exposed. The appearance of Adam and Eve in the flower scene at the end of "The History of the World" is a kind of clue to the fact that everything that comes before in the book really has been about the double-edged nature of the acquisition of knowledge and the accompanying loss of innocence.

KR: As a follow-up question, are there any particular challenges you found to imagining forward—to making an empathetic leap into characters who are much older than you, rather than mining your memories of childhood and adolescence to craft a character?

RB: For reasons I truly don't understand, I find that writing older characters comes very naturally to me. I grew up with my grandmother in our home and with many older relatives visiting frequently, and given a choice between listening to an elderly aunt talk about what forty years of marriage had actually been like or listening to a twenty-something talk about whom they planned to marry and how happy they would be, I always found the former infinitely more interesting. And, on a conscious level anyway, I have never been interested in creating characters because they're like me. In a way, part of the joy of creating characters for me is finding out about other people, putting myself in someone else's place. It's one of the most fun aspects of writing, having that break from my own life story and the chance to be in someone else's.

KR: So many of the stories in this collection focus on an emotional or spiritual blind spot—their characters' inability to accurately see themselves, or their failure to fully apprehend a lover, a parent, a child, or, in the case of the title story, the neighbor who lives behind your cunningly erected fence. I'm thinking of the sort of intimate one-upmanship of the conversation between Clara and her ex-husband, Harold, in "Immortalizing John Parker" or Jeremy's startling discovery in "A Country Where You Once Lived." How can we be so wrong in our judgments of those to whom we are closest—our parents, our children? What blinds these characters; in your opinion, what prevents them from truly seeing one another?

RB: I honestly think it's just how we all bungle through life. We make mistakes. We assume we know what's going on and we don't. Every person carries a vast number of secrets, even people who don't think of themselves as secretive. We withhold from one another as a kindness or to be in control of some situation or because we don't want to violate someone else's confidence. Or because it's not even theoretically possible to tell someone everything you know. So much of life is conducted in this kind of strange, murky darkness. I think I may be more attuned to that than some people or I may be naturally drawn to it as an area of narrative potential, but I think it's a condition that exists for us all. What's amazing to me, and continually beautiful, is that we manage ever to connect to one another at all.

KR: The final image in "The History of the World" is one of the most perfect and astonishingly beautiful endings that I have ever read—that image of a mosaic of flowers curling up the hillside at dusk, Adam and Eve extending their hands, and all the colors trembling in the wind. It's not obvious or tidy, we don't get an Aesop's moral or a fortune cookie scroll, Kate's fate is still hanging in the balance; and yet it feels like a real *ending,* a plateau where we can breathe deeply as readers and consider everything that's come before. What makes a great ending? How do you know when a story is finished?

RB: Thank you for that. I'll confess that's my favorite ending in the collection, which is one reason I'm glad that's the final story. But I agree it's kind of puzzling why it works as an ending since it's really just an image and not a conclusion of any kind much less a resolution. I think about endings a lot—I suspect every writer does—and more and more, I have the sense that the endings that work most powerfully on me are passages that might well be beginnings, that seem to open up more than they close down. And I think this has to do with the way those types of endings allow for the reader to keep a story alive in her imagination, her thoughts, even after the final words. I envision the ending of a story as the point at which I complete the process of handing the story over to the reader. It belongs to her by then. It's common for people to recommend starting stories mid-action or in media res, but there's at least as good an argument for ending them that way too. There's a kind of generosity to not closing a story down entirely, a way that includes the reader, and I aspire to that. Of course, like so much else, it's a tough balance to get right. Leave the wrong ends loose and it can feel like the exact opposite, ungenerous. It's for these reasons and more that endings are famously difficult to get right. And when you think you've got it, it's like walking out of the room where a baby is sleeping. You don't want to make a sound, not even breathe too loudly for fear you'll disturb it.

KR: In a collection where Death is a ubiquitous menace and your characters are grappling with everything from terminal cancer to vehicular manslaughter, I was surprised by how many times the dialogue made me laugh out loud. In the title story, Sam responds to tragedy with "a fistful of punch lines." Do you see humor as in some way aggressive—is laughter maybe a way, as Sam's dying wife puts it, to "resist erasure"? Or is it an analgesic? What role does humor play in your stories?

RB: I wasn't with my father when he died at eighty-five, but my brother, mother, and the health aide were all in the room. At some point in the days that followed, I asked my brother at what exact time Dad had stopped breathing and my brother cleared his throat, then paused, then said, "Well, that's a little hard to say because the three of us were busy trying to get a new light into the ceiling fixture." And after another pause I said, "How many deathbed vigil attendees does it take to screw in a light bulb?" Now, my father was eighty-five, and though his death was plenty sad, it wasn't tragic, and in the absence of tragedy there is a place for humor. There are some tragedies though that simply defy humor, but aside from those terrible cases, life is almost always a braiding of many tones, including irreverent, funny ones. And I would hate for my fiction to be devoid of the lighter strands because we need them.

KR: Numbness, both emotional and physical, is a recurring motif in the collection—Anna, in "The History of the World," complains of her boss, whose hands "have no feeling. From the stove, from being burned. He touches me but cannot feel." Jean in "Tableau Vivant" stares at her dead arm in the rosebushes: "It hung there limp, covered in dirt, as though it were already dead and had been dug from

the ground." Yet in "Pine," Heidi seems almost able to feel
her husband touch her prosthetic leg.

What numbs these characters—what frictions cause
their emotional or spiritual calluses? What does it prevent
them from experiencing, or conversely, allow them to experience? Is Heidi meant to provide a model for how we
might accept and move beyond a loss?

RB: You're so right to detect that theme. I think that for
any of us who have had terrible losses, there's a kind of seductive quality to the idea of numbing out and I'm
tempted to say that these stories are an argument against
that and in favor of the idea that the only way through pain
is to feel it and the only way to feel joy is to be open to feeling pain. But even as I type those phrases, I find myself
hoping that the stories are a little more complex than that
because I'm certain that some numbness is necessary at
times for us all. I used to believe that every truth had to be
faced head-on, all the time; but I've come to see that life is
very often just too hard for that approach.

In "Pine," Heidi functions as an example of what sur-
vival can look like. There's a kind of transcendent whole-
ness she has—the kind of thing that makes the caress of
a prosthetic leg meaningful to her—but she also isn't exactly as she was before losing her leg. Her gait, her way of
moving through the world, literally and otherwise, has
changed. There's this important line between resignation
and acceptance. Claire is resigned to a life of misery and has
numbed out a part of herself in the service of that unhap-
piness—arguably her heart. Heidi seems to have come to
accept a change of circumstance. And I think the reason I

put in that reference early on to her being on her fifth prosthetic is to give a sense of process. One doesn't adjust to loss right away. One evolves to accommodate it. This is how I understand the process, anyway.

KR: Judgment is a theme in every one of these stories— the characters are continually weighing their own actions, making judgments about other characters, trying to assess their own responsibility, trying to juggle their self-interest against the needs of their children and spouses. Yet the stories themselves are never judgmental; they are supremely compassionate portraits of complex, flawed, courageous, suffering people. How do you think about judgment as it connects to writing fiction?

RB: It's hard for me to find a way to express how profoundly uninterested I am in passing judgment on my characters, because I worry that it makes me sound like an amoral person, which I'm not. But truly, it never even occurs to me. I am so interested in why people do what they do. And to the extent that those acts hurt other people I think it's important as a writer to not shy away from depicting that. But the last thing I am interested in doing is making moral assessments of my characters.

I would like my work to suggest the possibility that we all gain more from understanding one another than we do from judging one another. So my task as an artist is not to reinforce notions of good and bad or put myself in some kind of holier-than-thou role, but to expand people's curiosity about each other. It sounds a bit grandiose and it's certainly not what's on my mind when I sit down at my keyboard—today I am going to increase the world's empathy quotient—but it's there behind what I do.

KR: "Helping" also seems to be a theme in so many of these stories—the help that we yearn for, and the ways that we attempt, often clumsily, unsuccessfully, to help our loved ones. Jeremy in "A Country Where You Once Lived" is hoping that he can atone for years of negligence by helping his daughter to slaughter a bird; Kevin in "Pine" helps Claire at great psychic cost to himself, despite the fact that she will only accept so much of what he has to give her. What are the moral stakes of refusing to help? Of refusing to *be* helped?

RB: I think that the acts of helping and accepting help can be tremendously intimate ones. To accept help from somebody, really for anything, you have to let them in on a vulnerability, an aspect of yourself that needs help. In "Pine" Kevin finally tries to help Claire by shocking her past her self-pity, but she can't accept that help because she can't admit to that weakness, so she pushes him away. In "Immortalizing John Parker" Clara offers to help Katherine Parker in her project of capturing something of her husband before he slips away to his dementia, but Katherine Parker has to admit that she wants that, as foolish as it makes her feel. It's a very intimate moment. And it's the sort of intimacy that interests me, the unexpected, strange kind that grows out of the sort of relationship we don't usually associate with intimacy.

KR: Memory, in your stories, feels so precious and so terri-fyingly fragile to me. These characters suffer losses in the present, but often it's their version of the past that is most at risk. In "Immortalizing John Parker," there is a wonder-ful dinner scene between Clara and her ex-husband when reminiscing becomes a heart-stoppingly dangerous activity: "Harold has just taken from her a part of George she thought she held . . . as effortlessly as she has just rewritten decades of Harold's life for him." Is this a loss or a betrayal that you wanted to explore in the collection—how even the past can be taken from us?

RB: Definitely. And also how memory can be preserved and how we conspire to create the past. In "Immortalizing John Parker," Clara robs her former husband of his version of events, but she also offers to preserve John Parker for his wife, agrees to try to keep the past alive that way. In "Tableau Vivant," Jean and her daughter tell and retell the story of a shared evening to one another because doing so preserves a moment of happiness. It's a kindness they give each other. I think there's something inherently hurtful to someone saying "Really? That's not how I remember it at *all*." It strikes a very deep chord. I imagine that we all want to believe we are reliable witnesses to our own lives. Maybe because it makes time itself seem more like something we are able to hold.

KR: In "A Country Where You Once Lived," there is a wonderfully tense moment at the kitchen table, where a family is gathered together for the first time in years: "This is one of those moments, Jeremy knows, at which he can pierce the social fabric and acknowledge what they are all thinking about anyway . . . an opportunity to be direct." A beat later, he asks, "Are those your potatoes?"

Dialogue is such a pleasure in these stories—you have such an ear for the way that lovers and parents and children speak to one another, all the old affections and hostilities and resentments coming to head in a single joke or off-handed remark. And I was impressed at the way that dialogue can *create* atmosphere, just as surely as any Virginia Woolfy description of dark clouds. Even when I was not yet privy to the characters' secrets, I could still feel a terrible tension building. It was almost like watching a thunderhead swallow a house, darkening all of its windows, and then suddenly burst, unleashing a torrent of rain. As a writer, how do you decide what and when a character should withhold versus accuse, challenge, confess?

RB: I have learned to love writing dialogue, though that was a long time coming. In general, I'm at least as interested in what isn't being said as in what is, or maybe it's more accurate to say that what really fascinates me is the interplay between the two. When Jeremy chooses to ask about his daughter's produce instead of acknowledging what they're all thinking anyway, I mean that avoidance to be every bit as informative about who he is and what it's like to be in that room as it would be if he'd gone ahead and said something more provocative. Learning to write dialogue for me has been a matter of learning to resist the impulse to have characters say exactly what they mean. That and recognizing how rude we all are to each other all the time. My characters interrupt and talk about their own interests out of context, and, sad to say, I think that makes them sound like the rest of us.

KR: There are so many concrete metaphors in these stories—the fence in the title story, the wooden leg in "Pine," the box of roses that appears "like a foundling infant on the front porch" in "Tableau Vivant." Reading the collection, I kept thinking about Flannery O'Connor's quote about the wooden leg in her own story "Good Country People"—"If you want to say that the wooden leg is a symbol, you can say that. But it is a wooden leg first, and as a wooden leg it is absolutely necessary to the story. It has its place on the literal level of the story, but it operates in depth as well as on the surface." Could you reflect a little bit on how you find these metaphors within your stories— how you let the objects accrete meaning and operate on both a literal and a figurative plane?

RB: Often, those images are the one aspect of a story that comes from real life. We really did have electric water, believe it or not, and our neighbor did build a fence practically in our driveway. I wrote "Tableau Vivant" after I planted bare root roses for the first time. And there is a real flower festival in Italy, just like the one at the end of "The History of the World." And so on. I think my mind tends to get snagged on potential metaphors in real life, they fascinate me, and very often they inspire stories. So maybe if those symbols aren't shouting SYMBOL on the page it's at least partly because they are so intrinsically at the heart of the stories that have grown around them.

Having said that, the proposed slaughtered chicken in

"A Country Where You Once Lived" is an exception because when I wrote that I was consciously playing with the
whole notion of symbols in fiction. For various reasons I
wanted that violent image in there, but I knew as soon as it
occurred to me that it was just too obvious and over-the-
top. If I'd actually written a story about a father and daughter making up over killing a bird, it would have been
capital B Bad and capital H Hokey. So I decided that the
way to have it both ways was to slip in the idea, but then to
have the central character acknowledge what a hackneyed
and embarrassing hope it was on his part that there might
be some kind of symbolic healing to be found through a
chicken slaughter. The only way I felt like I could get that
image in there was to make fun of it.

KR: What's up next for you, Robin? What are you working
on now?

RB: I'm writing a novel—and at the same time continuing
to write stories and also nonfiction essays. And I'm still trying to make some sense out of life—of course.

Questions and Topics
for Discussion

1. The title of this book is *If I Loved You, I Would Tell You This*. What are some instances in the stories of people deciding which secrets to tell and which to keep? What goes into these decisions? For example, in "Immortalizing John Parker," why does Clara finally tell Harold about her affair? In "Tableau Vivant," why does Jean hide her stroke from her family? What are the impacts of these choices?

2. Several of the stories are about women in their sixties or seventies. Clara in "Immortalizing John Parker," Jean in "Tableau Vivant," and Kate Rodgers in "The History of the World" are all dealing with the absence—or impending absence—of a longtime partner, but each of their situations is very different. We're told that Kate would have preferred losing her husband to death than to another woman. What do you think Clara and Jean would say about that? What kind of conversation might these three women have?

3. The book depicts more than a dozen marriages—some successful, others not. Which of the couples seem happy to you, and which do not? Do the stories share a common message about what makes for a happy marriage, or does it seem to be more unpredictable than that?

4. Every one of these stories is about a loss of some kind, yet there are almost no scenes in which anyone cries. Why do you suppose that is? With what other actions does Black demonstrate grief? Did you identify with the ways in which one or more of her characters experienced loss? Discuss.

5. These eleven stories were written over an eight-year period. Do you have any guesses about which were written earliest and which most recently? What makes you think so?

6. What do you think happens to the characters in the minutes and days after the stories end? For example, near the end of "The Guide," Jack learns that Lila knows exactly what's going on with her parents, but the story is over before they have a chance to talk about it—or *not* talk about it. What do you imagine their ride home will be like? And in "Pine," what happens next between Claire and Kevin? If she wants another chance at a romance with him, will he risk it? Should he?

7. Black pays a lot of attention to the houses in which these stories unfold. Why do you think she describes them in

such detail? What do the houses tell you about the different characters who occupy them?

8. None of the characters in this book are painted as entirely virtuous. It seems like everyone has made their share of mistakes along the way. Are any characters made out to be all bad? Which of them would you want to share a meal with? What would you ask them, if you could? Which would you rather not meet?

9. There are some pretty upsetting situations in these stories, yet the characters don't seem to have lost their ability to hope. What kinds of things keep them going? In "Immortalizing John Parker," why does Clara decide to paint the portrait as Katherine Parker wants her to? In "Tableau Vivant," why does Jean keep the bare root roses that she forgot to cancel? In "Harriet Elliot," why does the narrator feel "something like belief" on her last day at school? Discuss what you think this collection suggests about the capacity in people to survive loss.

These stories originally appeared, in some cases in slightly different versions, in the following publications:

"The Guide," *Indiana Review;* "If I Loved You" (as "A Fence Between Our Homes"), *The Southern Review;* "Immortalizing John Parker," *Freight Stories;* "Harriet Elliot," *One Story;* "Gaining Ground," *Alaska Quarterly Review;* "Tableau Vivant," *The Georgia Review;* "Pine," *Colorado Review;* "A Country Where You Once Lived," *Hunger Mountain;* ". . . Divorced, Beheaded, Survived," *Bellevue Literary Review* and *The Best of the Bellevue Literary Review* (BLR Press, 2007); "Some Women Eat Tar," *Brain, Child*. A portion of "The History of the World" appeared in *The Double Dealer* as winner of the 2005 Pirate's Alley Faulkner-Wisdom Writing Competition in the Short Story Category and appeared in full in *Colorado Review*.